NOTE TO READERS

A list of content warnings are on the next page, so skip that page if you'd rather not see them.

STAY

LANDMARK MOUNTAIN
BOOK 5

WILLOW ASTER

All rights reserved.
No part of this book may be reproduced in any form or by any electronic or mechanical means, including information storage and retrieval systems, without written permission from the author, except for the use of brief quotations in a book review.

Willow Aster
www.willowaster.com

Copyright © 2024 by Willow Aster
ISBN-13: 979-8-9880213-7-7

Cover by Emily Wittig Designs
Photo: © Regina Wamba
Map artwork by Kira Sabin
Editing by Christine Estevez

*Rocky Mountains
*Ski Hill
*Tiptop
*Glass Dome
*Gandola Ride
*Alpine House
*Summit House
HERITAGE LANE
*Landmark Mountain
Lodge & Ski Resort
*The Pink Ski
LANDMARK
MOUNTAIN
*Happy Cow
*Sunny Side
*The Dancing Emu
*The Dispensary
*Feathered Whims
*The Park
*The Gnarly Vine
*Hooked

CONTENT WARNINGS

The content warnings for *Stay* are a thirteen-year age gap and profanity.

CHAPTER ONE

LIE BY OMISSION

FELICITY

It's been difficult to think of anyone but Sutton Landmark since we had an online meeting over a week ago.

His dark hair and his dancing brown eyes offsetting the serious but sensual line of his full lips made me want to know all his secrets. His ridiculously long eyelashes made him look younger than I know he must be since he's a judge, and his gruff voice and all-business persona made my heart pound throughout the entire interview.

If I were a wiser person, I would've never agreed to a second interview with him. Especially after I looked him up online and fell down a Sutton Landmark picture trap for hours.

But if I've proven anything this year, it's that I don't always make the wisest decisions.

There's also the fact that I need this job, and more than that, I need to get out of my brother Weston's house.

I adore my brother, but he's a quarterback for the Colorado Mustangs and never lacks company. The allure of being around his teammates all the time was fun for a couple of weeks, but since Weston is adamant about me not dating any of them, that cuts the fun down by at least half. Not to mention, he has a steady stream of women coming in and out of his bedroom, and I don't think that will ever *not* be awkward.

I've only been back in Silver Hills for a couple of weeks, but it's felt so strange. Much different than all the times I visited when I was on break from Georgetown.

My parents can't figure out why I haven't just stayed with them, but I'm not ready to tell them that my plans have derailed considerably from what they're expecting of me.

I need time to work up to that.

And working for Sutton in Landmark Mountain is the perfect way to bide my time.

I feel that way even more as I drive into the beautiful mountain town. It only takes an hour and a half to get here, and I enjoy the view. Silver Hills is beautiful, but the mountains feel even closer out here, and after being in D.C. for so long, I'm living for the mountains. After a grueling course load over the past four years, I think I'd enjoy anything that doesn't involve my crowded room and cramming for tests. It's the first week in January, and shopkeepers are removing traces of Christmas from their sidewalks and front windows, replacing them with winter decor or Valentine's Day decorations. There are so many cute shops, places I'd love to spend the day browsing…and maybe I'll have a chance to do just that if I get this job.

When I pull into Sutton's driveway, I sit and stare at the gorgeous house for a few minutes. There's a small wooden sign out front that says Summit House, and the name is fitting for the regal house with unique roof peaks and windows galore. There's water alongside the house, so much that I'm not sure if it's part of the Blue River or a lake, but I could get lost in that view all day. Someone walks past the front window inside the house, and it spurs me into action. I get out of the car and walk up to the front door, knocking twice.

The door opens wide, and I stare unblinking for I don't know how long…long enough that Sutton clears his throat and holds out his hand. We shake and neither of us speaks right away.

He's the first to break the silence.

"It's nice to meet you in person, Felicity Shaw," he says.

It's ridiculous the way my body reacts to his hand and his voice…and his eyes on me. Who knew I was into older men? That's something I'll have to get over *immediately* if I'm going to be a nanny for his son.

"Nice to meet you, Mr. Landmark." I'm impressed with how calm I sound when my insides feel anything but.

"Call me Sutton," he says, his voice gravelly. "Come on in."

I follow him inside and take in the living room. The ceilings are high and there's a large sectional with a chaise lounge on one end. I've always loved those. Next to that is a massive chair that looks like it would fit two people, and over the fireplace is an enormous TV screen. Bookshelves line either side of the fireplace and I'd love nothing more than to walk over there and see what kind of books Sutton Landmark reads.

I don't even know the man beyond our one online meeting, but I think I've already figured him out in my head. He doesn't seem snobbish, but he does seem proper. Even now, at two o'clock in the afternoon, he has a three-piece suit on, not a hair is out of place, and he smells like a heady combination of cedarwood and vanilla. I bet he only wears designer clothes and drinks $100 bottles of wine. I wonder if when his son is with his mom, he loosens up? Someone as good-looking as he is must have women rotating out of his bed like clockwork.

What kind of women does Sutton Landmark like?

"Have a seat," he says.

My face heats with my thoughts and I try to focus on keeping this as professional as possible.

"Can I get you anything to drink?" He motions for me to sit on the couch, and it's then that I notice a long charcuterie board full of deli meats, cheeses, dried fruit, and chocolate sitting on the large square ottoman between the two couches. An elegant silver bucket of ice, two glasses, and a pitcher of water are on a tray next to the food.

Mr. Landmark has expensive tastes.

"This looks amazing."

"I can't take credit for any of it. There's a place in town called The Gnarly Vine, and I just toss everything on the board and call it a snack. I wasn't sure if you'd eaten with the drive, and I worked through lunch." He smiles slightly and motions behind him. "I have Coke, Sprite, apple juice, and water." He motions toward the water on the ottoman.

My image of him never included apple juice or him

saying the word *snack*, despite knowing he has an eight-year-old son.

"Water will be fine," I say.

"But would you *rather* have something else?"

His eyes narrow on mine and it's as if he can see right through me, down to all the intimate thoughts I've been having about him.

"Uh, I'd love a Coke."

He nods, as if pleased, and I lean back against the couch cushions needing to catch my breath. I feel winded.

"Thank you," I add.

He goes into the kitchen and is back within minutes, carrying two bottles of chilled Coke with the caps already popped off.

"Thank you," I repeat.

I'm not normally at a loss for words, but there's something about this man that makes me tongue-tied.

He motions for me to take one of the small plates I didn't notice behind the bucket, and I do, using the little fork on the board to pick out a couple of things. I don't know if I can eat right now, which is also a problem if I'm seriously considering this job…which I am. Meanwhile, he's using the other fork and piling food onto his plate like this is his first meal of the day.

Once we've settled back into our seats, Sutton directly across from me, he looks at me again with that direct gaze.

"I'm just going to be forthright…you'll find that I am, sometimes obnoxiously so," he says, a mischievous grin crossing over his face.

And wow, that smile. All the proper I was seeing before just flipped into pure sin.

I shift in my seat. I like that he's more down-to-earth than

I expected him to be, but I'm still unable to ignore the way the man affects me.

"Of course," I squeak.

I clear my throat and nod, picking up a dried apricot and taking a bite in hopes that it'll make me look cool and nonchalant.

"I've interviewed twenty-three applicants, and I have to say you were a top runner from the beginning, until—"

I stop chewing the apricot and let my eyes meet his.

"Until?" I ask, sounding like I've run a marathon.

"Until I realized you omitted something very important on your résumé." He sets his plate down and leans forward, his elbows going to his knees.

The visual is very, *very* sexy.

Is he aware of what this look does to women?

I swallow hard. "I did?"

He nods. "You did." His lips pucker and the place between his brow deepens. "Would you care to tell me why you didn't tell me the truth?"

CHAPTER TWO

SLIM PICKINGS

SUTTON

This girl is stunning, and I did my best to find someone else for the nanny position because of that fact alone, but the pickings were slim. Either they had no personality at all or were so hyper I knew I wouldn't be able to stand being in the same room with them.

No one stood out like Felicity Shaw.

Unfortunately, in more ways than one.

But I'm determined not to discriminate against her because she's beautiful.

When my friend Henley Ward from the Colorado Mustangs told me Weston's younger sister was looking for a job and she had already sent in her résumé, it helped even more. Henley is a single dad, newer to the single thing than I am, but nonetheless, he gets it—this need to cover all the bases perfectly when it comes to our kids.

I'm just curious about why she didn't tell me the truth. I wouldn't be the judge I am if I didn't look into any hidden motives, and that only magnifies when my son Owen is involved.

"Didn't tell you the truth?" she asks, eyes wide.

It's a little distracting, how blue her eyes are.

"Yes. You want to tell me why you failed to mention you graduated pre-law at the top of your class and could have your pick of any law school in the country?"

Her cheeks turn ruddy, and she sweeps her long blonde hair back before carefully setting her plate on the ottoman.

"I didn't think it was important," she says.

"Why not? As a judge, how would it look if I hired someone planning to become a lawyer?"

"That's just it...I'm not." Her hands clasp in front of her and she straightens before taking a deep breath. "However, technically, as long as I never appeared in front of you on a case, it wouldn't have mattered."

My eyebrows lift. She has a point. Still, it'd give the appearance of impropriety that I've worked so hard to avoid to have a soon-to-be-lawyer nannying my son.

"I didn't mention it because I'm not going to law school in the fall," she says. "I graduated a semester early and I-I don't know what I'm going to do for sure yet, but I know that I *don't* want to become a lawyer."

Well, that is not what I expected to hear.

She tries to make eye contact, but her eyes flutter down to her lap.

"Why not?" I ask.

"I'm not cut out for it," she says softly.

"Your grades and everything I found on you says otherwise."

"You did your homework."

I smirk and her flush deepens. "Always. And especially when we're talking about someone watching my son. So... what are you considering? And would it involve you leaving in the fall?"

"I'm not sure yet. Something that feels like I'm helping people..." Her eyes meet mine and I feel a flicker of pride when they stay fixed on me. She swallows hard. "During our first interview, you mentioned you need someone to take Owen to school and pick him up...someone to be there for after-school events, and that there's a room over the garage... did that mean you only need someone here until the school year is over?"

"I was hoping to have someone more long-term than that, but we could try it for that long and reassess then."

Her face brightens. "Does that mean I'm hired?"

"More than it did a few minutes ago," I admit. "It's important you're honest with me," I say.

She nods.

"Is it true that you've done a lot of volunteer work for local children's charities, both when you were in high school in Silver Hills and during your time at Georgetown?"

"Yes. Everything on my résumé is true. I just left out that I'd been accepted into law school because I didn't feel it was relevant."

I stare at her long enough that she squirms. I don't mean

to make her uncomfortable, but I need to know she's being upfront with me.

"One more question…" I start.

She swallows again and I watch her slender throat dip. She's wearing a delicate silver necklace with a tiny circle pendant that sparkles when the light hits it just right.

"Walk me through an afternoon after you pick Owen up from school."

She leans forward and wipes her hands on her jeans, one of her long legs bouncing up and down until she realizes it and then stops.

"Well, I'd want to know all his favorite things to do, so we'd have several options. But first, we'd get home and I'd give him a snack and let him unwind for a little bit before starting his homework. Depending on how much time is left between then and dinner, we'd either do one of his favorite activities, or while I'm making dinner—you mentioned needing help with that a few nights a week—he could either help me or he could set the table. I'd have him take a bath or shower after dinner since that would make mornings go easier, and we could read before bedtime…if you still needed me for that kind of thing."

I nod, happy with her answer. "Do you have time to meet Owen this afternoon?"

Her eyes widen and she smiles. "Of course. I'd love to meet him."

"I asked Grinny, my grandmother, to pick him up today. She'll be here in just a few minutes. She's helped a lot and is willing to keep doing so, but I want to give her a break. She's long overdue one." I leave it at that.

Grinny and Granddad never had the chance to just be grandparents. My parents died in a car accident right before my fifteenth birthday, leaving my three younger brothers, two-year-old sister, and me devastated but in capable hands. I tried to do my part to help out, but I was grieving and angry and I didn't always make the best decisions.

My ex-wife Tracy being one of those decisions.

We dated on and mostly off throughout high school and college, breaking up more than we were together. But when she got pregnant during a weekend we were contemplating getting back together, I asked her to marry me, and she said yes. Our marriage lasted a year and was a mistake, but she's the mother of the best gift of my life, so I don't regret it.

Our not-so-amicable divorce cured any desire I ever felt for her, and I've never gone back on that, despite her occasional efforts to seduce me. Sex was never our problem; it was everything else. She's going through her second divorce now and taking a new job in Arizona, so I'm hoping the attempts at seduction are a thing of the past.

Just then there's a tap on the door and it opens, Owen rushing in and Grinny right behind him.

"Is she here?" Owen asks. He comes to an abrupt stop when he sees Felicity in our living room. "Oh, hi," he says. "I'm Owen."

Felicity stands and reaches out to shake his hand. He grins up at her and she gives him a smile that I haven't seen from her yet.

"Hi, Owen. I'm Felicity. Did you have a good day at school?"

"It was okay. I was more excited to see if you'd be here when I got home. Dad said if he liked you in person, I'd get to meet you. And if not..." He makes a slicing gesture across his neck, laughing. "He must like you." He smiles over at me and I laugh, swiping a hand down my face.

Grinny's head falls back as she laughs. "I don't know whether to fuss at you, Sutton Henry Landmark, or to just laugh." She reaches out and squeezes Felicity's shoulder. "Hi, dear. I'm Grinny. You'll have to excuse the manners on this one, he's a judge and all, but sometimes he's more trouble than all of the Landmarks combined. I assure you, there will be no," she mimics Owen's slicing gesture across her neck, "while I'm around."

Between my son and my grandmother, I can't get away with anything.

Felicity's laughing when she glances at me too and I feel it like a sharp arrow pricking my chest. *Damn*, she's gorgeous.

"Good to know. Glad I'm in safe hands with you, Grinny. And hopefully you too, Owen." Her eyes are on me as she says it, and too many things in me spark to life.

Owen nods excitedly. "Don't worry. I've got your back."

"Already siding with her? I'm not sure this is a good sign," I tease.

I wait to see if Felicity has anything to add and when she just smiles sweetly at Owen and then me, I reach out my hand. "Looks like the job is yours if you want it."

She clasps my hand and there's an electric shock when our skin touches this time.

"Oh!" she says in surprise. I'm not sure if it's from the shock or that I've offered her the job. "Thank you so much."

"Don't make me regret this," I say, still in a teasing voice.

But she swallows hard. "I won't, sir."

And the way those words send a jolt of lust through me has me wishing I could take it all back.

God, I hope this isn't a mistake.

CHAPTER THREE

PANTS ON FIRE

FELICITY

By Saturday morning, I've almost finished packing and I'm feeling more confident about my new job. I'm leaving for Landmark Mountain as soon as I've tidied up a bit. I got here before the holidays and expected to be staying until at least late summer, but I'd barely unpacked, so it doesn't take long.

"I can't believe you're already moving out. You just got here." Weston stands in the doorway of my room—*his* guest bedroom—scowling at me.

"Tell the truth, you can't wait to have your freedom back," I say, stuffing another sweater into my suitcase.

He scoffs. "I've been plenty free with you around here."

"Exactly." I roll my eyes.

He makes a face. "Shit. That's why you're leaving, isn't it?"

"I'm leaving because I got a good job. The pay is great, and I'll have a cozy little place…"

"You really want to spend your time before law school away from home? Why even bother graduating early?"

I turn and pack a few more things into the last open box, hoping my brother didn't see me flinch just now. I can't believe Sutton found out about law school. I wasn't expecting to have to answer for that. I certainly didn't intend on carrying out the lie with him too. I feel awful for not telling my family the truth yet, but I just can't imagine it going well.

My parents have a practice in Silver Hills, and my sister Olivia has worked there since she passed the bar. I had every intention of following in their footsteps. Weston has been consumed by football since he was a child, and thankfully, he's always excelled at it, because otherwise, I don't think he would've gotten off the hook so easily.

My parents love me and want what's best for me. I know without a doubt that this is true. But the guilt I have about all the money they've put toward my schooling, not to mention the plans they have for my future at the Law Offices of Shaw & Shaw…it's overwhelming, and it's a weight I've been carrying for over a year now. The closer I got to graduation, the more anxiety I had over following that career path.

Especially since I haven't exactly nailed down a new career path just yet.

"Felicity?" Weston says.

I turn and he lifts his eyebrows in question.

"You really want to spend your time off this way?" he repeats.

"Oh…yes, I do. I think it'll be fun. Judge Landmark is nice, and I think I'll stay busy."

"Wait, you didn't tell me you were working with a judge." He tilts his head, looking impressed. "Okay. Very cool."

My hands ball into fists. And now I've let him think my new job is something related to law. No one in my family would understand if I told them I'm taking a nanny job. Not at this point in my life.

It would not align with what they expect of my future.

I don't remember ever consciously lying before, ever… until now. It's awful. I hate it. But it would also be much easier if everyone thinks that's what I'll be doing for a little longer. At least until I can save some money to repay my parents and figure out exactly what I want to do.

"Yes!" I say, injecting enthusiasm in my voice. "And Landmark Mountain is such a cute town. I can't believe we never went there growing up. It's not that far."

"This is a family of workaholics, sis, you know that." Weston laughs. "I'm gonna miss you. You just got back…and I liked having you around. Sorry if I made it too uncomfortable for you with the women…"

I walk over and poke his side. He grabs my arm and twists me into a half-hug, half-wrestle move.

"I liked being here…most of the time." I maneuver out of his hold and kick the back of his knee, making him jerk forward. Never gets old. I move out of the way before he can grab me again, laughing at his attempt. And then I smile over at him fondly when I'm at a safe distance. "All kidding aside, I've loved being here. Thank you for everything. And I'll still come to your games…as many as I can."

"Bring whoever you want as often as you want to be

there. Just give me an idea of how many ahead of time and I'll set you up."

"Thanks, West. I'll miss you too. Once the season is over, you can come visit me too."

He nods and turns when the doorbell rings. "I will, promise. Pizza's here. Take a break and come eat something."

When I go into the kitchen, my parents are there, and I shoot a look at Weston for not warning me that they were coming over. He shrugs and grins. I hug them both and get a plate, piling it with a couple of slices of Hawaiian. I called them about the job last night and they both got on the phone and had plenty to say about it.

"Felicity, you didn't tell us who you're working for," my mom says. "Now, it all makes sense!"

She beams at me, and I focus on grabbing a drink and balancing my plate.

"Weston said you're working for Judge Landmark. You should've told us that from the start," Dad says. "He's fair and committed, and from what I've heard, he's done a lot for his community and for this state. I wouldn't be surprised if he ran for office at some point. Your sister has different thoughts about him, but you know how she can be." He chuckles and I look at him in question.

"She doesn't like him?"

"Ahh, you'll have to ask her the specifics. If I recall correctly, she lost her first case when he presided."

I flinch. I remember it clearly now, her losing that first case…I just didn't realize he'd been the judge. I was visiting from school for Christmas right after it happened, and it was all she could talk about. My sister has a way of taking over the conversation when she's having a good day, but when she's having a bad one, *everyone* is going to hear about it… and hear about it…and *hear about it some more*.

"How about we keep it on the down-low that that's where I'll be working?" I suggest.

"Nonsense. You should be proud of this," Mom says. "I guess now would be the only time this position could really work since this time next year, you'll be in law school. What all will you be doing for him?"

I take a huge bite of pizza as she starts her question and prolong the chewing for as long as I can.

"I don't fully know yet. Just seemed like an opportunity I couldn't pass up," I finally say.

"Well, keep us posted," Dad says. "We'll want to hear all about it. Who knows? Maybe we'll get over there occasionally to see you." He grins and I bump his hip with mine.

"On all those days off you're taking?" I tease.

"I'm here right now, aren't I?"

I laugh. "Yes, you are."

I lean my head on his shoulder and then walk over to the island and sit on a stool, digging into the food. My stomach is queasy, but I eat anyway, feeling more and more like a fraud.

It's only for a short time, and then I'll explain everything, I tell myself.

Hopefully they'll never even have to know that this job is not exactly what it seems.

CHAPTER FOUR

HEART TO HEART

SUTTON

Owen has been excited all week about Felicity arriving today. She made quite an impression on him during their first meeting. Each day, he's brought up different activities, asking if I think Felicity would like doing them with him.

My discussion with Tracy didn't go as great. She thinks it's ridiculous that I'm hiring a nanny when I have plenty of family nearby that can help. And she's right. Our family is always willing to help, but everyone is extra busy with building their businesses…and relationships.

I'm the last Landmark down for the count, no love interest options on the horizon for me, and while I know my family would do anything for us, I don't want to ask it of them right now. They've already done their part, going above and beyond when Owen was a baby and Tracy moved out. Tracy hadn't been excited about the pregnancy, but that wasn't really a red flag for either of us. She hoped she'd bond with him when he was born, but it didn't happen. She said she didn't know until having him that she wasn't cut out to be a mother, and as hard as that was to hear, I respected her for telling me the truth. Her desire to be with Owen more hasn't changed much over the years. What started out as fifty-fifty custody quickly changed into her having him less and less.

For years now, she's had Owen every other weekend and for a couple of weeks in the summer. I've worked hard to keep the communication open with Tracy and to never say a negative word about Owen's mother to him, but she's difficult. The bottom line is she doesn't want her son most of the time, but she wants to have a full-time say in what he's doing. I get it because I want that too, but she doesn't get to tell me how to run my life when he's with me. Often it feels like she's using him as a bargaining tool with me, and I'll never be okay with that.

My brothers and sister deserve this time to build their new lives without too much distraction. Within the past year, less than that even, each of them has found their person, and I want their relationships to have a solid foundation, unlike mine and Tracy's.

"Do you think Felicity will like it here, Dad?" Owen asks.

The room over the garage is spacious and has a separate entrance from the rest of the house. It doesn't have a full kitchen, but there's a microwave and a fridge, and the bathroom is nice. Scarlett helped me fix it up a little bit over the past few days. She says it's cute, and I trust my sister's taste.

"She might miss having access to a kitchen up here," I say.

"But she'll be with us all the time and we have a kitchen," he says.

I pause and turn to look at him as he makes sure the TV is *working properly*, his words not mine.

"I wouldn't say *all the time*," I start. "Once I'm home, she can come out here or go into town or whatever she wants to do."

"But you asked her to take care of meals sometimes, so she'll eat dinner with us, right?"

"Well, yes, maybe sometimes…if she wants to. But if she'd rather eat out here, we'll need to be okay with that, okay, son?"

He tilts his head up at me and nods, but his expression is serious.

"I don't have to go to Arizona if I don't want to, do I?" he asks.

"Your mom will want you to come see her sometime in the summer, but she said she'll come here during the school year as much as she can."

He wrinkles his nose. "I don't like leaving you or our family, and I don't like leaving Landmark Mountain." He stands up and kicks the tip of his shoe on the hardwood floor.

I walk over and put my arm around his shoulder. "Your mom loves you and she'll be missing you a lot. I bet there will be things you love about Arizona. You need to give it a try before you decide you don't like it."

He buries his face in my stomach. He's still small for his age. The Landmark boys' growth spurts didn't come until a little late in the game, but once we started growing, we didn't stop until we were beyond six feet. I'm curious to see how it goes for my boy, although I'm in no rush whatsoever for him to grow up.

I hear sniffles and pull back, tilting his chin up. Tears are running down his face and it's so rare that he cries, I find my throat constricting as a lump forms inside.

"Owen, what is it? Talk to me."

He shakes his head and the tears keep falling. I lead him to the chair and sit down, pulling him into my lap. For a few seconds, he leans his head on my shoulder. It reminds me of all the nights I sat with him in the middle of the night, wondering how I could possibly be a good dad to this precious boy but promising him that I'd die trying.

"Mom acts like I'm in the way." It's muffled, his head still against me, but then he pulls back and looks at me. "You know how we have all these new people in our family now?"

I nod, feeling gutted by what he's just said about Tracy, but not wanting to do anything that might keep him from saying what he needs to say.

"They've only been around a little bit," he says, "but I'm more…I-I feel more like *me* around Uncle Jamison and Aunt Sofie and Aunt Marlow and Dakota and Aunt Ruby…"

He lists all the people my siblings are dating or married to, and Dakota, Marlow's little girl, who immediately took to Owen. Over Christmas, it was decided he'd call his aunt and uncles' partners uncle or aunt whether they'd gotten married yet or not. There's no doubt in my mind that it's only a matter of time before Jamison proposes to Scarlett, and Wyatt and Marlow are already engaged.

I'm the oldest of five, but Scarlett was the first one to fall in love, the baby of the family, and I never would've thought I could love the guy she chose as much as I do. He's been a great man for her from the beginning, but my brothers and I had always thought no one would deserve her. We were proven wrong with Jamison Ledger. And then Theo's high school sweetheart came back after eight years. Technically, I guess he was the first one to fall in love way back then. We'd all grieved when she left because she was like family to all of us—but once we knew the reasons behind her leaving and that she was here to stay, we welcomed her back with open arms. Theo and Sofie got married last fall. And in the middle of all that, Wyatt, my middle brother, hit it off with Sofie's best friend Marlow when she moved to town, and she has the cutest daughter in the world, Dakota. That little girl has all of us wrapped around her finger, and I suspect the baby they're expecting will too. Even my grump of a brother Callum has found love now. I would've never believed he'd find someone who made him want to come out of his cave, but Ruby is that person.

And every single one of them has made Owen feel more special than his mother has.

"And Pappy too," he adds.

Pappy is Jamison's grandfather, and we all love the man.

"Can't forget Pappy," I say, sounding choked up. I clear my throat and trace circles on his back. "Have you ever told your mom you feel this way?"

I've tried to talk to Tracy about this before myself, just from seeing how Owen is around her when she comes to pick him up. I've subtly suggested activities I thought they might enjoy doing together, or I've passed along books he likes, thinking she could read them so they'd have something to talk about…anything to develop more of a bond.

"She gets upset when I cry for home, so I try to not cry in front of her."

"I didn't know you cry for home. Why didn't you tell me?"

His little shoulder lifts and he lays his head back on my chest. "I didn't want you to think I'm a baby. And Jeff was okay. I wish they weren't getting a divorce. He was fun sometimes, but now that he's gone, it'll just be me and Mom again, and I don't—"

I wait, but he doesn't say anything.

"It sounds like we should have a talk with your mom. Would you be okay with that?"

"Would you ask her if I can just stay with you?"

My heart cracks a little more. "I think it'd be better if we talk about this, see if your relationship can get better. I don't want you to have any regrets later about missing out on time with your mom."

"I really don't want to go to Arizona," he says, his voice breaking again.

"It wouldn't be for long, son, but if you feel the same way when that time comes, we'll figure something out with your mom. I'll go with you or ask her to keep coming here. I don't want you to be anywhere that you're not comfortable."

"Thanks, Dad." He wipes his nose on the back of his hand, and I point to the tissues next to the bed.

"Why don't you go grab one of those tissues and then wash your hands? We don't want to spread germs in Miss Felicity's clean room."

"Do I have to call her Miss Felicity? She didn't say that the other day," Owen says, hopping up to do what I asked.

"I'll leave that up to her."

"Will she be here soon? I'm ready for her to get here." He stands in front of me and looks lighter already, his excitement about Felicity back in full force.

I glance at my watch and nod. "Pretty soon. Why don't we head to the house so we hear when she arrives?"

Owen bounds to the door and we jog down the stairs, just as a car and SUV pull into the driveway.

Proof that I've been too preoccupied with thoughts of Felicity since seeing her for the first time: I forgot all about her brother being Weston fucking Shaw, the best quarterback the Mustangs have had in years, until he steps out of the SUV and walks toward me.

It's still not enough to distract me from his beautiful sister heading my way.

CHAPTER FIVE

TWERPS AND BACKSIDES

FELICITY

Sutton and Owen are there to meet us when we get to the house. I practically swallow my tongue when I see Sutton in jeans and a black sweater. Saturday Sutton is even hotter than Tuesday Sutton and I didn't think that one could get any better.

Owen is the first to reach me, and he's adorable with his wide smile, hazel eyes that light up his whole face, and long, dreamy eyelashes.

"Hi, Felicity," he says excitedly. "Or should I call you Miss Felicity?"

"Absolutely not," I say, laughing. "Call me Felicity. And this is my brother, Weston."

"Hi, Weston," he says. "Wait. *Weston Shaw?*"

"That's me." Weston laughs. "Nice to meet you, Owen." He holds out his fist and bumps it against Owen's.

Owen stares at Weston in shock and glances over at his dad. "Wow."

Sutton smiles at him and Weston and then at me. "Afternoon, Felicity."

I say something resembling a hello. I've been a nervous wreck since Weston insisted on coming to help me get settled into my "apartment." I then had to clarify that it was just a room over a garage, specifically *Sutton's* garage.

I am not cut out for all this covert behavior.

Reason number six hundred and seventy-nine that I am not cut out to be a lawyer.

Sutton reaches out to shake Weston's hand. "Sutton Landmark. It's nice to meet you, Weston Shaw. Thank you for making it fun to watch the Mustangs again. My son and I are big fans as you can probably tell."

"Thanks, man." Weston's smile is easy, completely unaware that I'm over here freaking out about my whole cover getting blown.

Owen bounces up and down. "I cannot believe I'm meeting Weston Shaw," he says in one fast, breathless sentence. "This is *so* cool."

Weston chuckles and Owen is still looking up at Weston like he's going to preserve this moment in time forever.

And Sutton *is* a football fan. We didn't talk about it during either interview, so I wasn't sure. Since being back in Colorado, anyone who hears my name for the first time asks if I'm related to Weston Shaw. Since Henley is also on the team and is the one who told me about this job, I should've realized Sutton already knew I was Weston's sister.

"We've got a great team this year. I couldn't do it without my guys," Weston says.

"Henley Ward is a friend of mine, and he doesn't say anything negative about anyone…but I can tell you he's fuu—reaking happy you're giving him something to work with." Sutton chuckles, glancing over at Owen.

Owen holds out his hand and Sutton reaches into his pocket, tossing a quarter that Owen catches in mid-air. He glances at Sutton expectantly and Sutton shakes his head, laughing.

"You're lucky you got that much—I didn't say the word," Sutton says, lifting his shoulders.

Owen's eyes are full of mischief as he pockets the quarter.

"It was implied," he says.

It was implied? I bite the inside of my mouth to keep from laughing. This kid is smart!

Sutton wrangles Owen back to him, tickling his side. "Can't get anything past this guy," he says.

"Next time just go ahead and say the swear so I can get a dollar," Owen says, laughing as he gets out of Sutton's reach.

"My brother's fiancée has a four-year-old daughter, and since they got here, she's been cleaning up our language," Sutton explains. "I'm about to go broke now that this one's caught on."

"I totally missed whatever you said," I say, laughing.

"Eagle ears didn't," Sutton mutters, pretending to be annoyed, which cracks Owen up.

God, they are so cute together. How will I not dissolve into mush every time I'm around the two of them?

And note to self: *Clean up your shitty language.*

"Can we help you with your stuff?" Owen asks.

"Oh, I think Weston and I can get it all, but thank you," I say.

I need to limit the time my brother is around Sutton and Owen before he realizes I'm just the nanny.

"Nonsense," Sutton says.

"Please, we want to help," Owen chimes in.

"See? We want to help." Sutton grins. "What all do you have?"

"Not much," I say, just as Weston says, "A ton."

I roll my eyes at him and he smirks, lifting his shoulders.

"What? You brought an entire library," he says.

"Never too many books," I say.

Weston pops the trunk on his SUV and is already pulling out boxes. When Owen jogs over to help, Weston hands him a tall lamp.

"Yeah, but does everyone also bring their own fancy reading lamp to a fully furnished place?" Weston teases.

"You got that?" he asks Owen.

Owen nods, his brows and mouth puckering with the effort of lifting the lamp.

"People who aren't jocks do," I tease under my breath to Weston, but Sutton hears me and I see the corners of his mouth twitch.

When Weston's reaching in to get something else, I do the slight kick behind his knees that gets him every time, and sure enough, his legs jolt forward. This time, Sutton laughs out loud and the swarm of flutters in my chest take flight at the sound. I think I stare at him for a full ten seconds without moving. His eyes crinkle up at the sides and his teeth are extra white against the scruff on his cheeks. Scruff that I bet only makes an appearance on the weekends.

"Yep, you're gonna hit it off with my little sister Scarlett," he says, still laughing.

"Oh, how old is she? Does she live around here?"

"She's older than you…twenty-three."

"Not by much," I say.

"The little twerp is a pain in my backside, but I love her," he says.

"Sounds familiar," Weston mutters, giving me a pointed look.

I don't love the way this conversation is going. My brother is a measly three years older than me, so he can back the hell off of sounding like an authority on age, and I still have no idea how old Sutton is, but I'd rather him not think of me as a kid.

Sutton chuckles. "You guys remind me of us. And yes, all my siblings are here in Landmark Mountain," Sutton adds. "You'll meet them and their significant others soon."

But do you *have a significant other* is what I want to know.

"Is Scarlett the youngest?" I ask.

"Yes, and I'm the oldest, with three brothers between Scarlett and me." He hefts a heavy box of books up like it's nothing and walks toward the stairs leading to my room.

Weston sets the boxes of books and clothes on the ground and takes the bookshelf out. "I'll take this up there first and then you can start organizing your books," he says.

"Thanks, West."

"Nice guy," he says, nodding toward Sutton. "Much more laid-back than what I was expecting from a judge," he says under his breath. "Is it going to be weird for you though? Living so close and working with him?"

I turn before he sees my flushed cheeks and pick up a couple of boxes, following him. "Nah. I'll have space."

When I saw where I'd be staying the other day, I was relieved I wouldn't be staying in the main house. It'll be nice to come and go without running into anyone when I have free time.

Owen has the lamp plugged in and it's right where I wanted it—by the comfortable chair. The place is simple and cozy, with a queen bed and a single barstool by the counter. A pretty picture of wildflowers in the valley of gorgeous mountain peaks hangs near the counter, and when I step closer, I see Sutton's name on the lower right side.

"You're a photographer?" I ask.

He looks slightly embarrassed, a dimple tucking in when he smiles. "I dabble," he says. "Scarlett insisted on hanging that in here," he adds gruffly.

"It's *beautiful*," I say.

"Dad won awards for his photography," Owen says.

"In another life," Sutton says.

I can tell it's making him uncomfortable to talk about himself, but I want to know all the things.

"My two favorites are in my room," Owen adds. "They're *awesome*. One of them is at the top of those mountains right there," he points out the window, "and you can see our house and our family resort and *all* of Landmark Mountain." He grins up at his dad.

"My one and only fan right here," Sutton says, ruffling Owen's hair.

"Not true. *Everyone* loves your pictures, Dad. And then the other one in my room is of Lucia and Delgado," Owen tells me. "They're the best. Well, Fred is too, but I don't think Dad has taken a picture of Fred yet." He frowns at Sutton. "You should take a picture of Fred."

Sutton laughs and squeezes Owen's shoulder, leading him out the door. "You're right. Can't leave Fred out."

"Lucia and Delgado and Fred are my aunts' and uncles' dogs," Owen says over his shoulder as I follow them down the steps. "Lucia and Delgado belong to Aunt Scarlett and her boyfriend Uncle Jamison—so, he's not really my uncle yet, but I think he will be one day, so that's why I said *uncles*. And Fred belongs to Uncle Theo and Aunt Sofie...they're married now, so she really is my aunt."

"Someone is excited you're here," Sutton leans over and whispers once we're walking toward the SUV, and I feel a trace of his warm breath against my skin.

There's so much Owen said that I need to unpack. They have a family resort? And all the names. I need a chart to know who's who. But for now, all I know is that every hair follicle stands on end when Sutton whispers in my ear.

"I really, really, *really* want my own dog," Owen says. "And I've finally got my dad talked into it too." He glances back at Sutton, a worried look on his face. "See? I *can't* go to Arizona," he says quietly.

"We've got some things to figure out, buddy," Sutton says.

Owen freezes and looks stricken and then his eyes fill with tears. He takes off running toward the house.

Sutton's expression is grave when his eyes meet mine and he shakes his head. "He's not normally like this, but there's a lot going on right now. I'll explain more later. I better see about him. I'm sorry to bail on the unloading. Hopefully this won't take long."

"Oh no, please don't worry about this. There's not much more. Go be with Owen. I hope he's okay."

I watch as he hurries to the house and Weston moves next to me.

"Kids, man. Good thing you'll have your own place and

will be spending most of your time at the courthouse," he says under his breath.

I've said nothing about working at the courthouse, but as soon as Weston heard *judge*, he's assumed that's what my job entails.

How wrong is it to lie by omission?

"He's a sweet kid," I say quietly, wondering what's going on and if I'll know how to help Owen when it's just the two of us.

CHAPTER SIX

OKAY, MAYBE I AM

SUTTON

I find Owen in his room, sitting on his bed. He puts his fists over his eyes and wipes them.

"Sorry, Dad," he says. "I don't know why this is happening today."

"You never need to be sorry for how you're feeling. And knowing you're worrying about this move of your mom's just lets me know I need to talk to her. I'll call her tonight, okay? I want to put your mind at ease."

He nods. "Okay. But even if I have to go see her sometimes, can I still have a dog?"

I groan. "Can we see how things work with Felicity helping out around here first?"

Part of my hesitation in getting a puppy has been trying to train one with my unpredictable schedule, but having another adult around would help…if Felicity is even agreeable to being around dogs.

"Okay," Owen says, nodding excitedly. "I think she'll be great, and we should see if she likes dogs."

I sigh, knowing I can't resist this boy and his desire for a dog for very much longer.

"Do you think she saw me cry?" Owen asks softly.

"I don't know, but it's all right if she did. You don't have anything to be embarrassed about, okay?"

"Yeah. Let's go back out there and help. I only took up the lamp and there's probably lots more to do."

"We should give her time on her own to get settled too, but you're right…we can make sure everything's unloaded first."

He's already out the door and in the hall when he calls out, "Come on, Dad."

I brace myself on the doorjamb and follow him out, and we help with a few more boxes.

Weston heads back to Silver Hills for a party, but before he leaves, he invites Owen and me to the divisional round game against Houston in a couple of weeks. I tell him we'll be there, and then Owen and I go pick up food from Sunny Side. When we get back, it's dark, but the lights are bright enough to see Felicity near the gate overlooking the water. Her long blonde hair lifts with the wind and she wraps her arms around her sides.

We grew up in this house—the Summit House. When my parents got married, Granddad and Grinny moved from the big house to the smaller Alpine House on the same extensive property and gave my parents this place. When my parents died, Granddad and Grinny moved back in with us and stayed until I married Tracy. I tried to give the house back to them when Tracy and I divorced, but they wanted Owen to be raised here like I was.

My siblings and I learned to swim before we could talk because of all the water surrounding the side of the house. I've added a ton of lights along the edge of the water, but I'm still not comfortable having a bunch of kids over here. When Owen has a play date with a friend from school or Dakota, I take them to play at our family resort or the park.

With every person I interviewed, one of the first questions I asked was, *"What kind of swimmer are you?"* Felicity said she's an *excellent* swimmer, and I assured her that Owen is too, but that I still watch him like a hawk when he's outside.

I'll have to reiterate how important it is for her to never let her guard down when he's outside, but even as I'm thinking it, I'm telling myself to relax. I'm a control freak and an overprotective dad who's had to mostly do this on my own. Even admitting that I need help is hard for me.

Felicity turns when she hears our doors slam and walks toward us, running her hands up and down her arms.

"It got a lot chillier when the sun went down," she says. "Something smells really good."

"Sunny Side," Owen says, holding up the bag of burgers and fries.

"Would you like to eat with us tonight? You're always welcome to, but I don't want you to feel like you have to when it's your day off or…anytime you don't…just do what's most comfortable for you." It's awkward, but I felt like I needed to get that out of the way right from the get-go.

"With you guys would be great," she says easily. "Thanks for the food."

We go inside the house from the side and walk into the kitchen. Felicity looks around as we place the bags and shakes on the table.

"Is this your family?" she asks, pointing at the framed picture by the desk where Owen does his homework.

"That's at Uncle Theo and Aunt Sofie's wedding," Owen says. "And my Uncle Callum just got married too, but we don't have pictures yet." He points out who everyone is, and she stares at the picture for a long time, a smile playing on her lips.

"Beautiful family," she says.

She glances around and sits down at the table. I pass her food to her and she thanks me again.

"Do you have a housekeeper?" she asks.

"I wish," Owen says, sighing.

I nudge his elbow with mine. "I thought I'd convinced you to enjoy cleaning," I tease. To Felicity, I say, "We do not. It's rare for us to have anyone besides family in our home. But they're over plenty, aren't they?"

"Lots," Owen says.

"Well, I'm impressed with how clean your house is…at least the rooms I've seen. I can help too—I like to clean."

Owen's eyes light up. "Do you like cleaning toilets? Because that's the worst!"

Felicity and I both laugh.

"You're not getting out of cleaning the toilet when it's

your week, son. Your future spouse will thank me for it."

Felicity's eyes are warm when she glances at me. "Add me to the schedule," she says. "I want to do my part around here."

Conversation is easy between the three of us. With Owen around, it wouldn't be any other way. He's happy to have her here, all his earlier angst has dissipated, and Felicity seems to love getting to know him.

We go over the upcoming week's schedule, and I assure her that her time off on Saturdays and Sundays can be spent completely free of any work. I reiterate that she can use the kitchen as her own, anytime. When she yawns a little later, admitting she didn't sleep much the night before, I stand and clear the table.

"Let me give you my cell number before you head out for the night," I tell her. "And please, let me know if you need anything."

"We usually do pancakes on Sunday mornings," Owen says.

I give her an apologetic smile. "She probably wants her rest on Sunday mornings," I tell Owen.

She lifts a shoulder and smiles at both of us. "Pancakes sound great. What time?"

"Eight," Owen says.

"*If* you're awake and feel like it, you're more than welcome," I tell her. "No pressure." I squeeze Owen's shoulder as I say it and he just grins up at me.

We exchange numbers and Owen and I walk her to the door.

"Goodnight, you two," she says.

"Goodnight," we echo, both watching her out the window until she's out of sight.

"I like her," Owen says softly.

When I don't say anything, he looks up at me.

"Do you like her too?"

"I do."

"Mm-hmm."

We go through his nighttime routine and once he's in bed, I can't put it off any longer—I pick up the phone and call Tracy.

"Hey," she answers.

I can usually tell by Tracy's tone whether she's going to be snippy or flirty or—on the rare occasion, vulnerable.

It's easiest to deal with her when she's vulnerable, but tonight sounds like the snippy variety.

"I hoped we could talk about Owen," I start.

"We can always talk about Owen." She sighs, already sounding defensive, and I sit down in a chair in the living room, telling myself to be patient for Owen's sake.

"He has reservations about visiting you in Arizona, and I thought we could come up with some ways to make him more comfortable before the summer."

"Well, I'm sure after the first visit, he'll be just fine, Sutton. And that won't be for another, what—five months?"

"He's worried about it now," I say.

"What kind of *reservations* does he have?"

"I'm sure they're typical nerves about going to a new place. He's…not excited about the move and doesn't want to leave Landmark Mountain, so I think just telling him about the fun things you'll do when he visits, that type of thing."

"You coddle him, Sutton. And I shouldn't have to blackmail him with fun activities to excite him to see me. He should just be happy to spend time with me. He's overstimulated ninety percent of the time, with all the running around you have him doing. A little downtime with me is good for him."

I slide my hand down my face, determined not to argue with her. "I'm not saying you need to schedule every second of his time there. He's happy doing simple things. Talk to him about books he likes. Let him pick out a movie now and then. Just anything to make him feel like you're invested in him."

"Invested in him? I'm his *mother*. Of course, I'm invested in him. And you always say that about books like I have any time to read. I don't have a jillion family members on hand to take him, Sutton. Or a full-time *nanny*. When he visits, I'll be taking time off of my new job and I'll make sure he has fun. Okay?"

She makes it sound like I'm never with him…like someone besides me takes him to school and makes his dinner and puts him to bed. Grinny picks him up from school most days, and the guilt I feel over that is acute. It's important to me that he knows he's my priority. And I didn't hire Felicity because I want out of any of those things. *I just need the fucking help.*

"You never told me he still cries for me when he's with you."

"What the fuck is this, Sutton? I'm moving and now you're going to lay even more guilt on me than you already do? He cries because I don't *spoil* him."

"I've never tried to lay guilt on you. If that's what you think this is, I apologize. I do want to communicate about our son, and I'm telling you, he doesn't want to come to Arizona. So, either you talk to him and work on making it good for him when he's there, or I will be coming with him to make sure he's not uncomfortable…and if you don't like those options, you can come here to visit him this summer."

The silence builds for so long that I look at my phone.

She hung up on me.

I slam the phone down on the table next to me and find

myself hoping Felicity *does* come for pancakes in the morning.

I tell myself my desire for her to show up has nothing to do with me, and everything to do with not wanting my son to be disappointed.

CHAPTER SEVEN

SUNDAY FUNDAY

FELICITY

I just thought Saturday Sutton was a dream, until I see Sunday Sutton. When Owen excitedly opens the door and high-fives me, I look up to see Sutton standing in front of a long griddle flipping pancakes with an apron that has an emu on it saying, *Do I look emused?* His hair is messier than usual, and that scruff is even more pronounced today.

I feel like a cat flopping around in catnip with every new look he rolls out.

"That apron is fantastic," I say, laughing.

He makes a face. "My sister-in-law Ruby gave it to me for Christmas, and Owen loves it. Don't get me wrong, I'm very fond of Ruby and her emus, but I'm not sure this is my look."

"Oh, it's definitely your look," I tell him.

His eyebrows lift as he smiles at me. For the briefest moment, his eyes sweep down the length of me and back up, sending heat flickering through me, but then his jaw clenches and he looks down at the pancakes. His next pancake flip looks more like a slam dunk.

Well, that was weird.

"So, when you say Ruby and her emus…is that her clothing line or something?"

"Sort of," Owen pipes up. "She has emus *and* emu merch!"

Sutton laughs. "Listen to you, all up on the influencer lingo…*merch*." He chuckles again.

"Wait. Are you talking about Ruby Sunshine, the influencer with the emus and lumberjack boyfriend?" I ask.

"Yep, she's married to my brother Callum," he says. "The lumberjack." His smirk is so sexy I stutter on my next words.

"So, so c-crazy. I've followed her for a while. I can't believe that's your family. Small world. I've never seen an emu in person before." I let out a sharp exhale.

"They're my new favorite animal," Owen says. "We'll have to go over there so you can meet them. They're so funny when they run like this." He weaves across the room, looking like a drunk person.

He looks so pleased when I laugh at him, he does the same thing toward me, laughing and coming to an abrupt stop when he reaches me.

"You're hilarious. I've gotta see that," I tell him.

He nods happily. "They have cows and goats too, and Aunt Sof's got horses."

"And Aunt Scarlett has the dogs?" I attempt to get it right.

"Yep, and Uncle Theo does too."

"Does…who's left—Uncle Wyatt? Does he have pets? Or Grinny?"

"Nope. Uncle Wyatt says he takes care of too many people in the hospital to come home and take care of a pet—he's a doctor—but Dakota wants a pet real bad, so Dad and I think it won't be long before they get one."

He looks back at his dad and Sutton smiles at him.

"And I dog-sit sometimes," Owen adds. "Dad's making sure I'm able to take care of dogs before we get one of our own. Do you love dogs?"

"I do," I say. "But I've never had one of my own."

"She loves dogs," Owen yells back at his dad.

"I heard," Sutton says, amused.

"I bet you'd be a good pet owner," Owen says, nodding. "I mean, if my dad trusts you to take care of me, I bet you'd be even better with a dog."

I laugh. "Well, thanks for your vote of confidence. I'd like to think I would be."

I glance at Sutton again and his eyes meet mine, more serious than I'd expect, given this conversation. I feel overheated in my fluffy white sweater and jeans. He clears his throat and holds up a plate piled high with pancakes.

"Who's ready for pancakes?"

"Me," Owen yells.

"Me," I pipe up.

Sutton carries them to the table and nods toward the coffeepot. "I forgot to mention the coffee and there's juice on the table."

I grab a mug and pour a cup of coffee, adding cream and

sugar before I take it to the table. When I sit in the same spot as I did last night, Owen looks over at me and beams. He takes my hand, something he didn't do last night, and then takes his dad's. Sutton looks uncomfortable for a moment when Owen tilts his head for him to take my other hand.

"Uh, right," Sutton says.

Is that okay? His eyes ask, and I nod.

He holds out his hand and I clasp it, while Owen closes his eyes and says, "Thank you for this food and for Dad who made it and for Felicity who's living here now…and help us to have a good day and lots of fun and send all the dogs our way. Amen."

When Owen opens his eyes, he glances at me and leans closer. "On Sundays, I say grace."

I nod solemnly. "I like it."

He grins and I can't keep a straight face when he's looking at me like that.

"I especially liked the dog part," I whisper.

"Me too." He giggles and Sutton groans.

"I can already tell I'm gonna be ganged up on quite often," Sutton says.

Owen just laughs as he takes a huge bite of pancakes, his gaze meeting mine conspiratorially, and I get warm fuzzies over how sweet he is.

This is already the most fun I've had in a long time.

After a delightful breakfast where I try not to stare at Sutton too much and laugh nonstop at all the funny things Owen says, I ask if it's okay if I make a dessert for later.

"Of course. Do I need to pick up anything from the store?" Sutton asks.

"Can I look in your pantry?"

He grins and holds his arm out. "Have at it."

I called my mother twice earlier about this pie, just to make sure I really have it right.

"Yes," she'd said, laughing. "I've made it your whole life this way. It's that simple and it's right."

"And I really don't open the can?" I asked again. "You're *positive*?"

"No. You really don't. I'm positive!"

I find what I need and get started on the pie, making sure the water is high enough and the stove is on low when I put the can in the pan. Then I throw on my coat and boots to go grab my planner from my room when Sutton wants to discuss Owen's schedule. I'm happy about this—we barely scratched the surface last night. I could've put everything in my phone, but I like my massive planner where I write down every minute detail. It's half-calendar, half-creative journal, pages filled with pictures I love or doodles I draw and quotes I like, but it's what keeps me on track with *everything*. I'm lost without it.

I already have *Breakfast with Sutton and Owen* in this morning's time slot, and when I grab the bag of erasable colored pens that I use to fill in my planner and rush back to their kitchen, Sutton's eyes widen and Owen says, "Wow, what is *that*?"

Suddenly feeling about twelve, I glance at the planner I created. I can never find one that fits all my needs, so I make my own, and now I'm having second thoughts about exposing the level of my need for organization.

Sutton simply goes to the computer sitting at the built-in desk in the kitchen and opens up the calendar, handing me a small sticky note with the Wi-Fi and password.

"I didn't know you'd be so old school," Sutton teases, nodding at my planner. "But feel free to also use this computer whenever you need. I try to make sure all upcoming dates are in here and I'll add your email too, so you have full access," he says.

I nod and decide I'll add all the dates to my planner later.

"Besides wanting to give Grinny more of a break in the afternoons, I have a case coming up that might mean earlier mornings than I've had in a while. The bus comes early if I'm not able to take him, but if I have an extra hand getting him on the bus, that'll help a lot."

"Of course. I don't mind taking him too."

"That'd be great. He doesn't love the bus."

Owen makes a face and shakes his head.

"And the days I have a lighter schedule, I can pick him up, but as I said, it might be a little chaotic for the upcoming weeks, even in the afternoons," Sutton says. He glances at Owen. "I'll try my best to make it to all your hockey games and practices, but Felicity may have to get you there some of the time if I'm running late."

Owen nods like they've already discussed this.

Sutton glances at me again and then points out the Wednesday night and Saturday morning practices. "I can handle Saturdays with no problem, but Wednesdays are sometimes challenging. He likes to skate after school on Mondays and Tuesdays too, but I'll let you guys decide the days you want to do that. There might be other things you'd rather do, and that's fine, but it's an option. Games are typically Thursday nights or Sundays. During the week, I can let you know if it seems I might not be there to get him to the rink early enough, and then once I arrive, you're free to go. Does that seem doable?"

"Absolutely," I respond.

I feel Owen's shoulder sag next to me and I glance at him, seeing disappointment on his face. I frown.

"Am I not allowed to stay for the practices and games?" I ask.

Owen's eyebrows lift. "You can totally stay," he says.

My heart melts when I see his hopeful expression.

"Oh, well, then yeah. I'll just do that, especially on the days when I'm already taking you."

"Really?" Owen's eyes are like tiny starbursts, they're shining so bright. He's practically vibrating, and Sutton gives me a look I can't quite decipher.

"How about we wait and see how you feel about that once you're there?" he says quietly.

I feel reprimanded for some reason. It makes me wonder if I'll run into Owen's mom at the games and if that will be a problem, but Sutton mentioned something in our interview about her taking a job in Arizona. It must be a short-term thing though—I can't imagine her moving that far away permanently.

"Okay, sure." I shrug.

After we've worked on the schedule, they show me the rest of the house, how to work the remote, and a few ideas of what Owen likes to eat. I also find out Sutton is partial to Italian and Mediterranean food, which is fortunate, since I have a few favorite dishes that I think he'll enjoy. Over the next couple of hours, I keep checking the stovetop. The crust is ready, and everything else should be soon too.

We're playing a game of Bananagrams at the table when an ear-piercing explosion goes off.

"Get down," Sutton yells, pulling me and Owen under the table.

He looks us both over carefully to make sure we're okay before carefully peering over the table to look out the window. Owen reaches over and grabs my hand and I pull him next to me. I glance back at the window myself and don't see anything suspicious.

Sutton stands up and walks to the door and is about to open it when I hear him say, "Holy shit."

And then he lets out a laugh so loud, Owen and I stare at each other with wide eyes before carefully crawling out from under the table.

"It's okay." Sutton barely manages to get the words out. "You can get up." He starts laughing again and I look around, trying to figure out what's so funny.

I gasp. "Oh no," I cry, rushing to the stove to turn off the burner.

Caramel drips from every surface of the kitchen. Even the ceiling has patches of caramel. The can of sweetened condensed milk *exploded*.

"I'm so sorry. I can't believe it. I asked my mom over and over if this was the right way to make this caramel pie and she swore it is." I want to cry, but it's also hilarious, and when I look at Sutton, he's wiping his eyes from laughing so hard.

He meets my eyes and then comes over and sticks his finger in a big glob of it and licks it.

"Mmm, it is good," he wheezes.

I lose it then, and even more when Owen joins in, sliding his fingers in as much caramel as he can reach.

"It's one of my favorite pies," I say, when I catch my breath. "That I will never attempt to make again."

Just then, a dollop plops onto the end of my nose from the ceiling.

We stare at each other in shock for a few seconds before the three of us die laughing.

"I'd eat it," Sutton says, his eyes all lit up as he tries to hold in his laugh. "But I'll let you enjoy that." He points to my nose.

I apologize over and over as we start cleaning it up, and he tells me I don't need to apologize. Finally, when I apologize yet again, he says, "Felicity, I can't remember when I've laughed this hard."

"Never," Owen yells, laughing.

"Thank you," Sutton says so only I can hear, his expression so sweet.

Later that afternoon, after I've been on a ladder trying to clean the ceiling, there's a knock at the door. Amusement flickers across Sutton's face when he hears the door and I think he's going to start laughing again about the caramel because every now and then, one of us will start giggling again. This time, he makes a sound between a groan and a laugh.

"I have a pretty good idea of who this will be," he says, crossing the room to open the door.

Owen runs over and laughs in delight when the door opens wide, revealing Grinny and then what I imagine must be the entire Landmark family. They just keep trickling in. I'm still a little sketchy on everyone's names, but I recognize the faces from the wedding picture on the desk.

"When you said you were missing family dinner, we decided to come to you instead," Grinny says.

"Did you now?" Sutton says, laughing.

"We knew you'd do the same if you were in our shoes," Scarlett says, winking. She walks over to me and holds out her hand. "Hi, I'm Scarlett."

"I'm Felicity."

"Isn't she lovely?" Grinny says, smiling over at me.

"Absolutely beautiful," Scarlett says, grinning. "Sof,

Marlow, Ruby," she calls, glancing around and waving her arm for them to join us, "come meet Felicity."

They rush over and introduce themselves, and then the brothers and Jamison, Scarlett's boyfriend, come over one by one, introducing themselves. Once they pair off with their significant others, it's easier to tell who's who. I'm blown away by how gorgeous everyone is...and how *nice* they are. Even the brother that Sutton says usually only grumble-speaks, Callum, is really sweet and friendly.

When Marlow's little girl Dakota sees me, she gasps and clutches her heart. At first, I'm concerned for her, but then she says, "You're even prettier than Elsa!"

Owen leans over to whisper, "She's still in a *Frozen* phase."

"Elsa the *princess*?" I clarify.

"Yes," she says, nodding earnestly.

"I didn't even know I needed validation like that, but wow, way to give a girl a boost," I tell her.

"*And* she likes dogs," I hear Owen telling Scarlett and Sofie later. "She's *so* cool."

Okay, now *that* might be the best compliment I've ever been given.

"What are these brown spots over here?" Scarlett asks, pointing to a place we missed.

I groan and Sutton laughs.

"Try it, you'll like it," he says.

She looks at him like he's crazy, and he looks over at me and winks.

Okay, it's official. I've got it *bad* for Sutton Landmark.

CHAPTER EIGHT

THE BURDEN BAG

SUTTON

I chuckle to myself as the noise in my house goes up by several decibels. It doesn't surprise me at all that my entire family showed up. Hell, I should've expected it. Being the oldest, I can be a bit of a shit-stirrer with my siblings. They just make it so damn easy.

I'd say payback's a bitch, but when the payback is a night with my family, you won't find me complaining one bit. I don't care how meddlesome they are, they're my favorite people in the whole world.

And Felicity seems right at home.

Figures she would be since she's close to the same age as Scarlett and Ruby...and not too far off from Sofie and Marlow either.

I have to remind my brothers of that when they huddle around me later, giving me not-so-subtle eyebrow lifts and nudges in my side.

"She's great," Wyatt starts.

"I see you picked the beautiful one," Theo says under his breath. He was over here one day when I showed him the long list of people I was considering.

"Don't make it gross," I snap.

He looks wounded for a second and then laughs, holding up his hands. "I'm just proud you didn't *not* pick her for that reason. Knowing you, that seems more like something you'd do," he says.

"Hell, yeah, you would," Wyatt agrees, laughing. "She fits right in."

"Get your mind out of the gutter, you guys. She's younger than Scarlett," I hiss between my teeth.

"Owen's crazy about her already," Callum says.

I glare at him. "I expect it out of them, not you too."

He lifts a shoulder, smirking. *Bastard*.

"Will she be taking you to any games?" Jamison asks, grinning.

Jamison's brother is Zac Ledger, the GOAT of football, but I've even heard Zac say that Weston Shaw is the most talented player he's seen in a long time.

"It has come up," I say, relenting to a small smile then. "Weston helped her move in yesterday. Nice guy. Invited Owen and me to a game."

"That's more like it. It won't hurt you to have a little fun," Wyatt says.

"There will be no *fun* of the variety your dirty minds are thinking," I say, pointing at each one of them. "She's here to do a job and was the best qualified for it. Please don't make this weird."

"I was actually just teasing when I started," Wyatt says, pointing back at me, "but then the way you got defensive so quickly makes me think…" He juts his lips out and lifts his hands up and down like he's weighing something.

I give him enough of a shove that he stumbles back and he just laughs. I glance over his shoulder at the women across the room and he smirks.

"They're not hearing any of this, don't worry," he says. "Owen is also out of earshot."

"You're being ridiculous," I grumble. "And I'm being defensive because I knew you'd take one look at her and go there."

"You're making us sound skeevy, and we're not," Wyatt argues. "We're just ready to see you happy too, and we know better than anyone that it takes a lot for you to trust anyone with Owen. He's eight years old and this is the first time you've hired someone. So, I'd say she's already been thoroughly vetted and passed inspection." He laughs again when I glare at him.

"Sorry, brother," Theo says sheepishly. He's the tenderheart of the family and I squeeze his shoulder, letting him know we're fine.

I'm fine with all of them, but I want them to shut their fucking mouths and not make this a thing.

"You know you'd be doing the same thing if the roles were reversed. You *have* done the same thing to all of us," Wyatt says, laughing.

He's right about that.

"And what would be the harm if you *were* interested in something with her?" he whispers.

I look again to make sure no one else is anywhere close to hearing this conversation. Ruby says something and they all crack up, Felicity's head falling back as she laughs. My hands fist and uncurl when I see Owen and Dakota over by her, laughing too.

I look at my brothers and Jamison. "I'll say this once. I'm a judge. I have a moral responsibility to behave ethically. She's taking care of my son. She's thirteen years younger and fresh out of college. There's no fucking way anything will be happening between us. End of story."

"Wow, you've really mathed that out," Wyatt says.

When I glare at him yet again, he just shrugs with his dumb smirk.

But as I watch Felicity chatter easily with my family the rest of the night, my nerve endings on alert, I can literally *feel* where she is in the room at all times.

This day with her has been one of the best days I can remember.

I realize what I told my brothers was more for *my* benefit than theirs.

Nothing can happen.

The next morning, after tossing and turning all night, I'm up and ready for the day an hour earlier than usual. As I get my laptop and some files together, I notice that the light over the garage is on. It's still an hour and a half before Owen has to leave for school, so when he comes out of his room already dressed too, I call it.

"Happy Cow this morning?" I ask.

"Yes!" he yells, doing a little jump and hip bump against me. "Let's ask Felicity."

"Oh, I thought we could go and come back. We can get something for her."

"But if she goes with us, we can find out what she likes, and she needs to meet Lar and Mar," Owen says.

"It's so much earlier than we told her to be ready though." I shake my head. The plan is for us to drop off Owen together so she knows where the school is, and then I'll drop her back at the house afterwards and be on my way to work.

Owen's already looking out the window.

"But her light is on," he says.

"She's going to need time to herself sometimes too, son," I remind him.

Owen gasps. "She just walked outside!"

"She did?"

I'm torn between telling him to stop watching her and asking what she's doing. My brain trips over itself and I don't say anything.

"She's stretching," he says. "Come on, let's see if she wants to go with us."

He's pulled on his coat and is out there before I can stop him, and I groan. We'll need a more in-depth conversation about boundaries.

I grab my leather briefcase, the last gift from my granddad before he passed. When I step outside, I'm reminded of what he told me when he gave it to me. I've thought about it often, depending on how heavy my workload or the gravity of the case I'm working on.

But now, with Felicity's ass in the air, exquisitely wrapped in skintight yoga pants as she bends down to touch her toes, I find myself thinking about what he said for different reasons.

"When I saw what this briefcase was called, I knew it was for you. The Beast of Burden," Granddad said, chuckling. *"Could anything be more fitting for you, son? You don't make any decision lightly."* He shook his head and there was a glint in his eyes when he looked at me then. *"Keep trusting your gut. Your brain is sharp and wise, but let* this *carry the load."* He held up the bag when he said that last part and squeezed my shoulder. *"Lord knows you had to grow up faster than you should've, and when you become a judge—well, I just hope that every time you leave the courtroom, you'll remember to be that carefree boy you keep buried way down deep inside."*

Fuck me.

I can be carefree all day long when it comes to pushing Owen or my siblings to live their best lives, but when it comes to me, I don't have that luxury. Granddad and Grinny aren't the only ones who made sacrifices when my parents died. I did too, and I have no regrets about the way it shaped my life. It was my honor to help carry the load of raising my brothers and sister along with them. The *only* thing I'd change would be to have my mom and dad back.

I'll miss them every day of my life.

"Good morning," Owen calls out.

"Oh, hey." Felicity smiles at us with her head between her legs, still upside down.

My stomach hollows out, dick standing at attention despite the heaviness of my thoughts.

Felicity stands upright and tugs the bottom of her fitted ski jacket, her blonde waves cascading over her shoulders and down her back. She stands out like technicolor in a black-and-white film.

"You guys are ready bright and early," she says.

"We're heading to Happy Cow. Wanna come?" Owen asks, his cheeks rosy from the cold.

"Sure. I don't know what that is, but it sounds fun," she says.

"I love their donuts best, but they've got tons of other things too," Owen says.

He bounces around her like he's already on a sugar high.

"We can bring something back for you if you were about to exercise," I say. "It's still almost an hour and a half before Owen has to leave for school, so spend the time doing whatever you'd like before you're on the clock."

She waves her hand. "I can work out while Owen's at school. Now I'm curious about Happy Cow. That sounds like a place I'll like." She grins at Owen and slaps his hand when he comes over to give her a high five.

Lar and Mar are just opening when we walk inside. Mar's eyes sparkle when she sees us and then they widen when she notices Felicity.

"I don't know the last time I've seen you on a Monday," Mar says, smiling at me. "Must be a special occasion. Who's this?"

"This is Felicity Shaw. Felicity, this is Mar and her husband Lar."

"Nice to meet you," Felicity says.

"Hi, Felicity," Lar says, waving from the door of the kitchen.

"It's so nice to meet you, Felicity." Mar's smile just keeps growing as she looks back and forth between the two of us.

I knew this was a bad idea.

"Felicity will be helping out with Owen, so make sure

these two kiddos are taken care of if they ever come in without me, okay, Mar?" I say.

Felicity's head turns toward me, but I don't look at her. Mar clucks her tongue against her teeth.

"I sure will. But this beautiful woman in front of me is no kiddo, Sutton Landmark, I'll tell you that," Mar says, laughing as she taps the top of the counter.

Felicity laughs. Great. Everyone in this town is going to throw it in my face that I have a beautiful woman working for me. What the hell was I thinking?

She really was the best option, I remind myself.

"Would you like your usual, Owen?" Mar asks.

"Yes, please." He nods.

Mar hands Owen a donut with sprinkles and turns to Felicity.

"Do you see anything that suits your fancy, Felicity?" she asks.

"It all looks so good," Felicity says. "Owen says your donuts are the best, and I think I'll try that one right there." She points it out.

"Ah yes, the maple glazed," Mar says. "Anything else?"

"And a large flat white," Felicity adds.

Mar's eyes twinkle when she looks at me. "Why, that's exactly what *you* always order, Sutton. How 'bout that?"

"How 'bout that?" I repeat. "I think I'll mix it up today and have a bear claw."

Mar frowns. "And a flat white?"

"Yes, please."

"Have you *ever* come in here and not ordered a maple glazed?" Mar asks.

No, I haven't, but I'm trying to mix it up so no one gets any more ideas about how much Felicity and I have in common, thank you very much.

"I'm always mixing it up," I lie.

"Not around me, you're not," Mar argues.

Oh, for crying out loud.

"Stick a few more maple glazed and sprinkles in a box to go," I say.

Mar's face is triumphant as she adds them to a box, along with a bear claw.

My teeth grind together as I pay, feeling more out of sorts than I have in a long time.

I'm not sure this whole nanny situation is going to work out.

CHAPTER NINE

SENSORY OVERDRIVE

FELICITY

Taking Owen to school goes seamlessly—except for the fact that being in the car with Sutton is a full sensory experience. His tall, muscular frame takes over the small space. It's hard to keep my eyes off of him, but I try to not make it obvious that I'm staring at his large hands on the wheel, his thighs that only have the console between us…the way his chest fills out that shirt. Since the caramel incident, it's been more comfortable between us. Except I want to loosen his tie, bury my face in his neck, and inhale his smell, and that's not an option. He's all man, his cedarwood and vanilla scent mixed with cinnamon and coffee. His voice is lower and gravelly this morning and it scatters chills across my skin every time he speaks.

Keep it together, Shaw.

I tell myself that I'm just curious about the man, but the way my body reacts to him is beyond curiosity. It's like a switch has been flipped on inside of me and I am a receptacle to his current.

I could've gotten to the school without Sutton's help, but it's nice that he takes the time to drive us there. Once we arrive, I realize why he did it this way when he says he wants to introduce me to everyone in the school office so they'll know who I am when I come to pick up Owen.

From his meticulously clean and organized house to the way he dotes on Owen and their family, it seems that Sutton does everything with the utmost care. I don't know how he's managed to be a judge and be there for his son as much as he has. After I input everything from his color-coded online calendar to my physical planner last night and made sure it was all in my phone, it was more than evident that Sutton's a busy man. But even as he's dropping me back off at the house from taking Owen, he pauses and turns to look at me.

"Do you need anything from me before I go to work? Any questions?"

"I'll be fine. If I need anything, I'll figure out how to find it and take care of it," I assure him.

He nods briskly. "You can call me anytime. If I'm in court, my ringer will be off, but I'll have my phone with me. I might not see texts right away, but I'll respond if I do, and I'll call you back as soon as I'm free. And the list of the entire crew you met last night is in the kitchen," he reminds me.

"Thank you. Don't worry about me. I promise I won't try to make caramel pie in your kitchen." I smile and enjoy the way his laugh brightens everything around us. I open the door. "Have a good day," I say cheerily.

I can tell he wants to say more, but I don't want to make him late for work. I have a feeling it might take time for Sutton to relax with me filling this role. Time he doesn't have this morning.

I shut the door behind me and wave. He backs up but makes sure I'm safely inside before he pulls away. I lean against the door, needing a minute to catch my breath from being in his proximity. I've had two boyfriends, nothing too serious, and when both of those relationships fizzled, I decided to keep my romantic life lighter. In college, I went out quite a bit, mostly with jocks and artistic types because they're fun and also usually looking for something light.

But I can't say that a single guy I've met has affected me the way Sutton does.

The fact that he's a *man* surely contributes to this…but something tells me that if Sutton were my age, he'd still intrigue me and I'd probably feel just as trembly inside too.

I don't love the way he seems to think of me as a kid, but with the way I'm crushing on him like a lovesick child and his perceptive nature, I don't blame him. I'm not doing a very good job of hiding how attracted I am to him, and he's making sure I'm clear on the boundaries between us.

I'm not here to be friends with Sutton. I'm here to take care of his son.

I need to remember that and get a grip on my lusty eyes, especially on the days when he looks good enough to eat. So far, every time I've been around him has been that way, so it could take a while for this to sink in.

I get ready for the day and unpack my things, putting

everything away in a short amount of time. The space feels good, cozy. I slept decent, besides Sutton flitting in and out of my dreams all night. Despite being tired and amped up on Sutton's pheromones, I think I'll be comfortable here. Once I've tidied everything up, I go to the house and work on a meal plan for the week, taking stock of what they have and what we'll need, and then I head to Cecil's, the grocery store Sutton pointed out this morning. I definitely feel the need to prove myself capable in the kitchen after the explosion. I'm still finding caramel in surprising places.

There's more traffic than earlier, and the parking lot to the beautiful Landmark Mountain Lodge & Ski Resort that Scarlett and Jamison run is full. Scarlett mentioned last night that the lodge is undergoing renovations, but that they're busier than ever. Tourist season is going strong and will be for a while yet. I'll have to keep that in mind and give myself more time to pick up Owen this afternoon.

The grocery store is bustling, and I'm surprised by how well it's stocked. Not only are the produce, bakery, and meat departments top-notch, but there are all kinds of fun, random items I've never seen in a grocery store. I put a small potted ivy in my cart, along with a local brand of honey vanilla body wash and lotion that smells heavenly. Just as I'm telling myself I should get out of here before I find something else I love, I pass a large selection of unusual Hawaiian shirts and have a good laugh. And then it's too late, I see a pair of leggings that have cute detailing and are a velvety soft blend of spandex and suede and grab a pair of them in sage green and black. I need to gradually replace my grungy workout gear with cuter options.

When I finally make it to the line, I wait patiently, entertained by the cashier and the customer in front of me. The customer is a tall, adorable elderly gentleman, and he chats cheerfully to the grumbly, even older-looking man scanning the groceries.

"Fine day we're having," the tall one says.

"If you say so," the cashier mutters.

Now that I'm closer, I can see the cashier's nametag says Cecil. Ahh, this must be the owner. That thought makes me stifle a laugh. He can't be completely crotchety if he stocks Hawaiian shirts that have chickens getting suntans.

"Are you coming to chess night at the resort tonight?" the tall one asks.

"Pappy, you know I can't stand all the chatter at those things. I think you and I are the only ones who actually care about the game," Cecil says. "My tolerance for giggly ladies is not what it once was."

He makes a low *humph* sound and I try not to become a giggly lady myself.

Pappy. That sounds familiar. Is this who Owen mentioned the other day? I can't remember his connection to the family exactly.

"Oh, Cecil," Pappy chuckles. "You are hilarious."

When he says it, it sounds like *high-larious*.

Cecil looks up and makes eye contact with me, nodding slightly.

Pappy turns and his smile is friendly. "Hello there."

"Hi." I grin up at him. "I'm sorry to eavesdrop, but I think I've heard about you from the little guy I'm nannying now, Owen Landmark…"

Pappy's face lights up and he turns to fully face me while Cecil bags his groceries. "So you're the beautiful Felicity I've been hearing so much about. It's lovely to meet you."

My mouth drops open with his words. "You've…heard about me?"

"I've heard about you too," Cecil says. "Lar and Mar were quite taken with you."

"That was…just this morning."

Pappy laughs. "You'll find word travels fast around here."

"Landmark Mountain, where news flies and so do the bets at Sunny Side," Cecil says.

Pappy shoots a nervous look at Cecil before smiling back at me. I make note to ask one of the girls what *bets at Sunny Side* means. They each gave me their number before they left last night and asked if I was offended by group texts. I asked them to please add me to all the chats.

I like all of them so much.

"Owen's such a special kid," Pappy says. "He's my great-granddaughter's age and every time Ivy visits, she never wants to leave…thanks in large part to how much fun she has with Owen."

"Where does she live?" I ask.

"In a little town outside of Boston," he says.

"Oh…is that where you're from too?" I wasn't sure what his accent was until he mentioned Boston.

"I've lived there most of my life until now…and I still go back and forth quite often," he says. "Can't stand to be away from my family there *or* here for very long…but it's actually helped to be away from the house my wife and I lived in when she was still with us." He waves his hand and gives me a sheepish look. "Ignore my sentimental blathering. You've waited for your turn long enough." He picks up the bags and nods at Cecil, taking his receipt. He turns and winks at me. "I'm sure I'll be seeing you around very soon."

"I hope so," I tell him.

I watch Pappy walk away as Cecil rings up my groceries and wish I had more time with him. The pain that crossed over his face when he talked about his wife makes me sad and I wonder how long she's been gone.

"Looks like you've got some good meals planned," Cecil says, surprising me with the warmth in his voice. "That Sutton's always been a good egg. Helped raise his brothers and sister when their parents died and then had the worst luck of it with that wife of his." He lifts a hand to emphasize his next words. "Not a fan of divorce, but even I was glad when they parted ways." He shakes his head, getting back to work as he scoffs under his breath. "Best thing to ever happen was the day she left, if you ask me."

I wait with bated breath, half guilty that I'm hearing this information, yet not wanting to miss any of it.

He meets my eyes and nods firmly. "You'll be good for them," he says, as if he's giving his stamp of approval.

"Thank you," I finally say.

He doesn't say another word, obviously done sharing, and when I thank him again once the last bag is placed in the cart, he simply nods and glances at the next person who steps up to the counter.

When I've got the groceries in the car, I pull out my phone and am surprised to find a slew of texts. While I'm waiting for the car to warm up, I open the one from Sutton.

> **SUTTON**
> If everything goes as planned, I should be home by 5:30.

All business. Okay. I keep the same tone in my text back to him.

> I'll have dinner ready by 6.

There's a text from Weston too.

WESTON

Ready to come home yet?

Nope. I love it here!

WESTON

<side-eye emoji> I had a feeling you would.

I almost text him about a crazy idea I had last night. Not sure if it's too late to pull it off, but I'll still ask him about it later.

The group thread from the girls is definitely chattier than Sutton's.

SCARLETT

Hope your day is off to a great start, Felicity. Don't hesitate to text or call any of us if you need anything at all. We're really excited you're here.

MARLOW

Dakota is still talking about how pretty you are. She hopes her hair is as pretty as yours when she grows up.

SOFIE

My aunt and her wife are dying to meet you now too. They were with me when we saw Lar and Mar at Happy Cow this morning—you guys had apparently just left—and L & M talked you up good. They are FANS. And so are we, if you can't tell. Too much? Are we scaring you yet? <Crying laughing emoji>

RUBY

OMG. Callum and I were in Happy Cow this morning too! Yes. L & M were on a Felicity high! I'm so bummed we missed you guys. I'm the newbie to Landmark Mountain compared to everyone else, but you'll find it's such a welcoming place…especially this family. <Heart emoji>

MARLOW

What Ruby said.

SCARLETT

Between us and Lar and Mar, we're bordering on weirdly welcoming.

SOFIE

Oh God. We're a lot, aren't we? We can take five steps back if you need. LOL

My face aches a little from smiling so hard and I type back.

> Not scared even a little bit. I've been in the grocery store and I can't even tell you how happy this group chat just made me. How's this for too much? In my four years at Georgetown, I never felt like I connected with friends as much as I did in the short time we were together last night. I'm really happy to be here. And guess who else I just met? Pappy and Cecil! Pappy is a dreamboat and Cecil is a wealth of information.

SCARLETT

Sniff. That warmed my heart and I'm the hard-hearted one in this group. Pappy! One of the main reasons I'm dating Jamison is because of Pappy. Kidding, but he's a huge bonus. We adore him. And Cecil too! I snorted about Cecil's wealth of information. I think he gossips more than The Golden Girls—that's Grinny and her girlfriends Helen and Peg. You just wait. You'll fall hard when you meet them too.

It finally clicks as I'm reading it, still smiling like a fool. *Jamison's* grandpa. That's how Pappy's connected.

MARLOW

I vote we have a night at The Dancing Emu soon. We can make sure everyone's there to meet Felicity.

> Color me intrigued. The Dancing Emu?

SOFIE

It's Ruby's Uncle Pierre's place and you'll love it. Good food, crazy fun vibes, and karaoke.

> I have a hard time imagining Sutton…or Callum…or Wyatt doing karaoke. Theo and Jamison, maybe?

SOFIE

Nailed it. <Crying laughing emoji>

RUBY

Sorry I keep taking forever to respond! Apparently, I had peanut butter on my jacket. I couldn't figure out why Delphine and Irene wouldn't leave me alone. They chased me for a MILE before Dolly stepped in and blocked them! Once she started drumming at them, it got the others going, and I swear it sounded like a drum corps on steroids.

I stare at this one for a couple of minutes, trying to decipher what it could possibly mean.

MARLOW

Interpretation for you, Felicity. Delphine: Callum's naughty goat who's obsessed with peanut butter…and Callum. Irene: Callum's cow who can't seem to say no to Delphine's peer pressure. Dolly: Ruby's emu and number one stan.

RUBY

Oops, my bad. What Marlow said. LOL

> I had no idea Landmark Mountain would provide such endless entertainment.

SCARLETT

Stick around. We're just getting started.

> Oh, while I have everyone…can you tell me what Sunny Side bets are? I thought that's where Sutton got our burgers and shakes the other night…

MARLOW

I'll let you take it, Scarlett or Sofie. LOL

SOFIE

Oh my. Have they already started with you?

RUBY

I'm finding out that the bets at Sunny Side are LEGENDARY.

SCARLETT

Let's just say that the nosy britches in town love nothing more than to place bets on the love lives of the Landmark family. Things besides love lives are wagered on as well, but the romance really gets their knockers knocking. And it all goes down at Sunny Side, an otherwise lovely place to get the best pancakes, omelets, and hamburgers.

RUBY

And fries and shakes…

SOFIE

Is knockers knocking a saying? <laughing emoji> I'm filing that one away for later usage…

This is such a fun town.

SCARLETT

That's the spirit! Please don't get too offended when everyone you meet tries to pry information out of you so they can go tweak their bets. They do mean well.

Noted.

CHAPTER TEN

ACCLIMATED

SUTTON

By the time Friday rolls around, I'm more than ready for the weekend. This case is exhausting me already and we're only getting started. I can't wait to have a couple days off, and it has nothing to do with the fact that, in such a short time, Felicity Shaw has turned my house into a cozy, welcoming oasis. Each night I walk into the house, the aroma from the kitchen smells like heaven, and the smiles on Owen and

Felicity's faces when they see me make me feel like a fucking rock star.

Not only is Felicity beautiful, but she's sweet and easy to be around. And caramel pie debacle be damned, the girl can cook.

So far, she's made baked ziti, steak with garlic mashed potatoes, homemade mac and cheese that Owen and I lost our minds over, shrimp fettuccine, all with the most incredible salads, and tonight I watch as she pulls pepperoni rolls out of the oven.

I'm about to go on about how great the food looks when she steps out from behind the island and I notice that she's more dressed up than usual. My eyes wander slowly down her body against my will, taking in the fitted blue sweater dress, her long legs bare and her feet still in the cute fuzzy slippers she wears when she's inside.

She looks incredible.

When I reach her eyes again, her cheeks are flushed and she resumes her path to the table, pepperoni rolls in hand.

I swallow hard, setting my things down and moving to the sink to wash my hands. Sometimes I feel her curious eyes on me and I'd be lying if I said it wasn't flattering, but I'm doing my damnedest to keep this professional and not let my guard down around her. Hard to do when we're in my home and she's the one making it better.

It's even harder when her very presence snags something inside of me and rattles me around.

I'm thirty-five. I've seen plenty of great bodies in my lifetime, but fuck me if I've ever seen one that shakes me up like hers does.

It's been too long since I've been with anyone, but I can't even blame that.

I thought a mid-life crisis happened later in life, and that it meant you were sad about aging, which I don't feel at all. But maybe my crazy reaction to her could be chalked up to that.

All I know is that my hand is getting a helluva workout.

"Did you see what we made yet, Dad?" Owen asks, bouncing over to me.

Guilt and happiness permeate throughout me, both constants since Felicity arrived.

"You helped with these fantastic-looking pepperoni rolls?" I put my arm around him and he nods proudly at me.

"I couldn't have done it without him," Felicity says, beaming at him.

Owen hurries to the table. "We should eat fast. Felicity has to go soon."

"Oh." I glance at Felicity, trying to school my reaction to her in that dress. "You have a date tonight?"

She laughs. "Yes, I do."

My throat gets a tight, itchy feeling and I loosen my tie.

"With the girls," she adds. "Actually, I think your brothers are going too. At least Wyatt and Theo are…and Jamison too. You should come."

"Oh, I don't want to intrude on your plans."

She makes a face before handing me the pepperoni rolls. "It's a plan that came together while we were making dinner. I didn't want to interrupt you while you might be driving home or I would've invited you myself."

"Can we go, Dad? Can we?" Owen looks at me with pleading eyes and Felicity's expression turns apologetic.

"Sorry, I should've run it by you first," she says softly.

"I wondered why the guys called me back to back," I say. "Haven't had a chance to check messages yet." I take a pepperoni roll and groan when I take a bite. "Wow…amazing."

Felicity and Owen high-five each other and it's quiet the next few minutes while we eat.

"There might be a call from Ruby too," Felicity giggles, "to see if you can talk Callum into going."

I snort. "Fat chance in hell."

I dig a quarter out of my pocket and pass it to Owen before he points to the curse jar that Dakota introduced him to. She's only four and thinks Owen, at eight years old, is the master of all things, but he latched onto the curse jar like it was a revelation. Dakota manages to get more money out of everyone than Owen does in this house, but he's working on that.

"What time is everyone going?" I finally ask.

"7:30. Drinks and dessert," she says.

"You got enough energy to be out past your bedtime?" I ask Owen, knowing it's a pointless question.

"It's Friday night and I stay up till at least nine thirty on Friday nights!" he insists.

I chuckle and finish my bite of pepperoni roll. "True. I guess we could go for a little while."

"*Yes,*" Owen says, eating faster.

"Seriously, this food." I take another roll. "If you can't decide what you want to do next, you could always open a restaurant."

Her cheeks flush with my praise. "Thank you. I do enjoy cooking a lot. But my parents would kill me if I chose something like that…" She lifts a shoulder.

Her expression gets tense when any mention of her future is made.

"Is there anything you're considering?" I ask.

She bites her lower lip and shakes her head. Her expression is so forlorn, I feel bad that I've brought it up.

"Well, you've got time to figure it out," I tell her. "I don't have much advice on the matter except this: Do something you love."

"Do you love being a judge?" she asks.

"Some days," I say, laughing. "Do as I say, not as I do."

She laughs like she knows I'm joking, and I'm amazed again by how easy it is to be around her. Each day I brace myself, disarmed by her beauty and charm, but by the time we get to these dinners together, my defenses lower and it's impossible to not just enjoy being with her.

And Owen. He looks at her like she is the sun and the moon.

I should be concerned by how attached he's getting to her, but the laughter and warmth she's brought into our home has been invaluable. I'm soaking it up as much as he is and not willing to think about the day she's *not* here just yet.

Which has enormous red flags all over it, I realize this and yet, here I am, eager for any and all interaction with her.

After dinner, I change into jeans and a sweater and call Callum.

"No," he says, not bothering with a hello. Bastard never does.

"I expect to see your ass at The Dancing Emu," I tell him firmly. "If I have to go, so do you."

"No one's making you," he argues.

"The girls texted that it's a little welcome for Felicity, and Owen's all excited about it, so we're going and I don't want to hear you whine about it."

"Fine," he grumbles, hanging up.

I grin at myself in the mirror as I tame my hair and grab my toothbrush. That was easier than I thought it'd be. Ruby's had that effect on him.

Owen talks during the whole ride. Our usual haunts are Happy Cow and Sunny Side, with the occasional family dinner at The Pink Ski, or for the big nights, Tiptop. The Gnarly Vine and The Dancing Emu can get a little out of hand during tourist season, but it's usually harmless fun. We can bail if it's too much.

"If we have to leave earlier than you want, anyone in my family will be happy to bring you home," I tell Felicity as we walk inside.

"I'm not tired," Owen says, opening the door for us.

"Of course not." I ruffle his hair and he grins at me.

"As I live and breathe," Peg sings, flitting over to me and kissing my cheeks and then Owen's. She turns to Felicity and takes her hand, whistling. "You're even prettier than they said. And just look at the legs on you." She fans her face, her smile wide. "I need to up my wager," she says under her breath.

Confusion and then amusement flits over Felicity's face, but she's friendly to Peg and then distracted by Grinny and Helen walking over. Great timing. I don't even want to know what they're betting on over at Sunny Side. This town is full of a bunch of nosy, matchmaking busybodies who love nothing more than placing bets on everything from how many inches the next snowfall will be to who will be the next Landmark to get married. My brothers and sister have kept tongues wagging over the past nine months, and with Wyatt and Marlow engaged and Scarlett and Jamison going strong, I'd like to hope that my name is kept out of the shenanigans, but the people around here have a way of making something out of nothing.

Wouldn't surprise me at all if there's already a bet going on in this town about who will win the heart of Felicity Shaw.

I introduce Helen to Felicity, Helen's tightly permed hair bouncing slightly as she grasps Felicity's hand and smiles.

"I've been hearing wonderful things about you," Helen says.

Felicity looks so touched, it's endearing. "Likewise," she says. "I've been looking forward to meeting Grinny's besties."

Grinny hugs her and then reaches for me. "And how are you, my handsome boy?" She pulls back and pats my cheek. "You sure look swoony in your sweater."

I squeeze her hand. "For you, Grin. I know how you like me in a sweater." I'm like a kid when she laughs, her laugh has been my goal for as long as I can remember. "You look lovely tonight. You singing?"

"No, no. I'll leave that to you kids," she says.

Just then we hear a loud, "Stop! In the name of love," and look onstage to see Peg, holding up her hands when she gets to the word *stop*.

"And Peg," Grinny adds.

Our attention is drawn to Felicity and the girls when they start dancing with Owen. My son pulls out some impressive dance moves.

Grinny chuckles. "Where did he learn to do that?"

I turn to her with an ambivalent expression. "We may or may not have an occasional dance party at the Summit House."

"I see." Her lips twitch as she tries to stay serious. "I'd like to be invited to one of those Summit House dance parties sometime." She leans in. "How's it going with Felicity?"

I feel a heavy hand on my shoulder and look back to see Callum, his expression more droll than annoyed, which is a nice surprise.

Grinny gasps to see him here, hugging him, while Ruby kisses my cheek and whispers, "Thank you for working your magic," in my ear.

"We both know you're the one who got him here," I tell her, laughing.

She lifts a shoulder but grins like she knows I'm right. The girls cheer when she dances toward them and stops to hug Felicity first.

I'm struck again by how well Felicity already fits in around here.

CHAPTER ELEVEN

CAR CHATS

FELICITY

"While I have you all together, I wanted to mention," I yell over the music, "my brother said if they win the divisional round next week, you're all invited to the game the following week…" I see the excitement in everyone's eyes and laugh when Scarlett bumps my hip with hers.

Sutton's eyes are bright as he smiles and lifts his glass of Coke at me. I grin, lifting my vodka lemonade his way. I have yet to see the guy drink alcohol, even on a night off at home.

All that self-control makes me want to see what rules I can help him break.

He's looked at me more tonight than he has all week. I was beginning to get weirded out by the lack of eye contact, but even at the house before we came to The Dancing Emu, it was almost like he allowed himself to take me in.

And here I go again, reading more into things. Sutton Landmark is not checking me out, and I don't want him to anyway. That would make everything complicated and ruin this awesome arrangement.

I might not know what I'm doing with my life just yet, but I've been happier in Landmark Mountain with Sutton and Owen than I've been in a long time. The stress from my time at Georgetown lessens with each day, and even the weight hanging over my head with my parents not knowing the truth feels farther away the longer I'm here.

"Count us in," Wyatt says.

They all start chiming in at once, thanking me and Weston. Well, except Callum, who simply nods at me, his smile all the sweeter since they seem hard-earned.

"They have to win first," I remind everyone.

"Oh, they've got this," Theo says.

"Agreed." Jamison and Theo clink glasses.

"Dad and I are still going with you next week, right?" Owen asks. His hair is going every which way, his face shiny from dancing his little ass off. I lean down, still dancing, but so we're eye to eye.

"Absolutely. And we're going to have the full tailgate experience too," I tell him.

"What's the tailgate experience?" His eyes go wide.

"Oh, you just wait. You're gonna love it."

The following Sunday, we're on our way to the game, and the excitement in the vehicle is palpable. It's about an hour and a half to Clarity Field and we're borrowing Callum's truck. We left with plenty of time to make it to the tailgate party as soon as it starts. Sutton glances over at me, a smile playing on his lips.

"What?" I ask, surprised by my boldness, but something just feels different about today. Like we're coloring outside the lines a bit.

"Nice outfit," he says, his eyes wandering appreciatively down my ensemble.

"Gotta show support." I lift my shoulder in nonchalance, but inside, I'm doing a fist pump and kick-ball-changing all over this truck.

I'm wearing a teal jersey, number fourteen for Weston, of course, white pants with teal and grey stripes down the side, and a teal puffer jacket with the Mustangs logo emblazoned across the back. My knees are even wrapped in teal bands to look like the players, but my tight-fitting version of the outfit is decidedly more feminine.

"I didn't think he'd ever sleep last night," he says. "He's been so excited about today."

I glance in the backseat and Owen is bopping his head to the music on his game. He looks up for a second and gives me his wide smile. It hasn't been long since I started nannying, but I'm already so damn attached to this kid. I can't wait for him to see all the surprises I brought.

And if anything, I'm even more intrigued by Sutton than I was in the beginning. The more I'm around him, the more I like him. And the more I like him, the hotter he gets.

Full disclosure: I'm about to combust with lust for the man.

When I look at him again, his eyes are back on the road

and I allow myself to study his profile for an indulgent ten seconds.

"I've been excited too." My voice sounds shaky, and I clear my throat. "I've only been able to make it to two games so far. Christmas and New Year's Eve," I add.

"Those were great games," he says.

"They were." My voice must give something away because he looks over at me.

"You sure?" he asks, chuckling.

I make a face. "No, they totally were. My sister was just in a mood."

"Ah. I haven't heard much about her yet," he says.

"She's the oldest. Beautiful. Type A."

He chuckles. "Seeing your planner slash manual, I'd say you might have some of those tendencies as well."

"Hey, kettle," I tease. "You have a more color-coded life than my sister and me combined."

His expression is mock outrage. "What's wrong with a little color?"

"Not a thing. It's just entertaining that chores are grey, hockey is blue, and family events are pink." I tap my finger to my mouth and his eyes track the movement. My cheeks heat and he turns back to the road. "Work events are green, school is red, town events are orange…"

"Sounds like you've got it down." He laughs and I squeeze my legs together, my core responding a little too greedily to Sutton Landmark.

"I just have two questions," I keep teasing. "I'm still not sure what your favorite color is, which feels wrong given how freely you use color…"

He snorts and the sound, so uncharacteristic of how he's been with me before now, makes my heart gallop against my chest.

"And the second is...why isn't there a color on your calendar for fun?"

That makes him laugh and again, my chest feels like a thousand birds just took flight.

"Color for fun?" he repeats.

I nod, turning to face him, my boldness kicking in even more with his guard down. "Yes! What color are date nights or, you know, nights out with your buddies?"

His eyes are still laughing even as his lips go back into their naturally sultry pout.

"Well, my brothers are usually included in any *buddy* outings...even if Blake or Pierre or whoever else also shows up." His lips twitch. "So pink still works and is fun, I might add."

"Ahhh. Yes, but—"

"And I don't really date—"

"What?"

He shoots me a questioning look. "I don't really date?"

"No, I heard you. I'm just saying, *what*? Why not?"

His lips jut out slightly in thought, and I couldn't look away if I wanted to. This ride is turning out to be so much more informative than I expected.

"I don't have the best track record with relationships," he finally says. "Divorced." He lifts a shoulder like that explains everything.

"For a long time now though, right?"

"Yeah, but you know...failing that spectacularly can make you reluctant to try again."

I nod and then frown when it hits me. I look back at Owen and he's in his own little world, but I still whisper my next words. "Are you not over her?"

His next laugh is incredulous, and I file away all these

new expressions and sounds while anxiously waiting for his answer.

"Trust me, I am. *Completely*," he adds. He lowers his voice. "But being a dad comes first, and then there's the whole matter of being a judge. I'm busy, and there aren't exactly a lot of full-timers living here that are single, and it wouldn't look right if I went out with a different tourist every week…not that I'd ever have the time for that…"

I think on that for a moment. "So when's the last time you…went out?"

My cheeks heat with how close I just came to asking him when he last had sex.

Slow your roll, Shaw. You're getting way too comfortable around your boss.

"Hmm." He shakes his head. "It's been a while. About a year ago now, maybe less than that. Blake's wife Camilla has a friend who comes every year to ski and we…had dinner the last time she was here."

Oh, he totally had sex with her. I can tell by the way he grips the steering wheel, his gaze focused back on the road.

"No repeats with…Camilla's friend?" I don't know why I keep torturing myself with this line of conversation, but I'm compelled to find out everything while he's talking.

"She calls occasionally, but she lives in New York." He shrugs. "I think she'll be out soon for her annual ski trip though."

"Ahh. Are you gonna ask her out again? What's her name?"

"Gwyneth. I don't know. Haven't really thought about it." He lifts his shoulder again and then smirks over at me. "Your turn. When's the last time you…went out?"

My mouth parts and I gulp, caught off guard when his grin grows. *Is he asking me the last time I had sex?*

No way.

Right?

"Wait, I still don't know your favorite color," I hedge.

"Purple."

That makes me smile. Unexpected. "Purple, I like it. So… would a night out with Gwyneth be purple in your calendar?"

He glances at me, his eyebrows lifted. "You'll answer *my* question now, Miss Shaw."

His commanding tone makes me shift in my seat, certain I *cannot* handle Judge Sutton in such close quarters.

"Yes, sir," I say breathlessly.

His nose flares and he turns back to the road. I feel the sudden need to stick my head out the window and get some air.

"Uh, it's been about a month and a half since I—" I'm not sure what I'd call what I did with Drew. More of a drunk groping session than a date, and far less satisfying than getting dinner.

"Your boyfriend?" he asks.

"No. I don't have a boyfriend."

He glances over at me, eyebrows going up higher than before.

"You seem surprised?" I ask.

"Well, yes. I guess I am. You're a…nurturing person and —yeah, it does surprise me." His features are hard to read as he stares at the road.

"Thank you," I say. "The guys at school just weren't my type, I guess. I went out plenty, but I knew I didn't want to get serious about anyone there."

"What is your type? Wait—let me guess." He smirks, looking down at my outfit. "Jock."

I flush slightly. "I've gone out with more than a few jocks," I admit.

He studies my expression for a second, and I feel like he can read every dirty thought.

"We're going to the right place then," is all he says.

I make a face, shaking my head. "No. Not only would I not want to date a football player, but Weston would never allow it."

He chuckles. "That's a good brother."

I roll my eyes. "Scarlett mentioned you were always ridiculously protective of her too."

He pretends to be offended again.

"Nothing I do is ridiculous," he says, smirking.

Damn.

Again, I'm tempted to at least crack the window a *little* to cool down.

"Mm-hmm," I say, laughing.

He points at me. "You should trust your elders."

My eyes narrow on his. "Okay, Elder Landmark. So what you're saying is that I should only hope for a love life as fulfilling as yours?"

He chokes back a laugh and scrubs a hand over his face, suddenly looking a decade younger. "Scratch that. As the only divorced Landmark, I am in no way the relationship expert."

My laugh dies as I study him. He really carries a lot of pressure over that divorce. I'd like to help him get over that.

CHAPTER TWELVE

FULL EXPERIENCE

SUTTON

I've broken out in a sweat multiple times during the ride to Clarity Field, certain Felicity will be able to tell that I've been hard for most of the trip. When we step out into the crisp air and Felicity gets to work making the bed of the truck cozy, I take a few deep breaths before I start helping her. She got a parking pass at the stadium so we could tailgate. Callum dropped the truck off early, and I was surprised to find it already loaded when I went outside this morning.

She lifts the blanket and pulls out a small portable grill and then smiles when she registers my shock.

"I thought it'd be fun to grill our own hot dogs...or burgers. We have both in the cooler," she says.

"*Yes*," Owen says, bouncing around her.

"Incredible," I add. "I had no idea you'd brought all this."

The large cooler has root beer and bottles of Coke—our favorites—tons of bottled water, hard cider, and large veggie and fruit trays that she assembled, the dips covered with cling wrap. There's also some kind of dessert option that looks delicious. I can't tell if it's lemon bars or what, but I'm here for it.

The smaller cooler has the meat, and once the grill is going, she puts a few hot dogs and burgers on there.

"Looks like you've done this a few times," I say, as she gets another basket from the truck.

"I haven't been able to come to many games since Weston's been with the Mustangs—we did this more when he was in college. But I'll be making up for lost time," she says, smiling over at me. "Number one fan right here."

I set out the chairs and watch Owen's face light up when Felicity tosses a football his way.

"Felicity!" A high, sing-songy voice carries through the already noisy area, and I turn to see who it is.

Two Mustangs cheerleaders rush toward Felicity and hug her. Felicity returns their hugs but seems uncomfortable.

"I thought that was you," one of them says. "We haven't seen you around lately...think you could get us into the after-party?"

"I'm not going to the after-party this time," Felicity says.

"Oh," the dark-haired one pouts and then smiles brightly, "you could put in a good word for us though." She shimmies and bumps her arm against Felicity's. "Your brother is *so* hot."

Felicity's eyes meet mine and her annoyance is easy to read. Too bad these girls don't seem able to read the room.

The dark-haired one turns to see who Felicity's looking at and her eyes light up.

"Hello, sexy," she purrs. "I'm Lexi, and you are?"

Felicity rolls her eyes and I bite back a laugh.

"Sutton." I point to Owen and for some idiotic reason say, "His dad."

Lexi makes a show of checking out my left hand and when she doesn't find a ring, she fans herself. "*Love* a single dad."

I glance at Owen. He's watching with rapt attention.

The blonde one sighs and crosses her arms over her chest. "I really wanted to go to that party."

"Don't you have an automatic *in*, since you cheer for the team?" Felicity asks.

"Not always," she says. "Last time we went, we sort of… drank too much. It cost us."

"Ahh," Felicity says.

"You could make me forget all about the after-party," Lexi whispers in my ear.

I take a step back and she looks back at me like she doesn't understand what's happening. A frown puckers between her brows and she turns to look at her friend and Felicity. I glance over too and Felicity has her arms crossed in front of her, and she looks pissed.

"Oh!" Lexi points between the two of us. "Ohhh, I didn't realize you two were—"

Felicity's arms drop in front of her and she flushes, shaking her head. "Oh, no, we're not—" She gives me a desperate look, and I motion to the grill.

"Why don't I check those burgers?" I say and she practically sags in relief.

"Good idea," she says softly.

The girls see someone else they know and they wave over their shoulders, most likely off to find another way to get to the party.

She makes a derisive sound as she watches them fawn over a few guys.

"Not your favorite people?" I ask.

"They're probably fine. It just gets old, people using me to get to my brother. It was like that even before he was famous. I guess I thought it would get better when we got older, but—" She shakes her head and makes a face. "Lexi looked like she wanted to crawl inside your skin and make herself at home."

I swallow hard at that description and the way she licks her lips and looks me over as she says it. Like maybe she's considering the idea herself.

I scoff and turn my focus on the grill, assessing the meat like it's my job.

"Nah, she's probably like that with everyone," I say.

Felicity's the one scoffing now. "Yeah, keep telling yourself that."

After we've eaten, we walk around, the music from the nearby DJ keeping our steps brisk with the beat, and then when we're back at the truck, Felicity pulls out a game of Yahtzee. Before we know it, the afternoon has flown by and it's time for the game.

"Weston offered us a suite, but I like being a little closer to the action," she says as we take our seats. She points out to Owen that we're near the players' tunnel. "We can take him up on the suite when your family comes..." She smiles up at me, and I feel that rush of endorphins that I get every time she looks at me.

"Thanks for this," I tell her. "It's been such a great day. I don't often do things like this…"

"What, have fun?" she teases.

"Hey, sweetheart," someone says.

Felicity and I both turn and Felicity jumps up, hugging an older gentleman and the woman next to him. When I get a better look at them, I realize they're her parents.

"Mom, Dad! I didn't think you were coming today," Felicity says.

Is it my imagination or does she sound completely freaked out?

"We didn't think we could, but Francis and Ken had to pull out of the trip. We decided we'd rather stay home and come to the game than go on the trip without them." The woman peers around Felicity. "Judge Landmark, is that you?"

I stand up and hold my hand out to shake their hands. "David and Lane, it's been a long time. Good to see you."

"It sure has," David says. "Good to see you too. Thanks for taking our girl under your wing. We know she's in good hands with you."

I tug on my collar, a little unsettled with his words. Images of her in my hands race through my mind, those full breasts—God help me. I clear my throat. My guilty conscience has me feeling a little unsteady, but I try to recall what it's like to be a decent, upstanding *judge*.

"Yes," Lane leans in, her tone conspiratorial, "when she told us she'd be working with you, all our concerns about her future vanished." She does a *poof* motion with her hand, laughing.

Felicity's eyes flash to mine, but I can't read her expression. All I see is panic.

What the fuck is going on?

"We are very grateful for all her help," I say, nodding toward Owen. "This is Owen, my son."

"Owen, these are my parents, Lane and David," Felicity says.

"Mister and Missus Shaw," I tell Owen.

"Hello, Mister and Missus Shaw," Owen says, smiling up at them.

"Well, aren't you the cutest thing," Lane says. "I didn't realize you had a son, Judge Landmark."

What?

"Oh, I told you that, Mom." Felicity laughs, her hand clutching her neck. It's red and her face is too. She shakes her head.

"Are you feeling okay, sweetheart? Your cheeks are flushed," her mom says.

"It's really hot out here," Felicity says, grabbing a flyer to fan herself.

Lane frowns, putting her hand on Felicity's forehead. "It's thirty degrees. Are you sure you're okay?"

"I'm fine." Felicity laughs. "Where are you sitting?"

"We're down a few rows." David points to their seats. "We thought we'd wait and use the suite for the next game if they win this one."

"Felicity said that's where we'll go when our family comes too," Owen says excitedly.

I put my hand on his shoulder, wanting to rein him in a little in case the suite's not big enough for everyone or…I don't even know what, but Felicity's nervous energy is making me uneasy.

"Well, I can't wait," Lane says. "They're winning today. Let's just put that out in the universe right now." She winks at

Owen. "So I guess we'll be seeing you and your family again soon."

He nods happily.

"Do you need anything before the game starts?" Felicity asks him. "We can go now and be back before we miss anything."

He rubs his stomach. "I'm still full from all the food we just ate."

"Where did you eat?" David asks. "There's great food in here."

"We tailgated!" Owen says. "And Felicity made burgers and hot dogs…and S'mores. It was awesome!"

"I didn't know you were tailgating today," Lane says, looking at Felicity in surprise.

"I wanted Owen to have the full experience," Felicity says. "This is his first game."

She smiles sweetly at Owen and blood thrums in my veins, my pulse quickening. I scrub my hand down my jaw, unsure of what to do with all this pent-up energy.

Lust.

Not lust, I correct myself.

Don't confuse gratitude and attraction with lust.

But even as I'm having this internal debate with myself, my eyes track every movement Felicity makes. I notice the curve of her hip and how easy it would be to put my hand there and tug her toward me.

God, this is bad. If I'm thinking this way in front of her *parents*, there's no hope for me.

CHAPTER THIRTEEN

NOT SO NICE

FELICITY

The Mustangs win and the euphoria is tangible as we walk back to the car. Owen's feet barely touch the ground, he's so amped up from the game. It took me a while to calm down after seeing my parents with Sutton. It was a bit of a disaster, but it could've gone much, much worse. As it is, I think it might've been confusing to Sutton, but I don't think my parents suspect that I'm just Owen's nanny.

Once it seemed like I was off the hook, at least for

another day, I let myself enjoy the game and I haven't stopped smiling.

"That was *awesome*," Owen says again. "When Weston threw that last pass, I thought for sure he was gonna get tackled, but he—" Owen does some fast footwork, maneuvering between Sutton and me.

"Perfect reenactment," I say, laughing.

"I can't believe he took a picture with us too," Owen's still going. "He must be so tired."

"He's usually amped up for a while after a game, kind of the way you're feeling right now."

"Yeah, I'm not tired," Owen says.

"Mm-hmm," Sutton says, chuckling.

"Yep, that sounds like my brother too. When we were little, he'd play hard and swear he'd never be able to fall asleep, but as soon as he sat down, his mouth would be hanging open…asleep in seconds flat."

Owen laughs. "That's funny."

"Sounds like someone else I know," Sutton says. "It was nice to see your parents."

I nod, avoiding his gaze. "Yeah, it was."

He doesn't say anything, but I can practically hear his questions.

"No one's gonna believe I went to the game," Owen says. "And that I know Weston Shaw. I told Micah the other day, and he said I was lying."

"I'll print the picture tonight and blow it up big, so there's no confusion for Micah," I say, a little heated.

Owen's told me a few things about Micah here and there, enough for me to know he's sometimes a rude little jerk.

"You could do that?" Owen looks at me with wide eyes.

"Absolutely." I put my hand on his shoulder and he leans in, wrapping his arms around my waist.

"Thanks, Felicity."

"You're welcome, buddy."

When we get in the truck, Sutton blasts the heat and we take off our jackets. I use mine to lean against the window and it takes a while before we get through the traffic. By the time we're driving away from Clarity Field, Owen is sound asleep.

And to avoid any questions from Sutton about my parents, I pretend to fall asleep too.

When we pull into the driveway an hour and a half later, I've really fallen asleep and it's Sutton's hand on my shoulder that jostles me awake.

"Oh," I whisper.

"Hey, sleepyhead. We're home," he says.

I stretch and look back at Owen, who is still out. I start gathering things and Sutton puts his hand on my arm.

"Leave it. I'll take care of all this. Get some rest. You did all the packing, the least I can do is unpack everything."

"I'll help…"

"Please. Go to bed, Felicity. We had the best day we've had in a long time, and that's all thanks to you."

I put my hand on my heart, his words making me warm and heady. "I had a great time too," I whisper.

His eyes are shining from the lamplight and then he moves toward Owen, unbuckling him and lifting him in his arms like he weighs nothing.

"Good night," I say softly.

"Good night," he says, smiling at me as he walks past.

I walk up the stairs to my room and lean back against the door after I've closed it behind me.

Being around Sutton is like being on a nonstop roller coaster ride for my insides. It's queasy and exhilarating, and I never quite feel steady on my feet.

I wonder if I'll always feel this way around him.

Once I've caught my breath, I move toward the bathroom and take a long hot shower, putting on a tank and shorts afterward since I'm thoroughly warmed up. I even crack the window a little to let out some of the steam from the shower. When I turn out the light to the bathroom and walk toward my bed, a flurry of movement catches my eye and I scream.

There is a mouse in here.

"Oh my God, oh my God, oh my God," I chant.

I run around the room and scream again when the mouse runs toward me. I hear something outside but don't take my eyes off of the mouse because *hello, a mouse could run right into my feet and please God, no.*

I jump onto the bed for safety.

"Felicity, open the door," Sutton yells.

"I can't."

"You…can't? Why did you scream?"

I'm quiet for a second.

"Felicity, I'm coming in."

I hear the key in the door and then Sutton rushes inside, looking ready to avenge my honor.

"What's wrong?" he asks, breathless.

He looks around the room and when he doesn't see anything but me standing on my bed, shaking, he frowns.

"There's a mouse in here." My voice wobbles and I point a shaky finger toward the couch where I last saw him. "Under there."

His lips twitch and then his eyes wander down the length of me, his mouth parting slightly. I feel my nipples jut out and I wrap my arms around my waist, willing them to calm down.

He swallows hard and looks where I've pointed. "A mouse."

His voice is hoarse and he nods like he suddenly understands.

"Okay," he says.

He moves to the kitchen and gets a paper bag from the cabinet and then moves toward the couch. When he moves the couch, the mouse tries to escape and he scoops it into the bag.

"You made that look easy." I climb off of the bed and point to the bag. "What will you do with it?"

"I'll take it for a little drive and leave it in a field somewhere."

I smile. "You're a nice man."

"I'm not so nice," he says. His eyes drop to my arms again when I shiver, and I see his Adam's apple bob in his throat. "I was also gonna say I can set up some traps if it makes you feel better."

I wrinkle my nose. "I'd feel awful if we actually caught one. They can stay out there all they want." I point outside. "I just have an irrational fear about mice darting against my feet."

His lips lift. "Understandable. I'll call Scott. He's the local pest guy and he's helped with keeping them from coming inside. Maybe we need to block some holes up here or something."

"Okay. That would be great. Thank you."

"You okay out here for tonight? You can sleep in the guest bedroom if you'd be more comfortable there."

I must pause a little too long because he laughs.

"Come on. It'll be good for you to be in the house with Owen anyway while I drive this mouse out to its new house."

I hesitate again. "No, it's okay. I'll be fine. I already feel better—I just don't like them catching me by surprise. But I'll stay in the house with Owen while you're gone. Let me just grab my robe." I slip it on and follow him out the door.

We walk together until I reach the pathway to the house and then he veers toward the car.

"Go get warm. I'll be home in a few," he says.

I try to ignore the way his words make me feel all mushy inside, like I'm part of something bigger. *Home.* Like we're cohabitating in a home together, which is not even reality. I don't know why I can't seem to keep the strict lines between us in my mind. It's me, I know it is…being childish and letting a crush on an older man feel like everything he says is meaningful and that he feels something for me too.

It's just not true.

I'm doing a job for him—that's all this is.

He hasn't done anything but treat me kindly and professionally. He's become my friend too, and yet, I find myself making more of every gesture he makes, a romantic slant behind every word he says. It's ridiculous and it will end up backfiring on me if I'm not careful.

When I walk inside his kitchen and shut the door behind me, I turn on the tea kettle and pick out a mug and tea. The few minutes it takes to boil are a nice break from my warring thoughts. By the time I sip my tea and he pulls into the driveway, I've worked on a new resolve to be more professional myself.

I like this job too much to let my silly feelings get in the way.

He walks inside and hangs up his coat, pausing when he sees me sitting on the barstool.

I take another sip of tea and stand. "The water is still hot if you'd like some tea. I'll head out and let you get some sleep."

"You're not staying?" he asks softly.

Again with my thundering heart. I smile and shake my head. "It's late. I should get to bed. Tomorrow will come early."

He nods. "You're right. Sleep well, Felicity."

"You too. Thanks for rescuing me."

"Anytime." His voice sounds like he's smiling, but when I meet his gaze, he's more serious than I expected.

"Night, Sutton."

I slip out the door before I can do anything crazy…like try to kiss him.

CHAPTER FOURTEEN

REALLY NICE

SUTTON

Over the next few days, I can't quite put my finger on what's different about Felicity. Because we had such a great time at the game and before that, out with my family at The Dancing Emu, it catches me by surprise when she's not herself. Or not even that, just distant maybe. She's not in any way rude, but she doesn't take any extra time to chat, and the past few nights, she's prepared dinner but hasn't eaten with us.

Tonight, Owen and I were forlorn as we ate the amazing soup she'd made, without her.

"Do you think she has a date?" Owen asks as we clean up the kitchen.

I turn to look at him, surprised he'd thought of that and I hadn't.

"I don't know," I admit. "Did she say something about a date?"

He shakes his head. "No, but she's leaving and she looks nice."

He points toward the window and I go just close enough to see that she's getting into her car…and she *does* look nice. *Really* fucking nice.

"Good for her," I say quietly.

My chest twinges slightly and I rub it, feeling a slight ache there.

"Good for her," I repeat.

Maybe if I say it enough times, I'll mean it.

I do mean it.

I'm trying to mean it.

She's a great girl. She deserves a guy that can show her a good time, someone who will treat her right. Someone her age, obviously. Problem is, I don't know anyone like that around here. My sister dated a couple of the locals and they sure as hell weren't good enough for her, and every other single guy I know either enjoys the tourists a little too much or has no intention of settling down. There's no way I'd trust Felicity with any of them…

And that leaves the tourists.

That's a bad idea waiting to happen.

She deserves way better than that.

Owen and I play Mario Kart for a while and then he gets

his shower. When I tuck him in, he says, "Is Mom still coming next weekend?"

"Yes, if everything goes according to plan, she'll fly in on Friday night and be here until Sunday."

"It'll be weird staying at the lodge without you. Why can't we just stay here?"

"Because you and your mom need some one-on-one time together."

Tracy wanted to stay here, but I don't want to start that habit. It hasn't been that long ago since Tracy tried to kiss me after she dropped Owen off. Fortunately, he didn't see it, but it was about as awkward as it gets.

"Don't you miss us?" she asked.

"Please, Tracy. We don't need to revisit this."

It had been enough to shut her down that night, but I don't trust her to not try again if she stays here. And I meant what I said about the two of them needing time together. She owes that to Owen.

"I'd rather stay at the lodge without you than go to Arizona, though," Owen is saying.

I groan inside. He's still adamant about not going to Arizona, and I'm not sure how much to push him about it yet.

"She's willing to come see you during the school year, which is great, but during the summer, she wants you to come stay with her," I tell him. "You need to give it a chance. Maybe you'll love it there too."

He shakes his head. "Not the way I love it here."

"Well, no. This is the home you've always known. It's understandable, but…that's where your mom will be."

He nods, his expression grave. "Do you think you'll ever get another wife?"

My eyes widen and I think my mouth gapes too, as I try

to think of what to say. "Do you want me to get another wife?" I finally ask.

He rolls to his side, tucking the pillow under his cheek.

"I like our new family," he says. "If it was someone like Sofie or Marlow or Ruby...I wouldn't mind at all. They make our family better, like Felicity does. Do you think Felicity would want to be in our family?"

I swallow and feel the words stuttering in my chest before I even try to say anything. "I-I...people can be part of the family without marriage. Felicity is our friend. She works for us—she takes care of you and she also cares *about* you, but it has nothing to do with romantic feelings for me...which is what is needed for a marriage to work."

"Do you have romantic feelings for her?" he asks.

"Geez, son." I just barely manage to avoid the heavier curses running through my mind. "I, uh, I think Felicity is great and that we're lucky to have her working here." I frown.

Why can't I just say no to his question? That would take care of that. But every time I try to form the word, I pause and think, *do* I have romantic feelings for her?

No. It's crazy. I don't. I'm attracted to her. I like her. I like to be around her. But that's all it is.

Midway through a yawn, Owen says, "I hope she never leaves."

I kiss his forehead and turn off his light and when I walk out of the room, I whisper," I hope she doesn't either."

Later, I pause when I pass the window and see her walking up her stairs. I glance at the clock. It's after ten. Where has she been? Maybe she *was* on a date.

She goes inside and I freeze when she pulls her shirt over her head. Her blonde hair spills over her shoulders and my mouth waters even though I barely see her bra. The expanse of skin and the curve of her tits when she turns to the side is enough to have me cursing myself for still standing here, while also wishing the distance between my room and hers was closer so I could get a better look. She glances out the window and since my room is dark, I know she can't see me, but she pauses a second before closing her curtains.

I put my fist to my mouth, my heartbeat erratic. What the hell is wrong with me?

Instead of crawling into bed, I stalk to the shower and have it out with my dick.

But it doesn't drive the thoughts of her out of me. Not even a little bit.

I dream of her and wake up in the middle of the night fisting myself, ready for another round, and when I wake up before my alarm in the morning, I'm hard as a rock, imagining her riding me hard as I come with her name on my lips.

What the fuck am I going to do?

That evening, when I get home from work, Felicity hustles to get dinner on the table and Owen and I try to be helpful.

"Will you be eating with us this evening?" I grab plates to set the table but wait to see how many.

She pauses at the oven and turns to look at me. I've missed her this week, missed the ease between us.

"Uh, I'm not—" she says, the doorbell cutting her off.

I frown, setting the plates on the counter. "Were we expecting someone tonight?"

"No, I don't think so," Felicity says.

When I head to the front door and open it, I'm shocked to see Gwyneth. Blake and Camila must have told her where I live because I've never invited her here. But I'm not complaining. Maybe this is exactly what I needed, someone to distract me from all these thoughts of Felicity.

"Gwyneth, hello!" We move to hug each other and I lean back, smiling at her. "I didn't know you were in town."

"I've only been here since this morning. I should've called first, but I thought I'd surprise you instead. I hope that's okay."

"Sure. It's good to see you," I tell her.

She presses her hand against my chest and grins. "I'm glad you feel that way…because I've been thinking about this for a while now."

"This?" I echo.

Her hands land in my hair and she tugs it, her mouth on mine before I've even had time to process what's happening.

CHAPTER FIFTEEN

VYING FOR CONTENTION

FELICITY

When Sutton doesn't come back right away, Owen grabs my hand and tugs me toward the front door to see who's there. When we round the corner, it's just in time to see a woman dig her hands through Sutton's hair and pull him down to kiss her. I think my mouth drops before I remember little eyes are watching, so I try to back us out of the room.

Owen's feet remain firmly planted.

He clears his throat and lets go of my hand long enough

to cross his arms, just as Sutton takes a step back and starts to say something to the woman. But then the throat-clearing registers and he turns to look at us, an unreadable expression on his face. I can't begin to imagine what my face must look like, but since Weston says I have no poker face, I can only imagine it's not hiding anything. I wish the floor could swallow me up, but since that's not possible, I do the next best thing and turn, lifting my hand up in a wave.

"Sorry to interrupt," I say over my shoulder, as I walk out of the room.

When I've reached the kitchen, I hold onto the counter as I will my heart to calm down.

You were trying to create distance for a reason. You knew you needed to take a step back.

It all sounds reasonable in theory, but the way my stomach is turning over seeing Sutton lip-locked with a beautiful woman is another story.

You have no right to feel this way. You haven't known the man for long, and what you do know has given you no reason to believe he's interested. This kiss just confirms that.

Again, reasonable in theory, but it's like my heart is conferring with my stomach and they're in cahoots. I've lost my appetite, and that never happens. The baked spaghetti with a combo of marinara and alfredo sauces that I prepared for tonight is freaking delicious, and I can't even consider eating it right now.

He is your boss. Nothing more.

I get the ice for the glasses and find my purse on the desk just as Sutton walks back with Owen and the woman. She gives me a friendly but assessing smile, and I try to only look friendly as I smile back at her, but I probably fail.

"Felicity, this is Gwyneth Daly."

My heart thrums against my rib cage, hearing her name.

This is the woman he had dinner with when she was visiting last time…the one I just knew he'd slept with. After seeing that kiss, I'd say my intuition was hella on point.

I can barely hear Sutton saying, "Gwyneth, this is Owen's nanny, Felicity."

"Oh, you're the nanny. That's great," she says, her smile widening. "It's nice to meet you. What smells so good in here?"

"Nice to meet you," I say on autopilot. "Baked spaghetti."

"Felicity is an amazing cook," Sutton says. He glances at the pasta I've taken out of the oven and his eyes widen. "We haven't had this yet, but I can guarantee it'll be out of this world."

My cheeks warm with his praise. We still laugh at my disastrous first attempt in his kitchen, but he never fails to tell me how delicious everything is and to let me know how grateful he is for everything I'm doing here.

"Looks like I either came at the worst possible time or that this is my lucky day," Gwyneth says, laughing. Her eyes meet mine and I jump in to avoid making it more awkward than it already is.

"There's plenty, and I pulled out an extra plate for you already, just in case." I point to the plate next to the casserole dish and salad, the garlic bread steaming next to that. It brings me no small comfort to know they'll have dragon garlic breath when they kiss later. "I'm just heading out, but everything's ready to go."

"But you should stay," Owen says, his hand reaching out to touch my arm.

"Yes, stay," Sutton adds.

"I really can't," I say. I lift my hand over my shoulder. "I've got a…thing."

It's obvious I'm lying. At least to Gwyneth. She's looking

at me with a mixture of *yeah, right* and *you poor girl, you've got it bad, don't you*?

Yes, I freaking do, okay? I didn't realize just how bad until I saw Gwyneth's tongue down Sutton's throat.

And I don't really care what she thinks, I just want to get out of here.

"Have a great night!" I sound like a chipmunk, each word chirping higher than the last.

Sutton tries to say one more thing, but I pretend to not hear him, opening the door and rushing toward my place.

When I step inside, I'm tempted to crawl under the covers and stay there for the rest of the night, but I don't. I add a little more eyeliner and powder my nose. After I've added lip gloss and a spritz of perfume, I put on my jacket and leave before I can talk myself out of it.

Heritage Lane is the cutest street, lit with white lights and Valentine decor popping out everywhere. Every time I drive into town, more decorations have been added. There are heart garlands along the storefronts and red and pink decorations attached to the lampposts. The Hallmark card holiday is just around the corner and I don't even want to think about it right now, but the town sure looks festive.

As I drive down the busy street, I'm unsure of where to stop. I don't really care where it is—I just need a distraction. When I see a car pull out of The Dancing Emu's parking lot, I decide to try there. If it's too crowded, I'll go back to my place, but I'd rather not run into Gwyneth or Sutton again tonight.

I hear my name called and turn abruptly, running into someone as I do.

"I'm so sorry," I say.

When I look up, there's a good-looking guy smiling back at me, and I apologize again.

"You can run into me anytime," he says, giving me an easy smile.

I laugh awkwardly and then glance around, looking for who would've said my name.

Wyatt, Marlow, and Dakota are sitting at a table and Marlow waves me over. I exhale in relief, my mood already lifting as I walk toward them.

Marlow stands up and hugs me and Dakota quickly follows, her little arms wrapping around me.

"This is exactly what I needed," I say, smiling down at her.

"Hard day?" Wyatt asks.

I look at him, his smile and concern giving me a pang of homesickness for my brother.

"It's just really nice to see you guys," I say.

Wyatt looks around. "Sutton and Owen aren't with you?"

"Oh, no…it's just me." I'm embarrassed, realizing they must have thought Sutton would be here and that's why they called me over.

"Even better," Wyatt says. "We can talk about him while he's not here."

He laughs when I look at him in surprise.

"Kidding. But you can talk about my brother if you want. I tell him he's a bastard all the time." His eyes are twinkling with amusement as he looks up at me.

Goodness, these Landmarks could make a girl get woozy.

Dakota holds out her hand, and Wyatt startles.

"What did I even say?"

"B-word," Dakota whispers.

He sighs and fishes out a dollar from his pocket.

"Don't let him fool you. The brothers—and Scarlett— have each other's backs more than anyone I know. They all talk a good game," Marlow says, laughing. She motions toward the table. "Join us?"

"I don't want to interrupt," I start.

Wyatt pulls out a chair for me. "Don't be silly. Marlow was craving Pierre's wings and Dakota was hoping there would be karaoke."

I sit down, smiling at Dakota.

"Wings seemed like a reasonable pregnancy craving." Marlow grins. "Better than a middle-of-the-night request for something with pickles."

"I'm living for the day that happens," Wyatt says, reaching out to thread his fingers with hers.

They are so cute it gives my heart whiplash.

A throat clears and we all look up. I expected to see a waiter, but it's the guy I ran into when I got here.

"I hope it's okay that I do this," he says, his eyes on me. "I just…wondered if I could have your number."

"Oh." I look at him in surprise. "I—"

"If you need to think about it longer, here's mine," he says, pushing a piece of paper toward me that has his number. "My name's Ethan and I'll be here for a few weeks and coming through Landmark Mountain often. I…thought we had a good vibe back there." He tilts his head toward the entrance.

I'm not sure when there was time to have any kind of vibe since I just ran into him, but I pick up his number and glance at it. His name is above the number with a Colorado area code.

"Thanks," I say, waving it slightly.

"I'd love for you to join me for a drink. I'm right over there." He points toward his table with a few friends. He grins and nods at Wyatt and Marlow, smiling at me once more before he walks away.

"Well, well," Marlow says, leaning in. "Somebody's interested!" She laughs. "Didn't take long for Miss Felicity Shaw to make her presence known in Landmark Mountain."

My cheeks flush and I shake my head, laughing.

Wyatt sets his phone on the table and lifts an eyebrow. "Are you interested in that guy?"

I lift a shoulder. "A month or two ago I might've been, but—"

The waiter comes up then and we all order. Not long after that the karaoke starts, and we listen for a while, commenting here and there about who's good and exchanging looks when it's not as good. Our food has just arrived when I hear Owen's voice behind me. I turn and see Sutton and Owen walking to the table.

Owen starts to sit in the chair next to me and Dakota motions for him to sit next to her. He gives me a hug first and then goes to sit next to her. Sutton sits down next to me and I feel him glancing my way. I don't look at him. Seeing him kissing Gwyneth is still on repeat in my mind like a festering wound.

It's best I just pretend my boss doesn't exist.

CHAPTER SIXTEEN

COUGH SYRUP AND EXPLETIVES

SUTTON

I'd just managed to get Gwyneth out of the house when Wyatt texted me. It was a quick dinner, obvious to Gwyneth that I wasn't comfortable with the drop-in at my house, and at least she didn't prolong the matter.

WYATT

Your girl is here with us at The Dancing Emu, and a tourist stud has already hit on her. You better get over here.

> She's not my girl. Stop talking like that. And fucking take care of it. You know the tourists are only after one thing.

WYATT

Just to clarify. She's NOT your girl, but you don't want her spending the night with a tourist?

> Fuck no. It's not safe.

WYATT

Even if Ethan looks perfectly safe and seemed to have a pretty good strategy with his pickup line?

> Who the fuck is Ethan? Is that the fucking tourist?

WYATT

Better not let Grinny hear that mouth. Or Dakota.

> Shut the fuck up.

WYATT

I think someone's feeling things he's not admitting.

Oh, I'm thinking a lot of fucking things right now. Somehow, I manage to keep that to myself.

"Owen," I call, "get your coat. We're going out."

"Well, this is a fun impromptu get-together," Wyatt says, smirking at me.

I give him a deadly look, the kind that, as a kid, would've had him scrambling to get back on my good side, but the son of a bitch has gotten cocky as an adult. Especially now that he's found love and is so supremely happy.

"I hoped you'd stay for dinner," I say under my breath, looking at Felicity. "It was delicious," I add.

Her shoulders stiffened when I started talking, and she focuses on her food. I don't think she's made direct eye contact with me since I got here and it bothers me more than I want to admit.

"Felicity?" I say, louder this time.

She looks at me then and the usual warmth I see from her is missing. I frown. Decorum keeps me from leaning in and whispering in her ear the way I want to.

"Everything okay?" I ask out loud instead.

"Everything's fine," she says. "Where's Gwyneth?" She looks around, searching the restaurant for her. "She can take my seat when she gets here."

"Gwyneth is in town?" Wyatt asks, looking at me sharply before also looking around the room.

"She surprised me by stopping by the house," I say.

"Did you forget to add your purple night to the calendar?" Felicity says, standing up. "I'm gonna go have a drink with my friend."

I put my hand on her arm without thinking. "I'll buy you a drink."

She pries her arm away. "No, thank you," she says coolly.

She walks away and I look up to see Wyatt and Marlow's gaze ping-ponging from where she's ended up and back to me.

Fuck.

"Purple night?" Wyatt asks.

I wave him off. "It's a schedule thing."

"Ah, I'd forgotten how you color-code everything." He leans in. "Why does she look so pissed?" he asks quietly.

I slide my hand down my face and shake my head.

"Gwyneth, huh?" Wyatt lifts his brows.

He tilts his head toward where Felicity is standing at a high-top table, talking to a jock type that looks like he wants to inhale her.

"Are you *trying* to blow this?" Wyatt says under his breath.

"*This* is *nothing*. *This* is the *nanny* who's working for me to take care of my son," I say between clenched teeth, low enough so Owen can't hear me.

"Well, *this*," Wyatt says, waving his hand in my direction, "is a whole lot of angst going on for *nothing*, and *that* is the *nanny* who looks like she's either taking the tourist up on his offer or she's trying to make you jealous. I personally think it's the latter. What do you think?" he asks Marlow.

She nods. "Definitely the latter," she says and then shoots me a guilty look.

I swipe my hand down my face. "She saw Gwyneth kissing me earlier and left without eating the dinner she prepared. She's been doing that lately…at first she ate with us, but I guess I thought tonight…she might stay."

"Go back to the *Gwyneth kissing you* part," Marlow says.

"Dad says Gwyneth was just saying hello," Owen says, hopefully only picking up on the last part of the conversation.

I'm sorry, Marlow mouths.

I wave her off like it's not a big deal, even though I don't want to revisit this discussion with my son. The whole way over here, he grilled me about Gwyneth and why it looked like she was one of those fish in the aquarium that sucks the glass.

"And Dad said they went on a date once and Gwyneth

might have thought they were picking up where they left off, but he didn't think they were picking up where they left off because they haven't talked since then and he doesn't feel like picking up where they left off, so he stopped the kiss," Owen says, running out of breath as he tries to get it all out.

He gasps in a deep inhale, and I question my decision of giving him that much honesty when I answered his questions.

I try to be subtle as I watch Felicity throw her head back and laugh, cursing every word imaginable in my head. Why is this making me so angry? I've warned her that the tourists aren't the safest option—hell, they might be decent, but we don't know them, do we? I'm tempted to run a background check on the kid.

Owen and Dakota start playing a game on his iPad, and I hope it keeps them busy so they don't hear any of this. I turn back to Wyatt.

"Did you catch his last name?" I ask.

Wyatt snorts. "No, and listen, you're not gonna go all judicial system mode here." He leans forward and says so softly that I can barely hear him in this loud restaurant, "I haven't seen you interested in anyone in such a long time, Sutton. Maybe not ever quite like this—you're the *play it cool, never let them see you sweat* guy, and just so you know, I'm seeing you sweat. Go over there, tell her you're not interested in kissing Gwyneth, and take her home and make it right."

I make a face. "Do you hear yourself? Just because you and the rest of the family have found love in the span of—practically *minutes*—doesn't mean I'm feeling anything for this *girl* I hardly know."

"He's making fun of all of us for falling fast, did you hear that?" Wyatt says to Marlow.

"Yep, I caught that." She nods.

They both try to not grin, and I'm so annoyed, I reach out and take a long swig of Wyatt's drink, nearly choking when the cough syrup sweetness coats my mouth.

"The fuck is that?" I sputter.

The kids' eyes turn on me and I dig money out of my pocket, cursing again since I already have my wallet out.

"Marlow's turned me onto some of her favorite cocktails, just occasionally since they're full of sugar," Wyatt says, putting his arm around Marlow. "We obviously got virgin ones tonight since we've got a baby on the way."

"You're going through all that torture and there's not even alcohol in it?" I ask incredulously.

Wyatt picks up the drink and slugs it.

"Refreshing," he says when he sets it down. He leans back in. "I didn't miss what you were throwing out when you said *girl*. She's young, yes, but twenty-two is perfectly legal, and the way she keeps glancing over here to see if you're looking tells me she is more than interested."

"I'm just here because I feel responsible for her," I grumble.

"Okay, you keep telling yourself that and possibly miss out on something great. Don't tell me you're not as smart as I thought you were," he says.

"When did you get so smug?" I grind out, swiping my hand down my face again.

He just grins and lifts his glass. "I dare you to go get her. We can even take Owen home for the night."

I scoff. "It's a school night."

Who fucking cares? He mouths it so he doesn't get fined by the expletive police, otherwise known as Owen and Dakota.

The restaurant cheers when the song is over and Wyatt

says something, but I can't stop watching Felicity with that jock wannabe.

Wyatt's wrong. I haven't caught feelings. Felicity has become a friend in a short amount of time for sure, and okay, I have less than platonic thoughts about what I'd like to do with her body…but since I know that can't go anywhere, I'm just in this weird protective friend role that I'm trying to fill.

And failing horribly.

I look at her again, giving myself five seconds to get my fix, and her eyes meet mine. I stand up.

"Owen, let's get back home," I say.

"Already?" he asks.

"You're not going for it? Unbelievable," Wyatt says.

"Mind your business."

"Granddad would be busting your balls right now," Wyatt says, pointing at me.

I pause, knowing he's right, but then shake my head. "He'd be appalled that we're talking about someone like this who's Scarlett's age. *Younger*, even."

He shakes his head. "Scarlett is living with her boyfriend. As much as I hate to admit it, our little sister is an adult." He whispers, "We might hate it, but *gasp*, Scarlett and Jamison sleep in the same bed. Haven't you seen that lingerie she makes? That should clear up the matter in your head about your sister's age. She's not a little girl anymore, brother. And neither is that woman over there."

Marlow leans in and I can tell by the mischief in her eyes that she's about to say something rotten. "I've got a great idea," she says, voice low. "Get Felicity in one of Scarlett's works of lingerie art and you won't have any confusion about whether Felicity is too young or not."

I scowl at both of them and they just laugh, while I

motion for Owen to get up. He grabs his device while I kiss Dakota goodbye, and we get out of there fast.

The image of Felicity on her knees in my bed, dressed in nothing but one of those sexy scraps of lace just made me hard as a rock.

CHAPTER SEVENTEEN
SENSES ROBBERY

FELICITY

I can barely enjoy the night.

I was frustrated when Sutton showed up at the restaurant, but I'm even more frustrated when he leaves.

It's not rational whatsoever—neither my frustration nor the relief over Gwyneth not being with him—and that's what makes me the maddest, this irrational thinking.

I'm the problem here—me and my ridiculous romantic attachment that has robbed me of my senses.

Ethan was nice and cute, and I couldn't even enjoy his flirtation because my eyes kept wandering back to Sutton's, where his dark eyes were assessing me every time.

I drive back to Sutton's and besides the light by the front door, the lights in the house are off. My shoulders are so tense that I feel tight all over. I'm ready to be done with this day. I shut the door to my car quietly and walk toward the stairs.

"Felicity."

The low timbre in his voice sends chill bumps skittering down my spine. I pause and turn toward the house, not seeing where he is.

"Sutton," I say quietly.

"You're home late."

"Didn't know my hours off were under such close scrutiny."

"They are when you're under my care."

A snort escapes me before I can stop it. "Under your *care*?"

I walk toward the house, stopping when I see his shadow on the side porch. I click the flashlight on my keychain and can make him out a little better. He sets something down. It sounds like ice rattling against a glass.

"As long as you're living with me, you're under my care," he says.

"You're taking the employer/employee role a little too far. I'm under no one's care but my own, thank you very much."

He stands up and I've moved closer to him than I realized.

He takes another step toward me and I gasp when our chests touch. This close, I see him just enough to tell that his hair is disheveled, like he's run his hands through it a million times, and warmth is emanating from his body even though it's cold out here. He reaches out and gently touches my face, pushing my hair off my shoulder, and then he grabs it in his fist and tilts my face up. His nose brushes against mine.

He smells like whiskey and leather and something sweet and I just breathe him in, scared to move in case it breaks this spell.

"Did you let him kiss you?" he says, his forehead lowering to mine.

"Who?" I whisper.

I pull back slightly and he loosens his grip on my hair, his hand dropping to his side.

"You're asking me if I let a guy kiss me when your lips were all over Gwyneth's earlier?" I shake my head. "Nope, you don't get to do that."

I turn to walk away and his hands around my waist stop me. His mouth is against my ear now, his body pressed against my back.

"I stopped the kiss. She caught me by surprise," he says.

I lean my head back on his shoulder, intoxicated by the nearness of him.

"God knows I *should* be kissing her…or anyone else…to get the thought of kissing *you* out of my system." His voice is hoarse and gravelly, and I can't get enough of it.

I turn around.

"You think of kissing me?" I whisper.

"All the time." He touches my face and his lips hover near mine, the anticipation making my entire body feel weighted, like his arms are the only thing holding me up.

The sound of a distant coyote howling and then another joining in breaks the spell. Sutton takes a step back, his arms dropping off of me, leaving me cold.

But his words send me reeling.

"This is…so wrong," he says. "Felicity, I—"

"Wrong?" I repeat.

"I'm sorry. I've had too much to drink tonight. I was… please, forgive me. It won't happen again." He walks toward the door to the kitchen and stands there, looking back at me. "I swear to you it won't."

He says that like it's a good thing. Like him promising to not touch me again is something I *want* to hear instead of the truth, which is, *now that you've touched me, I'll be craving it more than I already was.*

I don't have the first idea of what to say. For a second, I experienced sheer euphoria, and the next, it was snatched away from me.

So I say nothing, and he nods at me once more before turning and going inside the house, leaving me outside, numb and alone.

The next morning, I'm exhausted after a night of tossing and turning. There are a bunch of texts on my phone, but not a single one is from Sutton. I bite back my disappointment and scroll through them.

> RUBY
> What does one wear to a football game?
> Asking for a friend. <Wink emoji>

Tomorrow night is the game and as promised if he won, Weston has tickets for everyone. I'm just glad it will be all of us.

> **SCARLETT**
>
> Jamison and I bought Shaw jerseys! I think Jamison did it just to tease his brother, but Zac sent back a text saying he's the biggest fan of Weston. <Laughing emoji> What do you wear, Felicity?

I still can't believe Jamison's brother is Zac Ledger. I freaked when I found out and so did Weston when I told him. We've followed Zac's career forever. There's talk about him retiring. He won the Super Bowl last year and he's had a great season this year too, but their defense just wasn't quite there.

> **MARLOW**
>
> I need to go shopping before tomorrow night. I'm outgrowing my clothes a lot faster than I did with Dakota.

> **SOFIE**
>
> Are jeans and a sweater okay?

> Anything you wear will be fine! Honestly, I embarrass my sister Olivia so bad because I try to match whatever uniform Weston's wearing. So this week will be the white jersey and the teal pants with white and grey stripes. I even have the matching knee bands and a Mustangs jacket.

> **RUBY**
>
> CUTE!

> **SCARLETT**
>
> Love it. Family pride all the way. I'm here for it.

> **MARLOW**
>
> Will we get to meet your sister?

> I'm not sure. I'll text her and see if she's coming.

I hesitate before texting Olivia. It's been a while since we talked and she has a way of seeing through me. If anyone mentions me taking care of Owen in front of my family, I'll act like it's not a big deal that I'm helping with Sutton's son. They don't need to know the details about what I'm doing for Sutton, but Olivia is the one who will dig if she senses anything is off. I still need time to figure out the whole law school conversation.

My alarm goes off and I startle, tossing my phone across the bed and jumping up. I get ready and make an extra effort because as tense as I'm going to be around Sutton today and as angry I am that he said that perfect moment between us last night was *so wrong*...I want to look *good*.

The surprise is once again on me.

When I get to the house, Grinny is there with Owen. They both turn and smile sweetly at me.

"Felicity," Owen says, his sleepy eyes brightening when I get closer.

"What a nice surprise!" Grinny says. "Didn't expect to see you on a Saturday morning. Sutton had to go in early this morning," Grinny says.

"Oh...I was texting the girls about the game tomorrow and my alarm went off. I lost my mind and got ready, not realizing it's Saturday." I laugh. "I'm a mess. But Sutton should've let me know. You didn't have to do all this. I'm right here."

I carry the rest of the food to the table and Owen starts piling it on his plate. This little guy likes his breakfast.

"Oh, it's all right. I was missing my boy, and Sutton didn't want to wake you up early on your day off. He knew

I'd be up. It's no trouble at all," Grinny says. She sips her coffee and beams at me. "You look so lovely."

"Thanks, Grinny." Her words and smile give me a boost. I was feeling a bit dejected after all my efforts to look good and he's not even here.

It's not lost on me that he wanted to avoid seeing me so bad, he went into work early on a Saturday morning.

How will I hold onto this job if my boss can't even see me?

I enjoy breakfast with Grinny and Owen. He can hardly contain his excitement about the game tomorrow, and his energy is infectious. After I help clean up, I decide to go out for a little while. I don't want to hog Owen from Grinny, and I may as well explore the town since I have nothing better to do.

I stop at the little boutique connected to the resort and then I go find the lingerie shop Scarlett's mentioned recently opening. I'm blown away by how beautiful the pieces are and buy a couple. I'm not sure when I'll ever have a chance to wear them and I don't need to be spending money on anything right now, but it does make me feel better. I don't often use retail therapy, but it works. For now, anyway.

After going into a few more shops, I see an adorable restaurant called The Pink Ski, but it looks too crowded to get in. There are skis of every different color making a fence near the restaurant and at the bottom of one of the ski runs, and I wonder what made them settle on pink for the name of the restaurant. When traffic starts creeping, I turn off of the main strip and see Sunny Side, a restaurant I've heard mentioned more than once. This is where the girls say everyone bets on things. It looks a little tamer than everything did on Heritage Lane and I find a spot and park.

When I step inside, it gets quiet and it's almost like the

whole restaurant stops to look at me, but then it quickly picks back up, and I think I've imagined the whole thing.

On a little bulletin board next to the counter, I start reading and then step closer to see if I'm reading it correctly.

Oh. My. God.

The bets were not exaggerated in the least.

When will Sutton Landmark find love?

Higher winnings if you guess right between Gwyneth Daly, Felicity Shaw, or Unknown.

My eyes widen. I'm on the list? I've never even been in here before. Has Sutton seen this? He'd be appalled that anyone's even considering this. Or maybe he has seen it and that's why he's concerned. I keep reading.

What month will Jamison ask Scarlett to marry him?

How much snow will we get in February?

Lindsey Carpenter, you are the winner of January's weather bet. Collect your prize by February 1st or it will go back in the pot.

I'm about to back out of there when a nice lady comes out and asks if I'd like to sit at the counter or a booth. I get a shake to go and get the hell out of there.

CHAPTER EIGHTEEN

SCANDALOUS

SUTTON

I know, I'm a coward.

But the truth of it is, I've desperately needed the space from Felicity.

It's not that I'm afraid of facing her.

The problem is she felt so damn good that I want nothing more than to touch her again, and I can't.

I absolutely can't.

Regardless of what my brothers say, she's too young.

It sounds okay in theory since she's legal, but when I'm fifty, she'll be entering her prime and I'll be ready to snooze.

Not to mention how completely immoral it would look as a judge to have a relationship with my son's nanny who is thirteen years younger than me.

What I did a couple of nights ago was so out of line.

And the fact that I haven't made it right in person makes it even worse, but I've needed to get my head on straight. I worked at the office and then went skiing with my brothers and Owen on Saturday afternoon. Felicity's car was gone, so I didn't have to make a decision about talking to her yet. Then Owen spent the night at Grinny's with Dakota, and I went to Blake and Camila's restaurant Tiptop. I don't see Blake and Camila often enough, but it's always great when we can hang out.

All I could think about was how much they'd love Felicity and how I wished I could take her there, so it didn't work to get her out of my head, but today's a new day. And I feel more resolute today than I did yesterday.

I picked Owen up an hour ago, and we came back to the house to pick up Felicity and go to the game. That's been the plan since earlier in the week…before I shot everything to shit.

But there's a note from Felicity on the kitchen island saying she got a ride with Callum, Ruby, Scarlett, and Jamison.

Fuck. I've blown it again.

Owen and I get on the road and Owen falls asleep, worn out from his sleepover, and I mull over what I'm going to say when I see Felicity.

We're in a suite this time, and when Owen and I get there, the party's already started. Callum is the first one I see, and he squeezes my shoulder after hugging Owen.

"Thanks for bringing Felicity," I tell him.

"Of course," he says. He frowns. "You okay?"

"Yeah."

When I sound anything but, he shoots me another look.

"I will be. I've just needed..." I shake my head and lean in, so no one else will hear what I'm about to say. "I'm not sure it was a good idea to have her live above the garage. There's no...space."

His eyebrows raise. "And you're needing space?"

I stare at him for a moment and nod slowly. Who am I kidding? My brothers know me better than anyone and for some reason, Callum has always been the one to drag things out of me with his quiet man sorcery. For a man of few words, he seems to always get to the heart of the matter.

"You like her," he says simply.

"More than I should," I admit.

"She's a good person. What's wrong with liking her?"

"I've already—"

He holds up his hand. "I've heard your reservations, but some of that is you holding yourself to a higher standard than you have to."

I shake my head. "I can't, Callum."

He nods. "Okay. Then you probably shouldn't see her tonight."

I've already been looking all over the room for her. It's crowded, but if she were in here, I'd have found her by now.

"Why not?"

He grins. "She came dressed to kill."

"Fuck. Me."

"Yep."

Ruby comes over and leans her head on Callum's shoulder.

"My wife did as well," Callum adds.

She lifts her head and kisses him. "I did what as well?"

"Came dressed to kill," he says.

Ruby grins. She's in the Mustangs colors and looks great.

"Hey, Sutton," she says. "Have you seen Felicity yet?"

"Hey. Uh, no. Where is she?"

Ruby's grin widens. "Behind you."

I turn and my mouth parts, all the mental clarity I've been working on for the past couple of days where she's concerned going out the window. She's wearing a tiny white jersey crop top, inches of her toned stomach showing underneath, and her pants are like a second skin. This is the rated-R version of what she was wearing when we came to the game with Owen. There's nothing inappropriate about what she's wearing today, except where it takes my thoughts.

"Hi," she says, nonchalantly. As if she can't tell that I'm struck speechless by her.

"Hey. Sorry if there was confusion about getting here. I'd planned on bringing you."

Callum and Ruby move to talk to someone else and I step closer to Felicity. Her cheeks are slightly pink, her full bottom lip sliding through her teeth for a second.

"Not a big deal," she says. "I thought it was best if I had a backup plan since I haven't seen or heard from you in a couple of days."

Why do I feel like the child here?

"I'm sorry to leave you hanging. I've had a busy weekend."

"I'm sure," she says.

Her tone isn't sharp and neither is her expression, but I still feel her anger.

I glance around the room. Everyone is talking and laughing and eating. Owen and Dakota are playing with a few toys they brought. I reach out and almost touch Felicity's arm before I think better of it.

"Can we talk?" I ask. "Somewhere private?"

Felicity looks around and then nods. She turns and walks to the side of the room. There's a small hall connecting the suite to the bathroom.

"Is this okay or would you rather go outside the suite?" she asks.

"This is fine. Felicity, I just want to say I'm sorry."

"You've already apologized," she says.

"And yet, it doesn't feel resolved. I can't tell you how sorry I am for putting you in that position. You've done nothing to warrant that behavior, and I'm ashamed of myself."

A crease forms between her brows. "You make it sound like you did something scandalous."

"Well, it was. I shouldn't have—"

"There was *nothing* scandalous about it," she says, her voice rising, and the anger that I've been feeling from her finally shows. She points her finger at me but brings her voice down to a whisper. "I can't decide if you think I'm too young or you don't want to jeopardize my working with Owen. But either way, the only thing you did wrong was not finishing what you started."

And with that she turns and walks away, and I stand staring after her, wishing I could fuck it all and follow.

CHAPTER NINETEEN

CHEESE AND GRUDGES

FELICITY

I've managed to avoid deep conversations with my parents, asking them for no shop talk at the beginning of the night, and it's been the same with my sister, but near the end of the game, Olivia corners me when I stand to get a drink.

"Why didn't you tell me you were working for *him*?" she spits out. "You know how I feel about him. How did this all come about? What exactly are you doing for him?"

I sigh and pick up a cheese slice and two crackers, taking a big bite to stall a little longer.

"I thought maybe you'd gotten past that first loss," I say.

It's a lie. Olivia carries grudges *forever*.

She rolls her eyes. "I presented a good case and in his final instruction to the jury, I'm telling you, he slanted it in Joe Sellers' favor."

Maybe because he thought Joe made a better case is what I want to say but don't. She would not take that well. Especially not from me.

"So, what's happening? This is why you graduated early, so you could work for Judge Landmark?"

"My finishing early had nothing to do with this job. I just wanted to be done, so I worked hard to finish. I needed a break," I tell her.

"And...?" she prods.

"And what?"

"What are you doing for him?"

My head falls back. "Can we not talk about work tonight? This game is a big deal."

"They're winning," she scoffs.

"I don't want to miss the game."

"Are you finding out any sordid secrets about him?" she asks under her breath. "Anything illicit under that by-the-book facade?"

His fist in my hair comes to mind, the way his body felt against me...

I swallow hard and take a long swig of my vodka tonic.

"He's a nice man. He's been good to me, and I like his family. You've met everyone tonight, right?"

"Yeah, they're nice enough, but I don't feel like they're very forthcoming. When I asked something about the courthouse, it was like they shut me down."

"What did you ask?"

"If it was still old as sin…"

"Olivia!" I glare at her. "Why would you say something so rude? No wonder they shut you down."

"It was a legitimate question. Don't you think the courthouse needs a major redo?"

I haven't been inside the courthouse yet, but when I've passed it, I've thought it looks charming from the outside. Olivia doesn't appreciate historical buildings the way I do though.

I roll my eyes. "I can't believe you."

"What? I'm simply stating the truth."

"Sometimes you need to keep your thoughts to yourself."

Now she's rolling her eyes at me. "I've hardly lost a case since that first one, so I think I'm doing just fine."

"Maybe that loss motivated you." I lift a shoulder and stare her down when she glares at me. "Come on," I say, after a long sigh. "Let's watch the game."

I don't want to miss a second of this game, and I also can't deal with my sister right now. She's hard when I'm in a good headspace, and I'm still off after that conversation with Sutton. Knowing her, she'll circle back around to my job.

Owen and Dakota run over when they see me walking toward my seat. They show me the small LEGO set they've built since they got here. Owen's been dividing his time between watching the game and playing hard.

"This is so cool," I tell him. "You guys did that fast."

"We had to so I could still catch the game," he says, smiling up at me before he's off again.

He's so cute sometimes it makes my heart squeeze.

I feel Sutton's eyes on me and when I turn to look, he's close, and I was right…he's staring at me. He looks away when Olivia turns toward him.

"He's way hotter than I remember, I'll give him that," she mutters under her breath. "Anyone who can look sexy in those black robes has got some serious swagger. Too bad he's a prick."

"Olivia!" I hiss. "He's not a prick. The fact that you lost your first case probably has very little to do with him and everything to do with you. Get over it and move on."

I walk away and in doing so, I nearly run into Sutton. He steadies me and we exchange a heated look before I move past him, going to sit by my parents since the girls are by the food now. Sitting here feels safer than going near Sutton or my sister again, and my parents want to watch the game as badly as I do.

For the next hour, I get lost in the game and it's an exceptional one. The Mustangs win by fourteen and I can't even believe it—my brother's going to the Super Bowl! We dance around the suite, and when the game is over, after the awards and all the celebrating, we meet Weston on the field. His teammate Penn Hudson is next to him, and both are happier than I've ever seen them. Since meeting Penn, I've had a little crush on him, but when I see him this time, I don't feel that same rush of attraction.

I hug Weston and then Penn, congratulating them both, and then I hug Weston again, crying when I tell him how proud I am of him.

"You did it. I knew you would," I tell him.

Penn huddles with us, his arms around us, and I think all three of us cry a little bit. It's a sweet, emotional moment.

When we break apart and they move to hug my parents and the rest of their friends gathering around, I stand back and laugh as I watch them. I've never seen Weston this excited. I congratulate a few of the other players I met when I was staying with Weston and then turn, and Sutton is there.

"Sorry," he says. "I don't want to rush you, but I wanted to let you know I can take you home."

I start to argue but stop myself. It's most convenient for everyone involved if I ride with Sutton.

"Okay." My voice is resigned, and I don't miss the look of hurt that crosses his face.

"Take your time. We'll be over here when you're ready," he says.

And he turns and walks away before I can respond.

"I think we're going to take off," Scarlett says behind me.

I turn to face her and Jamison has her back pulled against his chest. They look like a sexy romance novel. For that matter, so do Callum and Ruby when they walk hand-in-hand toward us. Next to them, Wyatt and Marlow are sneaking in a kiss while Dakota and Owen chat, and Sofie's leaning against the wall of the arena while Theo talks to her, his forehead on hers.

My God. How do people live around this and not lose their minds with lust?

"This was incredible, Felicity. Thank you so much for making this happen," Scarlett says. "We had the best time."

"I'm so happy it worked out," I say, hugging her when she moves closer.

"Hey, you're okay, right?" she asks.

I pull back and nod. "Yeah, I'm good. Just a little weepy for my brother." I laugh and hope that I pull it off. I feel like crying for entirely different reasons.

"Do you need a ride back with us or is Sutton taking you?" she asks.

"Sutton's taking me."

She nods and smiles, but she still looks concerned, like maybe I'm not being quite as convincing as I'd hoped.

I hug everyone, saving my parents for last.

"Love you," I tell them.

"We love you…and we're missing you. When are you coming to visit?" Dad asks.

"I'm not sure. It's been busy so far, but hopefully I'll get there soon." I hug my mom next. "Where's Olivia?"

"She had to leave. Early morning tomorrow. Big day at court," Mom says proudly. "You're still planning on going to the Super Bowl, right?"

"Wouldn't miss it," I say, grinning at her.

Weston's eyes meet mine across the field and he smiles, pounding his fist over his chest. I do it back and almost cry all over again.

"All right. I better go. Love you," I say, squeezing my dad's hand again.

"Love you, honey." His brows pucker. "It's really something seeing Judge Landmark at two of the games. I wouldn't have thought he'd be out socializing so much."

"He's a normal guy, Dad."

He nods. "You're right. Is—are you riding back with him?" He's looking at Sutton over my shoulder.

Sutton's paranoia has me nervous and wanting to paint him in a good light, despite how much I disagree with him. So again, I evade the truth. I'm getting too good at this.

"I came with his brother and sister and their partners, so I better make sure I don't get left behind."

"All right, honey." My dad puts his arm around my mom's shoulders and watches as I walk toward Sutton.

Scarlett's not far from him, so I'm hoping my parents will think we're all leaving together.

"I've said all my goodbyes," I tell Sutton.

He nods and lifts off of the wall he's leaning against.

"Everyone want to head out together?" I ask hopefully.

"That's a good idea," Scarlett says. "You probably know your way around here much better than we do."

So everything works as planned. I don't have to talk to Sutton yet. My parents see us leave as a group.

Until we separate in the parking lot and I'm with Sutton and Owen, whose energy is quickly winding down. The tension amps up, and I don't know how I'll survive the hour and a half back to Landmark Mountain. When we reach the car, Sutton opens my door and Owen's, waiting as we both get in. As he walks around the car, I put my seat belt on, hands trembling as I click it into place. I lean my head back against the seat and look out the window.

And then I hear someone talking and look out Sutton's side to see who he's talking to.

Olivia.

Dammit.

She bends down and peers into the window, giving me a knowing look.

Sutton opens his door and Olivia grins.

"Well, this is cozy," she says under her breath.

I ignore her and look back at Owen. He's looking at Olivia with curiosity.

"This is my sister Olivia," I tell him. "Olivia, this is Owen, Sutton's son."

Her eyebrows rise when I say Sutton's name and I realize my mistake too late.

"Nice to meet you, Owen," she says.

"You too. Are you the oldest?" he asks.

Annoyance flashes across her face and even though I know Owen didn't mean anything negative with his question, I want to laugh because he managed to find a sore spot. She can't stand that she's twenty-nine and single. Absolutely cannot stand it.

"Yes, I'm the oldest, but not by much."

"She's six and a half years older than me," I answer before he can ask.

"That's a lot!" Owen says.

Olivia scowls at him, and I shoot her a look to knock it off.

"And Weston is older than you too, Felicity?" he asks.

"Yes, Weston is between me and Olivia."

"I wish I could be the oldest. I bet you loved it," he says to Olivia sweetly.

And anyone else would melt—I certainly do when he says it. But Olivia stands up straight and we hear her say, "It's not that great," before she walks away.

CHAPTER TWENTY

A LITTLE BIT OF TRUTH

SUTTON

Felicity's sister is a piece of work.

Earlier in the suite, Olivia Shaw reminded me we'd been in court together, and once she said a little more about the case, I remembered. She was a new lawyer and not prepared enough. I'd felt bad for her. She hadn't presented the facts well, and the way she bristled over the verdict, trying to convince me later that the jury hadn't given her a chance, made me wonder if she had what it took to stick it out.

Perhaps that doggedness and the curt demeanor have served her well in court with time.

But seeing her carry that over into life outside of work and hearing the way she talks to her sister and my son makes me think my first impression was right.

She's so different from Felicity and the rest of the family, I have a hard time believing they're related.

I get into the car and turn to Felicity. She looks stunned and a bit distressed. In the light of the parking garage, I can see how glassy her eyes are.

"Felicity?"

She shakes her head and wipes her eyes. "I'm fine. She just knows how to get to me. She's always been..." She shakes her head again.

"Jealous?" I start up the car and since we were in special parking and lingered afterward, it's not crowded the way it usually is.

"No," she says. "She doesn't have anything to be jealous about with me. You saw her. She's gorgeous, has a great career, and enough confidence to run the country." She laughs and wipes her face again.

"She doesn't have anything on you," I say, my voice firm.

I look at her and she's staring at me in surprise.

"She doesn't," I repeat emphatically. "You're so much more—" I clench the steering wheel. "*You're* gorgeous and smart, and kind, and your personality alone makes you a thousand times more appealing. I'm sorry if that's rude, but… I didn't like the way she talked to you. She has *every* reason to be jealous of you, but I know you'd never wish for that. You're not the type of person who's in competition with every woman you meet or the women in my family wouldn't already love you so much."

She's quiet for a moment and just when I think I may

have gone too far, she says, "Thank you. I've never been able to pinpoint what it is about me that my sister doesn't like, but what you said about competition…that's exactly it. She's been competitive with me our whole lives and I'm so not that way, I haven't even known how to define it. It's part of why I don't want to be a lawyer. I'm always seeking peace and trying to keep everyone calm. I hate to ruffle feathers or make people unhappy, and she thrives on being on an opposing side, looking for every opportunity to prove her point. And not that there's anything wrong with that, she just…she's never been able to get me to fight back the way she wants, and I think she hates that. She resents me for it."

"I'm sorry it's a tumultuous relationship. I wouldn't wish that on anyone. I can't imagine."

"I envy the ease you have with your siblings," she says. "I haven't picked up on any of that edge with you and…any of them."

"It's not there," I say. "I would say we've had to stick together more because our parents died, but I was fifteen when that happened, and our bond was already strong. I think that just solidified what was already there, you know?"

"I wish your parents could have seen how spectacular all of you turned out," she says softly.

"That's…a really sweet thing to say." My voice sounds raw and I clear my throat, focusing on the highway for a moment.

Owen is already out in the backseat, and I'm glad because I'm enjoying this time with Felicity, this openness between us. It gives me hope that we can get back to the friendship we'd started.

"I let my family believe I was riding back with your family instead of you…to avoid casting you in that bad light you're so concerned about," she says.

Okay, maybe we're not quite back to smooth sailing just yet.

"Why would it be bad for you to ride with me?"

"Besides avoiding the appearance of *scandal*," she says in a deep voice that I think is supposed to mimic mine, "they think I'm working for you as a pre-law student."

"They don't know you're Owen's nanny?"

"No."

"Shit."

"Yeah."

"Why would you let them think that?"

She sighs and turns to face me. "I told you they don't know I'm not going to law school in the fall…"

"Yes, but I didn't realize that entailed lying to them about what you were doing for me."

"Don't make me feel guiltier about it than I already do," she snaps. "It's killing me to lie to them."

"Then don't." I try to soften my tone with my next words. "They love you. I've only seen them with you a couple of times, but it's obvious. They want what's best for you, and even if it's hard for them to swallow, they'll support your decision. What they won't be happy about is finding out you lied to them."

"I've omitted the truth."

"Felicity…"

"Okay, if you want to talk about the truth, let's do it. What are you so afraid of?"

"Afraid of?" I echo, uneasy about where this conversation is headed.

"You heard me."

I chuckle. She's right—I think I am afraid.

I could use two fingers of whiskey right about now.

"I'm afraid of what you make me feel," I start slowly, "and what it could cost me."

"What do I make you feel?" Her voice is breathless.

I glance at her, her eyes luminous with the car lights and the streetlights that flash over her skin as we pass them.

I glance back to make sure Owen is still asleep and his head is bobbing. Out.

"Everything. You make me feel everything, Felicity, and it scares the hell out of me. After the other night, I don't think it's a secret that I'm attracted to you." It comes out in a rush, and yet it still feels like I'm copping out.

"Then why are you fighting this, Sutton?"

"That's all it can be."

She shifts, turning away from me, and I know I've let her down.

I rack my brain for something to say to make this better, but nothing comes, and the rest of the ride is silent.

CHAPTER TWENTY-ONE

POSSIBILITIES

FELICITY

I feel like an exposed nerve the next morning around Sutton, but I manage to act professional. He's nice, but his eyes are constantly reading me, like he's trying to figure out what I'm thinking. Everything is so *careful* and it makes me sad. The comfortable vibe that was between us before is now shaky and strained. But it's not long before he leaves for work, and Owen and I have fun finishing up breakfast and getting him to school.

"I can't believe you haven't met Lucia and Delgado yet," he says.

"I really want to. They sound amazing."

"Delgado spins around when he's excited and the best part is, Lucia lets him ride on her back."

I laugh. "That I've got to see. She's a Husky and he's a Chihuahua, right?"

"Yeah, and Uncle Theo's dog Fred is an Irish Water Spaniel. He's so funny. He looks like he's smiling all the time."

"They all sound so cute. I don't think I've ever seen an Irish Water Spaniel."

"Do you think Dad will ever let me get a dog?" he asks.

"I don't know," I admit. "But I tell you what, I'll put in a good word for you with him about it, okay?"

"Really?" His hopeful voice melts me.

"Of course, I will. You'd be an excellent pet owner."

"Thanks, Felicity. I think so too."

We pull into the school parking lot and get in line. It's more orderly than I remember my school drop-off line ever being.

"Don't forget my game's tonight," he says before he gets out.

"I won't forget, I promise."

"You're coming, right?"

"I wouldn't miss it."

He grins and hops out of the car, and I head back to the house. After I've cleaned the kitchen, I pull out the supplies I picked up last week after one of Owen's practices and work on the sign I'm making for him that says *Owen's #1 Fan* in huge letters. I draw hockey sticks around the edges and color in the letters so they stand out, and when I'm satisfied, I go back to my place and look at job options for hours.

What Sutton said about telling my parents the truth is staying with me, and I know he's right. I have to tell them my decision and figure out what I'm doing with my life.

Sutton and Owen are going out for pizza with the team later, so I don't need to make dinner. When I get stir-crazy from sitting so long, I look at the clock and make a spur-of-the-moment decision, texting Ruby to see if now is a good time to stop by. On the way to the game last night, Ruby told me if I ever needed to get out of the house, come see her. Scarlett piped up and said I should come see her too, but from what I can tell, she's always on the go at the lodge. Ruby's busy too, but it sounds like a different kind of busy. And what she said about the animals and how being around them is almost like therapy is what draws me over there.

Ruby's thrilled when I show up and I already feel a thousand times lighter when I see her surrounded by emus, goats, and cows. How she manages to look like a fashionista in the middle of all the snow and manure is truly astonishing. There's one emu, Dolly, that is Ruby's shadow, and watching her skitter around like she's dancing after too many drinks has me laughing my head off.

I've seen them on TikTok before, so seeing Ruby in this environment with Dolly is surreal.

"Sofie's stopping by too." Ruby comes over to stand by me near the fence. "She'll be excited to see you. When she needs a break from the horses, she comes over here, and I go to her place when I need to ride a while. We've got you covered if you need some animals in your life."

"Perfect," I say, laughing when a goat comes and burrows into my side.

"That's Delphine. She'll do anything to have her ears scratched."

I scratch Delphine's ears and wave when Callum walks out of the barn. He's carrying an ax.

"Wow, I feel like I'm seeing one of your videos but in real time."

Ruby laughs. "A day in the life." She winks at me. "It's a fun one."

Her eyes track Callum and I pet the cow that walks over.

"So, how are you adjusting to Landmark Mountain?" she asks.

"I love it."

"And what about you and Sutton?"

"What about us?" My voice sounds sharper than I intended and I shoot her an apologetic look.

"Oh, I just meant, has it been easy working for him? Is it weird living there too, or are you comfortable? I know how it was when I ended up here, alone with Callum in that house. It was incredible, but…a lot. Those Landmark brothers—they are a sexy breed," she says, fanning her face.

I laugh and I'm certain my cheeks flush, but hopefully she'll think it's because we're out in the cold.

"They sure are."

Especially the one I happen to be living with, I think to myself.

"Not that I'm insinuating you're interested in Sutton like that," she says. "I don't even know—maybe you have a boyfriend?"

"No. No boyfriend." I smile.

"Well, if you ever need space to breathe, I'm here." She laughs, and I relax.

"I'll probably be taking you up on that," I tell her. "I'm glad for my place over the garage. It's nice to have a separate place to go, and it's cute and cozy. For the most part, things have gone okay with Sutton. He's—"

It's a good thing Sofie shows up then because I don't know how far I would've divulged. Ruby is easy to talk to, and I can tell Sofie is too, so I need to keep the subject off of Sutton and me.

"I'm so glad you're here too, Felicity," Sofie says. "I've been wanting to come over and see about you, but I was hesitant to just drop by. Now that we're talking about it though... I just might do it sometime." She laughs. "I'll text first to see if it's a good time."

"I'm pretty open right now. And I didn't give Ruby much warning today," I say, making a face.

"You're welcome anytime," Ruby says. "And I promise I won't make you stay outside the entire time if you don't want to. You can come in and have a hot tea or hot chocolate..."

"That goes for my place too," Sofie says, smiling at Dolly before she pets her. "And Marlow and Scarlett would say the same even though they're not home as much during the day. As for me, I don't get out enough, so going to the game last night was great. And they're going to the Super Bowl!" She raises her fist in the air.

"It hasn't fully registered yet!" I shake my head. "Weston has dreamed of that for as long as I can remember. It was so fun having all of you there. I've loved being able to go to the games since being home from school. It's usually just me and my parents, sometimes my sister. Olivia and I don't exactly get along," I add. "Having backup was nice."

"I thought I was maybe picking up on that," Sofie says, crinkling her nose.

I laugh. "Yeah, she's sometimes a bit of a shit-stirrer." I make a face back. "I was mortified when she told me what she said about the Landmark Mountain courthouse."

Sofie waves her hand. "Don't worry about it. We're all

thick-skinned around here, and the courthouse could use an update. She's not lying." She laughs.

"Speaking of court—you're going to be a lawyer?" Ruby asks. "Your dad said something about you going to law school in the fall, and I hadn't realized that was your plan. That's amazing. We'll miss you though."

I groan. "That's what my parents are expecting of me, but it's not what I'm planning to do. I just haven't found a way to tell them yet."

"*Oh,*" Ruby says. "Ugh. That sounds stressful. If you need to talk any of that out with us, feel free. Sofie and I… and Scarlett and Marlow too…we're huge advocates in doing what you love. I have nightmares sometimes about what would've happened if I hadn't gotten out of what was expected of me. I'd be living an entirely different life right now. A miserable life."

"*Me too,*" Sofie says emphatically. "Neither of us would be here right now, married to the loves of our lives and with jobs we're passionate about."

"How did you know what you wanted to do?" I ask. "Which future to pursue?"

"What are *you* passionate about?" Ruby asks.

I bite the inside of my cheek. "That's been hard to figure out. I was good in school, and I could be a good lawyer, a great one even. But the thought of doing that filled me with such anxiety, I know I'd be miserable. The only thing I'm passionate about is organization and planning." I roll my eyes and laugh. "And what kind of career could I possibly do with that?"

"I'd give anything to be good at organization," Sofie says. "And I can't plan anything too far ahead to save my life. I'm opening a horse rescue, but all the red tape and paperwork involved with starting something like this has been exhausting."

"I could look over any legal jargon or help organize… whatever you need," I offer. "Or…you probably have Sutton do that."

"He's always willing to help, but sometimes I feel silly asking him about the minutia."

"Well, ask away anytime. I'm happy to look at any paperwork, and I literally get giddy about organizing. Put me in a hoarder's home and let me have at it, I'd be in heaven. Or color-coding someone's schedule…or labeling everything in the pantry—I wonder if Sutton would mind if I did that. His pantry could use it and he's organized!"

They laugh like they're not sure if I'm serious or not, but then Ruby says, "I bet he'd love it. Do it. And I'm going to take you up on this. Come over sometime this week and look at these papers and charge me an hourly rate."

"No way. I'm not charging you."

"We're watching a business coming to life right here in this pasture," Ruby says. "And I could use help organizing my website orders. I need a system to make the process simpler."

"You guys, I'm happy to do this just because," I insist.

"Yeah, but you'll need capital for your business expenses, such as your website, and whatever else comes with organizing," Ruby says.

"You're great with kids too. Have you ever thought of pursuing that beyond nannying?" Sofie asks.

I pause and turn to look at her. "You know…I've always liked being around kids but didn't know how much until Owen and Dakota. It's been so fun. And recently, I had a memory of when I was little—I told my parents I was going to be a teacher when I grew up. My parents corrected me and said being a lawyer was my future…to carry on the family business and all that. It was the first time I heard what was expected of me. I let go of all thought of being a teacher and hadn't even considered it again."

"You'd have to be organized and an excellent planner to be a teacher," Sofie says, lifting a shoulder, her eyes smiling.

Ruby reaches out and squeezes my arm. "Maybe it's time to dream again."

I nod, feeling like I might cry for some reason.

"Thanks for indulging me. You both have me thinking about the possibilities." I rub my arms and look at my watch. "Oh wow, I can't believe it's so late. I need to run and pick up Owen. This helped today, thank you. I didn't know how much I needed to talk about some of this."

"Anytime. We're happy to help you hash it out," Ruby says.

Sofie nods. "Absolutely. And tell Owen that Theo and I will be at the game tonight cheering him on."

"Callum and I are coming too," Ruby says, doing a little dance.

They both hug me goodbye, and I leave feeling much better than when I came.

CHAPTER TWENTY-TWO

MAMA BEAR

SUTTON

It's a rush to make it to the game on time, and I don't pull it off, pulling into the parking lot fifteen minutes after the game's started. I jog inside, feeling like a shit parent for being late. The first thing I hear is a whistle and then Felicity cheering, *"Go, Owen!"* at a pitch I didn't know she had in her. I chuckle under my breath and round the corner, pausing for a second at the sight she makes.

Surrounded by my family, she's front and center between Grinny and Dakota, holding up a sign that says, *Owen's #1 Fan* in huge colorful letters. I wouldn't be able to hide the massive grin on my face if I tried.

I quickly glance out on the ice and my boy is scrambling out there. They're up by a point and the other team is making them work for it. When the puck is passed to Owen, he flies with it, but he's offside and the play stops.

"What the hell was that, Landmark?" Lance Hicks yells. "Get it together, you little twerp."

At my kid.

My blood starts boiling. Lance is Micah's dad, and from what I can tell, Lance is raising Micah to be just like him, a little jerk.

I move in closer. No one has seen me yet, but I'm going to make sure Lance knows I heard him and don't appreciate him calling Owen out like that.

"*Hey*," Felicity yells, walking over to Lance. "You've been yelling rude things to these kids since they started playing, specifically Owen when he's playing a *damn good* game. They don't need to hear you talking like that. You have something to say, take it up with the coach later, but keep your foul mouth shut."

"Who the fuck are you?" Lance yells back.

"I'm Felicity Shaw, and I'm—" She holds her sign up in his face.

"Ah, figures you'd be with the Landmarks," he sneers.

"Lance, you really want to act like this at your kid's hockey game?" Wyatt asks, moving next to Felicity.

Callum moves to the other side of her and Theo is behind her, all of them looming over Lance.

Lance groans and covers his face. "He should've been

paying attention, so he didn't cross the line before the puck," he says, softer this time.

Callum growls at him and Lance looks terrified. He holds both hands up like he's backing down.

"It's a *game*," Theo says. "And they're freaking eight years old. They're still learning."

I move between people until I reach them and stare Lance down. He looks at me and rolls his eyes, cursing under his breath.

"Do we need to take this outside, Lance?" I ask.

"No, I'm good," he grumbles. He starts to walk away and then turns to look back. "You freaking Landmarks don't think your shit stinks, but you're no better than anyone else here."

"I assure you, we all know our shit stinks," Wyatt says, and I hear Theo snort behind him.

"Speak for yourself, brother," he says.

Felicity's eyes meet mine and she still looks like she's about ready to explode.

"Can we please act like civil adults and watch this game?" I ask Lance, exaggeratedly pointing out to the rink.

He doesn't say anything, just shakes his head and walks away. Marlow and Ruby are closest and check in with Felicity to make sure she's okay. When I move toward her, they go back and sit down and Felicity looks at me with concern.

"I'm sorry," she says, her voice low.

"Why are *you* sorry?" I frown.

"Your reputation is important to you and I just made you look bad, getting all up in that guy's face. He just made me so mad," she says between gritted teeth. "Here I was talking last night about how I'm all for peace," she groans, shaking her head, "but he was being awful and when he went there one last time with that assholery, I couldn't take it."

She looks so upset that I feel bad for almost laughing, but she sees me holding back my smile.

"What?" she says, the crease between her brows deepening.

I want to reach out and smooth it away.

"Thank you for standing up for Owen," I tell her.

"That was so badass." Scarlett leans on my shoulder for a second and beams at Felicity. "I was about to get in his face myself and you took care of it before I'd even gotten out of the bleachers."

Felicity makes a face and laughs, and someone calls Scarlett and she's off again.

"I've never felt that level of anger," Felicity tells me. "If that's what it means to go all Mama Bear, I guess I was there." Her eyes fly to mine and her mouth parts. "I-no, that's not what I meant. I don't think I'm…I know I'm not…"

I lean in a little closer. "I didn't take it in any kind of negative way," I tell her. "I appreciate you being protective of him. He needs all of that he can get. I also want you to be careful, confronting people like Lance…especially when my brothers and I aren't around."

"I can handle myself," she says, her teeth sliding over her bottom lip for the briefest second.

I have to look away. We watch them play, and they're doing great. Eventually, I glance around and Lance has moved away from all of the parents, looking sulky. The kids play better than ever.

Owen scores and we all go crazy. Jill, Dougie's mom comes over and thanks Felicity for putting Lance in his place.

"He's had it coming. I'm so glad you said something," she says. "I haven't met you yet, but I've seen you around town and in the school line. I'm Jill." She holds out her hand and Felicity shakes it.

"I'm Felicity," Felicity says, giving her a friendly smile before turning back to the game.

Jill looks at me and brightens.

"Hey, Sutton," Jill's voice turns flirty and Felicity turns to look at her again, her eyes widening.

She glances at me and I swallow uncomfortably. Some of the moms, single and otherwise, are often forward. The single ones though, like Jill, damn…they can be relentless at times.

"Hi, Jill. Dougie's looking good out there."

"Thank you. Owen is killing it. He's made all the goals tonight," she says excitedly. She leans in and her breasts touch my arm. I take a step back. "Maybe we could have them skate together while they're off the next couple of weeks."

"I've been bringing Owen to skate a few afternoons a week," Felicity jumps in when I don't say anything. "I could give you my number and let you know when we're going to be here."

"*Oh*." Jill's head tilts. She looks between Felicity and me, and I can see her wheels turning. "Now I know where I've heard your name." Her eyes are shrewd now as she assesses Felicity. "Sunny Side."

Shit. I haven't done anything but takeout from Sunny Side for a while, and there's a good reason for that. The bets that take place in this town are both comical and a huge nuisance. I don't want to even think about what they're betting on over there right now. It seems like there's always one about me going, whether I'm in there or not. They make jokes about it at the courthouse all the time.

"Don't believe everything you hear," Felicity says.

Her tone is sweet but sharp enough that Jill gets the point.

But she can't seem to leave well enough alone.

"So, you're the...nanny?" she asks, looking back and forth between Felicity and me again.

I want nothing more than to walk away from this conversation, but I don't want to leave Felicity alone to deal with the sharks. It's a good thing I don't because Lisa, who makes Jill look tame, walks up then.

"Sutton," she coos, running her hand up and down my arm. "We missed you at the fundraiser this weekend."

I cross my arms so her hand drops, and I take another step back. Felicity watches with a somewhat hostile expression—probably still fired up from her confrontation with Lance.

"I heard it went great," I say. "New uniforms for next season."

"Thanks to you," Lisa gushes.

"Thanks to Blake and Camilla Gamble," I correct. "Tiptop has generously covered the uniforms and then some."

"Well, I'm sure you had something to do with that." She winks. "I know you're close with them. I heard Gwyneth is in town," she says and then she acts like she's just now seeing Felicity. "Hey, I'm Lisa, and you are?"

"Felicity."

Lisa's eyes roam up and down Felicity and when she looks back at me, she lifts an eyebrow. "Has Tracy met her yet?"

I frown. "Why do you ask?"

She gives me a knowing smirk. "Because I can only imagine how that went over." She throws her head back and laughs. "Look at you, Sutton Landmark, finally living on the edge." She winks again. "I *like* it. Call me if you want to *explore* that dangerous side."

My eyes narrow and she just grins and walks away.

Felicity points her thumb over her shoulder. "I'm gonna go sit down now."

I nod and watch the game from where I'm standing, my mind whirling.

The rumors have already started.

Just fucking great.

CHAPTER TWENTY-THREE

PUBLIC OR PRIVATE

FELICITY

I'm invited to get pizza afterwards numerous times, but with Sutton's deer-in-the-headlights look after he heard the insinuations from Jill and Lisa about me and him, I didn't want to add to his stress. I already yelled at one of the parents. I think I've done enough for the night.

Owen was ecstatic about their win, and I'm afraid I might've disappointed him by not going out with them, but I think he and Sutton needed a night together.

The truth is, I didn't want to add to the gossip by showing up.

And I'm trying to make up for how I acted at the game by making a cake while they're gone.

Both Sutton and Owen are obsessed with peanut butter. I've never seen two people love it more, and I have a moderate addiction to it myself. So I decide to make them the chocolate cake with peanut butter frosting that Weston always wants me to make for him. I've made it as a sheet cake and a three-layer cake, but tonight I use my trusted Bundt pan that my grandma gave me. It never fails me. But it's really all about the peanut butter frosting.

I'm interrupted by my phone buzzing and turn to see who it is. Olivia. My nerves kick up a notch before I've even read it.

> OLIVIA
>
> Seems like you're getting along great with your boss. I didn't know football games with an employee were the perks of being a judge!

I roll my eyes and toss my phone aside, choosing to ignore her.

I'm just frosting the cake when I see the headlights shining down the long driveway, and I hurry, trying to finish before they come inside. I place the cake on the island where the *You did it!* helium balloons I bought before the game are sitting. I added a weighted bag at the bottom, making them the length I wanted and then added little plastic hockey sticks and ribbon around it. Right before they walk through the door, I wash my hands and try not to fidget. I'd hoped I could just leave the cake for them and be gone by the time they got home, but…didn't happen.

"Surprise!" I say, waving my hands in the air.

Owen bounds toward me. "What's this?" He gasps when he sees the cake. "When did you get that?"

"I made it while you guys got pizza."

"You *made* it?" He throws his arms around my waist and squeezes. "Thank you, Felicity."

"You're welcome." My eyes meet Sutton's and his smile is sweet, but he's quiet. "I hope it's okay that I made a dessert. Did you guys have some already?" I laugh awkwardly.

"No, we didn't," Owen says. "Can I have some cake, Dad?"

"Of course." Sutton hangs up his coat and takes Owen's from him.

"Way to go tonight. You played such a great game," I tell Owen. "You were amazing."

"I think I played great because you were there and Aunt Scarlett and all the uncles and everyone," he says happily.

He really is the sweetest. I cut a piece of cake and hand it to him.

"Would you like a piece, Sutton?"

"This is the best cake I've ever tasted," Owen gushes in one breath. "Dad, it's got peanut butter frosting!"

"I will definitely be having a piece then," Sutton says.

He thanks me when I hand him a piece and then we listen to Owen rehash his favorite parts of the night. He's animated and so happy that it's hard to stop smiling. Sutton laughs in all the right places too, but he's still quieter than usual. I can't read his mood, so I just focus on Owen.

"I want this cake every holiday," Owen says.

I laugh. "You sound like Weston."

"He loves it too?" Owen asks. He's fanning even more over Weston after seeing him play again last night.

"It's his favorite."

"It's *my* favorite," he says.

"Mine too," Sutton says.

I glance at Sutton and his eyes are gleaming in the lowered kitchen lights. I shiver and he notices, eyes widening.

"Are you cold?" he asks.

I shake my head.

"Why aren't you having cake, Felicity?" Owen asks.

"I had a lot of frosting while I was making it. I think I had my fill."

He laughs and eats the last bite, sighing and rubbing his belly. "Can I have another piece?"

"That's probably more than enough sugar for tonight," I tell him. "Or…whatever your dad says." I flush when I look at Sutton.

There I go again, inserting myself when it's not really my place.

I have cringed a thousand times since calling myself a Mama Bear.

"Felicity's right," Sutton says. "Thank you so much for the cake though. I want another piece too, but I'll save it for tomorrow."

I smile at them and start gathering my things. "I'm glad you like it. I'll see you tomorrow, okay? I hope you sleep well. Congratulations again on that game, Ace. You went out with style." My hand crashes with Owen's in a high five.

"Is that my nickname?" His eyes are so bright and excited, I can't take it. My heart is a melty lump of mush.

"If you want it to be. I think it fits," I say.

"I *love* it."

"Why don't you go get your shower, Owen? It's late, so

don't take a long one," Sutton says. He looks at me and his eyes are warm. "Can you stay for a minute?"

"Sure."

Owen gives me another hug before he goes upstairs.

There's a pregnant pause when it's just the two of us.

The sound of Owen turning on the water comes through one of the monitors and then he's singing as he showers.

Sutton takes the plates to the sink and then leans against the island. He's still in his dress pants and button-down shirt from work, his tie pulled loose. It's one of my favorite looks on him. His hair is messier than usual, and I want to sink my fingers through it and tug it the way he did mine that night.

He stares at me, his eyes dropping to my mouth for a second before meeting my eyes again, and I wonder what he's thinking.

"I just wanted to make sure you're okay," he finally says. "That was quite a night, and…I wanted to thank you again. I don't want you to ever put yourself at risk and thought it might make you feel better to know that, besides a shitty attitude, I think Lance is harmless. That being said, well…I think I already said it earlier," he chuckles, "but please don't do anything like that if me or my brothers aren't around. I don't know what I'd do if…"

He's quiet for so long, his eyes boring through me.

"If what?" I ask quietly.

"If anything happened to you," he says.

He stalks toward me and the next thing I know, my back is against the wall. His hand skims my neck until his fingers are lifting my jaw, his body hard against mine. His eyes are intense, as he looks from my eyes to my lips, and hovers so close we could almost kiss. I barely breathe.

"I can't stop thinking about this mouth," he whispers.

"I'm such a hypocrite, warning you to be careful of other men when I'm no better…"

"You're nothing like Lance," I say, my hands landing on his waist and then trailing up his chest. His muscles are taut and I explore them, unable to believe this is happening, but while it is, I'm going to enjoy it.

His eyes squeeze shut and when he opens them, they're haunted. "The town is already talking about us. It's just little whispers here and there, but it'll build. It always does around here."

"Well, when we're in public, we'll just have to be aware and keep our distance from each other, I guess," I say, my voice practically a purr.

His thumb drags over my bottom lip and he tugs it down, sticking his thumb in my mouth for a second and then dragging the wetness across my lips.

I lean on my tiptoes and whimper when his erection hits me in a better place. He puts his hands on the wall on either side of me and thrusts against me once. I gasp his name and finally get my hands in his hair. He closes his eyes again when I drag my hands through his thick, wavy hair and then tug on it. When his eyes open, he reaches down and runs his fingers over my nipple.

"What about when we're not in public?" he asks, moving to my other breast and tweaking until they're both hard pebbles.

"I think we do whatever we want," I whisper.

He grips me tighter, his lips whispering against mine. I want him to kiss me so bad it hurts.

"Yeah? Whatever we want? What if I want what can't be mine?" he asks.

The need in his voice makes my insides tremble.

"Tell me what you want and maybe it can be," I whisper.

His hands drop off of me and he takes a step back, leaving me cold once again. He swipes his hand across his face and lets out a ragged breath.

"I'm giving you such conflicting messages, I wouldn't blame you for hating me," he says.

"You are," I tell him, stepping closer to him. "But I promise I don't hate you. Not at all." I tug his tie, pulling him toward me, and I do what I've wanted to do since the first time I saw him.

I kiss the hell out of him.

CHAPTER TWENTY-FOUR

NO ONE ELSE

SUTTON

Her kiss is every bit as addicting as I knew it would be. Her full, pouty lips are my favorite thing, the taste of her sweet tongue, it's exhilarating. The way her body fits against mine is a heady experience, and her hands roam my body like she's just as hungry for me as I am for her.

I can't get close enough.

It's the sweetest heaven, even while I feel like I'm surely diving into hell.

I take the kiss deeper and she whimpers into my mouth, her tongue tangling with mine. I start to pick her up and wrap her legs around my waist when I hear Owen's shower turning off.

Fuck.

I've clearly lost my mind.

I set her back on the ground and loosen my grip on her, my lips reluctantly leaving hers. We're both breathless as we look at each other and I start to tell her it can't happen again, that I'm so sorry I can't seem to get a grip around her, but I will…when she points her finger in my face.

"That was undeniably the best kiss either one of us has ever had. Try to tell me differently," she says, chest heaving up and down. Her nipples look like they're trying to break free of her shirt, just like my dick is jamming against my pants right now.

I'm so stunned by what she's said and distracted by her phenomenal tits that I give my head a slight shake.

"I can't deny that." I smirk and wipe my lower lip with my thumb as I finally meet her eyes again.

She grins and then she starts laughing, and I run my hand through my hair, sighing loudly before I start laughing too.

"Fuck, Felicity. What the fuck am I gonna do with you?"

"Lots of dirty, dirty things, I hope, Mr. Landmark," she says.

Yeah, my dick really goes crazy with that.

"You…I—" I groan, holding the bridge of my nose with my fingers. "You're not playing fair," I finally say, laughing again.

"If that's what it takes," she says, shrugging.

My eyes narrow on her and she presses her lips together, trying to keep a straight face.

"I'm trying to do the right thing here," I say hoarsely.

"The right thing would be to show me a little fun," she says. She runs her finger over her lips and I watch spellbound. "And since it'd only be in private anyway," she lifts her shoulder again, "what could it hurt?"

"I don't want to hurt *you*," I tell her.

Her eyes flash in defiance. "What makes you think I can't handle myself? I'll remind you again, Sutton—I'm not a child. We're both adults here. We can decide what this is and keep it just that."

What she's saying sounds fucking fantastic in theory, but it's just that, conjecture. Feeling all keyed up the way I do over a kiss? It could get sketchy real fast. And she's young and it could get confusing once sex is involved.

There I go again thinking about her age, but *fuck*, I've got thirteen years and a lot of life on her.

"You could do that?" I ask.

"Could *you*?" she asks, putting it back on me.

And dammit, part of me is not sure if I could, but I want her bad enough that I'm willing to try.

"Yes," I say.

Her eyes brighten and her lips lift in a grin so seductive, I almost take back my answer.

This is probably a really bad idea.

But something tells me we'll be right back here repeatedly until we try this out.

"I'll put Owen to bed and make sure he's out. We'll have to be careful. He can't think there's anything going on between us." I look at her pointedly and she nods.

"I agree."

"Okay. If you still want to do this, stay, and if not, I'll know your answer."

"You already know my answer. I'll be back in half an hour," she says, moving toward the back door.

I race up the stairs, heart pounding in anticipation. Are we really doing this? Owen is in his room, picking out pajamas.

"Did you brush your teeth yet?" I pick up his wet towel and give him the parental *what was this doing on the floor?* look.

He grins and takes it, passing me to hang it in the bathroom.

"I brushed my teeth," he says over his shoulder. "Can I have cake for breakfast?"

I laugh and motion for him to get in bed. When he does, I tuck him in and lean over to pat his cheek and kiss him on the forehead. "I'm gonna say yes because I really want cake for breakfast too." I start to laugh again.

He loves that, his face crinkling into his full-body laugh that is the best sound on earth.

"I love that cake and I love Felicity," he says.

I nod solemnly. I could say the very same thing.

Not *love* love, but I love her for the joy she's brought into our home.

And the cake speaks for itself.

"I'm so excited we won," he adds.

"I am too. Your playing was stellar. I bet your dreams will be awesome tonight."

He nods, grinning. "I bet they will. I hope your dreams are awesome too, Dad."

My breath catches and I feel a wave of maniacal laughter bubbling up. "I think they're gonna be, son. We better get after that sleep. It's after ten, *way* past your bedtime."

His mouth stretches into a big yawn and his eyes are closed by the time I get to his door. I shut it and go to my room, checking out the window to see if I can catch a glimpse of Felicity. The light is on, but I don't see her. She said half an hour, so there's time for me to take a shower. I take the world's fastest one and brush my teeth, eyeing myself in the mirror as I do. I flex my chest muscles up and down—it always makes Owen laugh when I do this—and look down at my arms and abs.

I still got it.

Fuck. Who am I kidding?

Am I really doing this?

The excitement in my gut tells me I am, but since I haven't done anything impulsive in a very long time, I will likely overthink it to death.

Later. You can do that later.

As Felicity said, we're both adults.

But the fact that she lives here now and is nannying my son and he loves her—

Fuck. What am I thinking?

I hear the back door and jog down the stairs to tell her we can't do this and stop dead in my tracks when I see her. She steps out of her Uggs, her feet bare. Her long blonde waves stand out against her black shirt that hangs over one shoulder, more cleavage showing than usual. She's not wearing a bra and my dick is freer in my sweats, rising to attention just looking at her.

She notices, her eyes taking me in, which only makes me harder. But when her gaze meets mine, her expression changes.

"Have you talked yourself out of this?" she asks.

"How do you already know me so well?"

"I'm not sure. I like how you're such a straight shooter with me and have been from the beginning, but it also means I can read your expressions now." She sighs and looks down, wrapping her arms around herself.

I move toward her and lift her chin. "I was about to talk

myself out of it until I saw you. And only because of how much Owen loves you. I don't want this to wreck that."

"I hope that I can be close to Owen forever. I don't ever want to do anything to sabotage that. We just have to agree that we won't let that happen. We have to communicate and put him first. And when we're ready to move on from this, we'll still be friends."

Part of me doesn't like how easily she talks about moving on from this, but most of me is relieved.

"I can agree to that. How did you get so wise?" I ask.

She grins. "Maybe having lawyer parents who dissect everything."

"I want to dissect everything about *you*," I say, laughing as I pull her against me in a hug.

I hear the intake of her breath when she feels me against her and the only thing that could stop me now is if I thought she didn't want this.

When I pull away and brush her hair back, I lean in and kiss her. It's softer this time. Like we have all the time in the world, even though my body could easily be talked into hard and fast and reckless.

"We'll have to be quiet," I tell her, taking her hand. "Do you think you can do that?"

She nods, and we walk toward the stairs. "Do you?"

"Remind me if I forget," I whisper.

We walk up the stairs and I put my finger to my lips as I quietly open Owen's door and see him sleeping peacefully. Felicity puts her hand over her heart when she sees how sweet he looks and we back out of there, moving toward my bedroom at the end of the hall.

Once the door is closed behind us, she puts her hands on my waist and drags them up under my shirt, making my abs tense with her attention. My hands slide up her back and then I lift her shirt over her head, pausing to take her in.

"Felicity," I say, my voice reverent.

She lifts my shirt over my head and her mouth parts, as she smooths her thumb over my tattoo. "Sutton Landmark, you have a tattoo. I can't believe it."

I grin like the devil. "Didn't think I had it in me?"

"Oh, you have it in you, but I'm still surprised you went for it. It's beautiful. I've never seen anything like it."

"Thank you. I got the compass after Owen was born and then after Tracy left, I added this part." I point to Owen and me, walking away together, hand in hand.

Her eyes fill with tears and she leans in and kisses my chest, right over the tattoo. "That's the sweetest thing I've ever seen...and the sexiest."

I laugh, my hands skimming her waist. She has the softest skin. I lean down and take her nipple between my teeth, my eyes never leaving hers as I suck it. Her eyes glitter with want, and when I knead the other side with my hand and give her nipple a tug, she sinks her hands into my hair and pulls me closer. Her head falls back when my hands move down to her ass, sliding her leggings down so I can feel her bare skin, and she gasps when I lower them enough to press a kiss against her wet center.

"Is this for me?" I ask.

"Completely."

I groan and she smiles down at me, all inhibition suddenly gone. She looks powerful like this, like she has me exactly where she wants me.

I pull her leggings off the rest of the way and straighten, my hands never leaving her body. "You're so beautiful, I could get lost in you."

"Please do," she whispers, her cheeks lifting with her smile.

I shake my head. "You're trouble, aren't you?"

"You're just now figuring that out?"

"Get on the bed, Felicity." I smack her butt playfully, and she startles but grins back at me.

"Do you like to be spanked?" I ask.

Her cheeks flush slightly and she moves to the bed.

"I don't know. I never have been."

"Hmm. Noted." My teeth press against my lower lip and her eyes dart to my mouth as she licks her lips.

Her nipples pebble and I can't wait to get my hands on her. I kick my sweats off and have to grip my dick to contain myself. I've never seen anyone so beautiful.

She stares at me, eyes wide. "I tried to imagine what you must look like, but I have to say, this surpasses that."

"What were you imagining?"

"Something great, but I couldn't have imagined anything this great."

My laugh is low and I move over her, bracing my hand on either side of her.

"I've been thinking the same thing about you," I say, bending down to kiss her.

She kisses me and then pulls back. "Sutton. While we're doing this…no one else, okay?"

"There's no way," I tell her.

"Okay," she says, smiling up at me. "There will be no one else for me either."

And so help me, when she says that, I want to make her feel that way forever.

CHAPTER TWENTY-FIVE

SAVING UP

FELICITY

I expected him to slide a condom on once he was leaning over me, but he leans back, sitting on his feet, and spreads my legs. His hands slide up my thighs and I'm so relieved when he doesn't tease me but goes right for my center, spreading me apart and then gliding my wetness over me before dipping down inside. Again and again, until the sound of my arousal is so apparent, I'd be embarrassed if it didn't feel so good.

I squirm against him, already feeling so close, but he

takes his time, staring at where his fingers dip inside me. When I start moaning, his eyes meet mine, and he leans down to kiss me quiet. His fingers pick up and I thrash against him.

He breaks the kiss and says, "I want my mouth on you when you come. Can you be quiet?"

I nod, my breathing erratic.

"Good. If you're quiet, I'll make it so good, I promise."

His words. His touch.

"Please, Sutton. I'm so close," I tell him.

"I know. Wait until I can taste you."

He shifts, moving down my body, but his fingers never stop. When his tongue flicks across me for the first time, I cry out and he puts his hand over my mouth and then slides his finger inside. I suck it and then bite it and he laughs against me, then pulls my bud between his teeth and sucks. I see stars. I pull his finger out of my mouth and he drags it down my breast while I grab his pillow and put it over my face, giving in to the waves washing over me. When the pulses slow down, he gently pulls his fingers out and dips his tongue inside, moaning when I start coming again.

Finally, I pull the pillow away and he lifts his head, his lips and chin wet. He wipes some of it off and the smile on his face could send me to my knees. He kisses his way up my body.

"You taste so sweet," he says. "I'm only sad that I didn't get to see your face. You covered it up," he whispers when he's leaning over me. "Are you tired?"

"No. I don't want to miss a second of this."

He grabs a condom out of the side table and slides it on. I still can't get over the way he looks without clothes. His body is flawless. His cock…I've never seen such a gorgeous man. How in the world has anyone ever let him go?

"Tell me the second it's too much," he says, sliding in his tip.

"Mmm," I sigh, "it won't be too much."

Despite how wet I am, it takes time for him to sink all the way inside. He keeps pulling out and that slide over my clit as he goes in a little deeper each time has me out of my mind. My walls keep clamping around him and he hisses that I feel so fucking good.

"You're gonna make me come again," I whimper. I've never come twice in any sexual experience, and I didn't think three was possible for me.

"Not yet," he says, his voice low and authoritative.

It does something to me when he's bossy. I had no idea I'd love that, but I do. At least when it's him.

He goes deeper the next time and when my head falls back, he thrusts in all the way and we both go still. His face hovers over mine, as we stare at one another, our hearts pounding frantically against each other.

He flexes inside and I moan.

"Felicity?" he says.

"What?" I whisper.

"I don't want this to end."

His eyes are piercing straight to my soul and I couldn't look away if I tried.

"Me either."

I'm not sure if he means the sex right now or this between us, but as far as my answer goes, either works.

I knew before he took his clothes off that I was in too deep and I dove in anyway. When this whole thing with Sutton breaks my heart, I will have had this night of ecstasy and it will be more than worth it.

He kisses me, slow and deep, his tongue fucking me while his body lies flush against mine. When he starts moving, slowly thrusting in and out, his movements mimicking his tongue, it's almost too much. My body is fevered, my heartbeat thundering inside, and the whole time, I'm thinking, *I can't believe this is happening. This feels life-changing. Is it feeling anything close to this for him?*

He rolls us over so I'm on top and his hands slide around to my ass. He closes his eyes when he squeezes, and when he opens them again, his eyes are dazed.

"I love your body so much," he says. "Does it feel good like this?"

I nod. It's even deeper and when I get used to it, I start circling my hips over him.

"Fuck, you're beautiful," he says.

"Sutton," I whimper. I bite my lip to stay quiet.

"That's it, sweetness. God, I wish I could hear you scream my name." He presses his thumb against my clit and rubs. "Mmm, you're close, aren't you."

"I can't believe it," I gasp.

"I love it. Let me see you fall," he says.

I don't know if it's his words or how he knows just how to play my body, but I fall apart around him and he keeps our rhythm steady the whole time, prolonging my orgasm. Right as I think it's ebbing, he drives in deeper and when I feel him pulse inside of me, it only makes mine better.

He groans, his eyes squeezing shut and then he sits up to kiss me, his chest against mine as he lifts my hips up and down. He whispers my name as he swells inside of me, filling me so completely that I feel every movement. When we finally stop, we stare at each other in wonder for a long time.

"Wow, I never dreamed it'd be this good," he finally says. "Is it just me feeling this way?"

"No," I tell him emphatically. "I'm right here with you. That was…heaven."

"I want to stay right here," he says.

"Okay," I say.

"I'm not kidding."

"Neither am I."

"I guess I have to take the condom off, but…"

"Take it off and come back," I tell him.

I slowly lift off of him, both of us wincing with the loss, and he moves to dispose of the condom. When he comes back, we lie facing each other and he's still hard.

"It's like I've been saving up for you," he says, chuckling.

I slide another condom on him and we stay right where we are, facing each other, our movements slow and deep.

The connection is emotional, like we both know we're crossing into uncharted territory. A flicker of fear sends warning signals to my brain, but my heart and my body are already in too deep.

I don't know why I'm surprised when I come again. It's obvious that he's experienced, but I'm still impressed that he learns what I need so quickly. I've never been so in tune with another person and knowing that I'm not the only one he's made feel like this makes me want to burn things down, but for now, I try to pause those thoughts and just enjoy that he's only with me right now. He said there's no way he'd be with anyone else.

"What has you smiling?" he asks when he comes back from throwing away the condom.

I don't want to tell him, so I just say, "The way you make me feel."

"I want to make you smile like that every day," he says, leaning in to kiss me.

He tucks me against his chest, his arms around me. My body is languid and sore in the best ways. I'm also sleepy.

"I should get back to my place," I tell him.

"Do you have to go yet?"

"I don't want to fall asleep…Owen."

He kisses my forehead. "We could set the alarm and you could go before he wakes up."

"That feels too risky."

His hand roams from my hip down to my ass, as he squeezes my cheek. I arch against him and he gives me a heady kiss.

"Sutton," I warn.

"Just one more time," he says.

I freeze and pull back and so does he. He frowns when he sees my face.

"What's wrong?"

"I should go," I whisper.

"Okay. Did I say something wrong?"

"No." I shake my head. "This was amazing." I get up and gather my things, hurriedly putting my clothes on.

He gets up and puts his sweats on.

"You don't need to get up."

"The least I can do is walk you to the door and make sure you get home safely," he says, grinning.

"I'm *literally* in your backyard."

He shrugs. "I want to see you for as long as I can."

The things he says. My heart gallops away with me and I try to keep up, walking down the stairs. When we get near the door and I slip into my boots, he tugs my hand and pulls me back against him.

"Hey, slow down. You sure you're okay?" he asks. He smooths my hair back and stares intently at me.

"I'm great," I tell him. "Thank you for an incredible night. I'll never forget it."

He lifts my hand and kisses my knuckles. "It was my pleasure," he says, smirking.

"And mine."

"I sure hope so." His smile is pure debauchery and I get lost in it. "If you give me another night, I'll try to make it even better than this."

I sag against the door. "I thought you'd changed your mind and just wanted one more time tonight."

He frowns, his brows crinkling in the center. "That's why you ran out of my bed?"

I nod and he laughs, opening his arms wide.

"Come here," he says.

I step into his arms and he engulfs me in a huge hug.

"Do you want to know a secret?" he whispers in my ear.

I nod.

He leans back and looks at me. "I'm not going to stop wanting you, Felicity. Tonight was…that doesn't just happen with everyone. We're—" He puts his hand up and does an exploding gesture. "When this ends, it will be because you're ready to move on and I'll let you go because you deserve the best kind of life. I will never hold you back." He tilts my chin up, his gaze more intense. "But in the meantime, I plan on fucking you so good, you can't see straight. Understood?"

There's so much I want to say, but I think I'm lust drunk and speechless.

I lick my lips and nod, and he smiles.

"Good. Night, sweetness."

I turn and open the door before I can talk myself out of it and feel his eyes on me the whole way to my place. When I reach the top of the stairs and start to open the door, I turn and he lifts his hand. I do the same and walk inside, sighing against the door as I lean against it.

What the hell was *that*?

I knew it would be good with Sutton, but there's no way I could've imagined it being like *that*.

CHAPTER TWENTY-SIX

PINK LACE AND ALOE VERA

SUTTON

I thought I'd have a hard time falling asleep, but I'm so sated that I conk out not long after Felicity leaves. I dream about her and wake up wishing she was in my bed more than anything.

I've never been comfortable enough to put anything in writing with a woman, not even the woman I married—maybe *especially* the woman I married—but I trusted Felicity enough to take care of my son, to bring her into my home and my bed, so I trust her with this too. I grab my phone and text her.

> Woke up wishing you were in my bed.

I see the three little dots and wait, feeling ridiculously excited to see what she says.

FELICITY
I feel every place you've been and I like it.

Fuck me.

> So naughty, sweetness. Do something for me, okay?

FELICITY
Okay.

> No panties today.

FELICITY
...what?

> You heard me.

I grin as I get ready for work, looking like a schmuck in the mirror, but I don't fucking care.

Being with Felicity was earth-shattering.

I could freak out about it if I let myself, but once I was inside her, I decided to not even go there.

What I said when she left last night is true. I meant every word. I know myself. I've lived long enough and have been with enough women to know that what we shared last night was unique. And I'm going to enjoy every second I get with her. I'll count it as a gift and a privilege while she's mine, however long it lasts.

Owen is already dressed when I walk out of my bedroom.

"Good job, Ace," I say.

He grins when I use the nickname Felicity gave him.

"I'm surprised you didn't sleep in after your late night."

"I woke up pumped about the game and thinking about that cake," he says.

I laugh. "How could I forget the cake?"

He gives me an incredulous look like he can't believe it either, and then he tilts his head. "You look pumped today too," he says. "Are you sure it's not about the cake?"

"You're right." I laugh. "It's all about the cake."

We're cutting large slices when Felicity knocks twice and walks in. She flushes when she sees me, smiling shyly before squeezing Owen. She looks radiant today, like she's been thoroughly and completely fucked.

"Cake for breakfast? What have we here?" she says. "You know what that means, right, Ace?"

"What?" Owen says, his face lighting up even more when she calls him the cute nickname.

"You're getting extra veggies in your lunch."

"Aw man," he groans, but he's laughing.

"I'll put some Ranch in there too, don't worry."

"Whew," he says.

I enjoy the cake maybe more the second time around and after I've brushed my teeth again, I grab my bag and hug Owen. I want to hug Felicity too, but I settle for pretending to bump into her, my arms going around her waist to steady her.

"Excuse me," I say.

She smirks at me, lifting an eyebrow. "Clumsy this morning, Your Honor?"

"Feeling a little unsteady, like my world's been tipped upside down."

"Interesting. Vertigo, maybe?" she teases.

"Maybe," I say, laughing. "Have a good day, you two."

"You too, Dad," Owen yells as he runs up the stairs to brush his teeth.

I take that opportunity to tug Felicity's waist toward me and kiss her.

"Good morning," I say against her mouth when we break apart.

"Good morning," she whispers, breathless.

"Did you do what I asked?"

She lifts a shoulder, her expression seductive but aloof. "You'll have to wait and see."

She straightens my jacket and pats my chest. The whole thing is oddly domestic and I get a wave of longing. What if we could have that?

Don't ruin this, I tell myself.

She opens the door and waves sweetly before motioning for me to go out the door. "Have the best day, Judge Landmark."

My eyebrow lifts hearing her innocent tone when her expression is anything but. I wish I could stick around and kiss her senseless, but work is calling.

"You too, sweetness," I say under my breath.

Her cheeks flush again and I freaking love it.

Miss Eleanor is already at work when I get there; she typically is. The woman's work ethic is fierce. She's been the judicial secretary for as long as I can remember, working with the two judges who preceded me. All business and supremely private, Miss Eleanor has never been married and is one of the few people in town who consistently keeps to herself. I've tried to break the ice with her, make her comfortable with more of a relaxed environment, but she never cracks.

I don't have any idea if she has family nearby; she never shares personal antidotes. Because of this, I don't talk about my family with her, and my family doesn't know much about her either. She doesn't ask any personal questions about them. It's very professional, and at times exhausting, the sheer effort it takes to remain so proper and detached.

"Good morning, Miss Eleanor. How are you today?"

"Very well, thank you, Judge Landmark. And you?"

"Very well."

We go through our daily routine exchange and as she hands me the files for the day, I sneeze, startling her.

"Bless you," she says.

I thank her and look around for the tissues that are normally within reach but don't see them. I sneeze again and grab my pocket handkerchief out of my jacket to blow my nose in case another sneeze comes. I don't even register the color or texture of my handkerchief until I feel it against my nose, and pull it away, frowning. When I look up, Miss Eleanor's cheeks are bright red. I glance down again to see Felicity's pink lace panties and my own face flames.

"Excuse me, Miss Eleanor," I say with as much dignity as I can muster.

She nods, her eyes staying trained on one of her files.

I rush back to my office, trying to hold my laugh in until I've shut the door. I hold up the pretty underwear and stare at them for a minute before putting them back in my pocket. It's hard to stop laughing as I pull out my phone and text Felicity.

> I'm glad I didn't discover your surprise in court. However, I don't think Miss Eleanor will ever recover.

She answers my text within seconds.

FELICITY

<Crying laughing emoji>

> I'll need another pair, please. Before I realized what I was doing, I almost blew my nose in your pretty pink panties.

> I'd imagined blowing something else entirely.

FELICITY

o.O The mouth on you! Hold on a second while I fan my face. I'm at the grocery store and Cecil just asked if I'm sunburned.

FELICITY

There are plenty more where those came from.

> Now I'll be thinking of my mouth on you the rest of the day.

FELICITY

Cecil just handed me an aloe vera plant. Have mercy on me, Your Honor.

My laughter rings out in my office, and for the rest of the day, I try my best to focus, but it's an uphill battle.

About fifteen minutes before I leave for the day, Grinny messages.

> **GRINNY**
> I should've asked sooner, but this all worked out at the last minute. I'm taking Dakota to Sunny Side for a burger and shakes. Would Owen like to go too?

> I'm sure he would. I'll call Felicity to make sure that works and she'll call you.

> **GRINNY**
> Okay, my boy. Love you.

> I love you too, Grinny.

I don't hesitate to call Felicity, and she's in the middle of laughing when she answers. I can hear Owen in the background chatting away and it makes me happy hearing the two of them.

"Hey," she says.

"Hey. Sounds like you're having fun over there…"

"We are. We built a snowman and are standing by the fire trying to get our hands warm."

"Thanks for being so great with him," I say.

"Of course. He makes it so easy. I've never known such an amazing kid," she says.

I swallow, unable to put into words how much it means to hear her say that. My voice is hoarse when I speak again. "Uh, Grinny called and has Dakota. She wondered if Owen would like to go to Sunny Side with them."

"Oh, let me ask." She puts her mouth away from the phone and I hear them talking. He asks if she can go too and she tells him she needs to finish making dinner. He says something else I can't make out and she comes back on the line. "Okay, he's in."

"You don't need to miss out because of dinner," I tell her. "Especially if he won't even be around."

"I've already started. We can always save it for tomorrow night, but I should finish what I started here."

"Okay. Sorry to mess up the plans so late in the day."

"Don't be. It happens. This is fun. He'll have a good time."

"All right. Would you mind calling Grinny and letting her know?"

"I'll call her right away."

"Thanks, Felicity."

"You're welcome, Sutton," she says, matching my tone.

We hang up and I head out, walking past Miss Eleanor who is also about to leave for the day. Her cheeks turn pink when she sees me. I guess we're not over the panty incident yet.

Before, I would've been concerned about how this could affect my job, but at least I know with Miss Eleanor, it's not going beyond these four walls. But even imagining it happening anywhere else where it could have royally backfired, I start to laugh, the levity of the situation far outweighing the possible pitfalls.

She almost makes me want to throw caution to the wind and not care who knows about us.

Almost.

CHAPTER TWENTY-SEVEN

BEAUTIFUL SPECIMEN

FELICITY

Sutton comes in while Owen's still home, and he smiles at me over Grinny's shoulder as he hugs her.

"That chili smells delicious," Grinny says. "Oh, you made cornbread too? My goodness. My boys are eating like kings over here."

"You don't know the half of it," Sutton says.

"You've gotta have her cake, Grinny." Owen pulls Grinny over to see what's left of the cake.

"That does look good," she admits.

"Oh, and if you hear Felicity say Ace, that's me," Owen says proudly. "She calls me that sometimes."

"Ace, I like it," Grinny says, nodding. She looks at me and winks.

"Come on, have some cake, Grinny. It's so good," Owen says.

"Thanks, guys." I wave off the flattery, but inside I'm thrilled that they seem to like whatever I make. I was worried they'd be picky eaters. "Stay and eat, Grinny. There's more than enough."

"I think Dakota's got her heart set on Sunny Side. We should get over there to pick her up. You were closer, so I stopped here first." Grinny smiles down at Owen and then looks at me again, her smile widening. "Let me know the next time you make chili though."

"You've got it." I laugh.

After the goodbyes and watching them get in the car and drive away, Sutton turns to face me.

"Hi," he says softly.

"Hi."

I feel shy around him all of a sudden. Alone with him in the light of day…after thinking about our night together every second…

"You've distracted me nonstop today," he says.

He rubs his thumb over my bottom lip and my nipples pebble with the way he's looking at me.

"I might've thought about you once or twice." I lift my shoulder nonchalantly.

He growls and I laugh, and his lips are on mine in the next second, claiming me, owning me. He turns so I'm against the door as he presses his body against mine and I'm a goner. Our lips and tongues and teeth are wild and urgent, and when he thrusts against me and I moan, he suddenly pulls back, chest rising and falling.

"You made dinner and I come in here and try to ravish you." He laughs, running his hands through his hair.

"I love your hair messy," I say, lifting off of the door and putting my hands in his waves.

His eyes gleam and eventually drag from my lips to my eyes.

"Yeah?" he says, his voice raspy.

"And I've been thinking about you ravishing me all day. Why did you stop?"

His lips quirk up. "You're not starving?"

I nod. "For you...the food can wait."

He groans and grips my hips. "We do have the place to ourselves."

"What if we go to my apartment?" I ask. "Just in case they come back before we expect them to."

He nods. "I like it."

I move past him and turn off the stove, cover the cornbread, and am by the door before a minute has passed. His low, rumbly chuckle washes over me like a crashing wave and I shiver. He takes my hand and we go outside and up to my apartment. When he shuts the door behind him, he stalks toward me, looking even bigger in this smaller space. I sigh, loving how he towers over me.

"What are you thinking?" He runs his hand over my cheek.

"What a beautiful specimen you are."

"Specimen?" He laughs. "Beautiful? Hmm. And that's a good thing?"

"Would you rather I say hot? Sexy? Drop-dead gorgeous?"

"I'd think you were talking about you, all of that." He

leans his forehead against mine. "It's scary how much I want you," he whispers.

"I know," I whisper back. "Me too."

I don't know what else to say to let him know that I'm right here with him, a little overwhelmed with how perfect this feels.

I loosen his tie and watch him undo it the rest of the way, while I unbutton his shirt. When I see his skin, I run my fingers over his tattoo and kiss him there, against his heart. It's pounding so hard I feel it beneath my lips. My hands move to his belt and I slowly unbuckle it, sliding it out of the loops of his pants as we stare at each other. He takes the belt from my hands and tosses it aside, lifting my sweater over my head. He curses when he sees the pretty pink bra I'm wearing.

"Do I have the matching panties?" he asks, unable to hide his smirk.

"I have a few that match." I lift my shoulder and he bends down to kiss it, his fingers rubbing circles over my nipples. "Where are those panties, by the way?" I gasp when he tugs on my peaks.

"In a safe place," he says, smiling up at me. "You take my breath away, Felicity," he says. "So beautiful."

He kisses me over the lace, reverently, once on each side, and then he straightens.

"Let's see what's under those jeans." His tone is firmer now and every time he's used it so far, I get a gush of wetness between my legs.

I undo my jeans slowly and pull them down and he frowns when he sees my dark pink lacy panties.

"You *didn't* do as I asked," he says.

I shrug and he growls, which makes me giggle. His eyes narrow.

"It was already more than I could take to see you this

morning in front of your son. If I hadn't had on my underwear?" I put my hand on my head and laugh. "I would've been one giant red splotch the entire breakfast."

He tries not to laugh, but it bursts out anyway. He reaches out and tickles my side and I jump away. He pulls me against him and nuzzles my neck. I'm surprised when he pulls away.

"Panties off," he says.

I can just imagine that voice in court, firm and authoritative, and I shiver again but do what he says.

With his hands on my hips, he lifts me up and puts my legs around his waist. He sits down on the bed and circles me over him, his expression intense. I moan when I feel how hard he is underneath his pants. His hands slide over my cheeks and we both groan.

"I'm feeling a little too wild for your sweet softness," he says.

I rub against him for more.

"I want it," I whisper. "All of it. I'm ruining your nice dress pants though."

"You think I care about that?" He smirks, pushing my hair back as he arches into me and slides his fingers down, dipping inside of me.

He hums when he feels me. "So wet. Let's make you come this way."

The combination of what he feels like underneath me and what his fingers are doing makes me delirious. I jerk against him, feeling the sensations everywhere all at once. He's relentless, his eyes pure focus, and it doesn't take long for me to come so hard, my vision goes dark for a few seconds.

"Sutton," I cry out."

He doesn't stop until he's wrenched out all of my orgasm and when I finally catch my breath, I open my eyes and stare at him. And my God, the sight of him is almost too much. He's flushed and his eyes are shining with lust.

His breath hitches and he pulls my face back, his hands on either side as he stares at me.

"Slow me down if it becomes too much."

I nod. "It won't be. I can't get enough of you, Sutton."

My words send a fire through him. He stands, lifting me with him, and turns, tossing me on the bed.

"On your hands and knees," he says, grinning.

I turn and get in place, watching over my shoulder as he grabs a condom out of his pocket and takes his pants off. In the light of day, seeing his body, muscular and toned with that beautiful tattoo and the worthiest cock I've ever seen, makes my heart nearly jump out of my chest. He tears the wrapper and slides the condom down his length, his expression as he looks down my body eating me up.

He puts his knee on the bed and then pauses to press a kiss on my ass. He goes lower and exhales, sending warm air against me and I arch into it. He groans and moves over me, his tip pressing against my entrance.

I put my head on the bed and moan when he goes in deeper. He does a slow drag inside and out, going deeper each time, and it's unlike anything I've ever felt. Everything in me aches for more of him, all of him, and he's taking his time, building the need in me until I'm unhinged.

"Sutton," I cry.

"Tell me what you need."

"I want you…wild," I gasp.

He jerks with my words and smacks my ass as he does, and it's so perfect, I cry out. It unleashes something in him, and he moves, his thrusts becoming hard and smooth. The slap of his thighs against mine is intoxicating, and the way his fingers slide across my clit again and again makes pleasure wrap around me like ivy. I look at him over my shoulder and he moves harder and faster, holding my hip and watching the way he thrusts inside. He's still restrained and I want to see him lose his mind the way I'm losing mine.

He smacks me again and then squeezes my cheek and I arch into his hand, wanting more.

"I want to see your face," he says, hoarse.

He pulls out and turns me over, and drives in so deep, I yell his name.

My orgasm crashes over me, and I grip his ass so hard it'll probably leave marks, but I see the victory in his eyes when I crest over the edge.

It unleashes his wild.

The headboard bangs against the wall with his thrusts, and I'm there, matching his rhythm.

His muscles are tense, and his head falls back a little before he buries his head in my neck.

"Oh God, Felicity," he groans, his chest quivering slightly as he comes.

I relish every sensation, the way he stays in so deep, the pulses inside and my walls squeezing him back, making him groan again.

When he finally lifts his head, his expression is almost shy.

"Was that…too much?" he asks.

I frown. "It was so good I can't believe it."

He smiles and kisses me, and our lips lift when he jerks inside me.

"I don't want to leave this perfect place," he says, making a sad face as he slowly pulls out.

I don't want him to *ever* leave my body, but I keep that to myself.

He goes to the bathroom and a few minutes later, walks

out carrying a washcloth. He sits next to me and drapes the warm washcloth between my legs, carefully sliding it over my skin.

I run my fingers over his arm and his chest as he cleans me, and he gets hard. I wrap my fist around him and he hisses.

"You do this to me," he says.

I lean up on my elbow, sliding my hand up and down the length of him, and then I bend down and kiss the tip before putting him in my mouth.

The sound of car doors shutting make me pause and Sutton curses, laughing.

I pop my lips off of him and grin. "Looks like our time's up."

"You've given me a *lot* to fantasize about." He motions to us and the bed and then presses his fingers against my lips. He stands up and then leans down to kiss me one more time. "I already miss your warm heat wrapped around me." He reaches down and cups his hand between my legs, sighing when he pulls away.

CHAPTER TWENTY-EIGHT

FOCUS

SUTTON

I grab some clothes I'd planned to donate from my trunk and change in the garage, leaving my work clothes near the back door. I grin when I see the wet marks on the front of my pants. I'll take them to the cleaners this week. When I step inside the back door, I apologize for being outside when they got here. They're fine. Grinny's sitting on the couch and Owen is bringing books over to show her. I move to the stove and turn the chili on.

"You didn't eat yet?" Grinny asks in surprise.

"No, some things came up, so we paused dinner."

It's not a lie. Let's just hope my face didn't turn bright red when I said that. My grandmother is observant, and she'd jump on this with both feet.

Fortunately, Owen is distracting her with books.

But as I pull out a bowl, Owen turns and notices. "Is Felicity coming back?"

"I don't know," I admit.

"You should tell her to come eat," Grinny says.

I pick up my phone and text her.

> The consensus over here is that you should come eat this chili with me.

FELICITY

Is that right?

> It's more than right. It's a necessity.

FELICITY

I'm not sure I can look at you around Grinny and Owen without giving everything away.

> So don't look at me.

FELICITY

Not possible. I'll come eat because chili sounds good.

> You sound good.

FELICITY

Nuh-uh-uh. None of that.

> What? It's true. I especially love it when you whimper my name and say more and harder.

FELICITY

There's no way I can come over now.

> I'll behave! I swear. The chili's warming up. Come eat.

FELICITY

Okay.

I turn so Grinny and Owen don't see the ridiculous grin on my face as I pocket my phone and stir the chili. By the time Felicity walks in, I've heated the cornbread and have our silverware and glasses set up on the island. I dish the soup into the bowls and put them in place and motion for her to have a seat. She pulls out the stool and sits down.

"Thank you," she says, not maintaining eye contact with me.

I chuckle and Owen calls out, "What's funny?"

"Felicity just made a funny face," I tell him.

Her eyes shoot to mine and narrow.

"Can I see?" Owen says.

Felicity turns to him and makes a silly face and Owen cracks up, Grinny too.

"Did you have fun at Sunny Side?" she asks.

"Yes. It was yummy," he says.

"We would've stayed longer, but it filled up with tourists and I didn't want to stress Jo out by hogging the table." Grinny frowns. "Not many venture too far off of Heritage Lane, but it's been happening more and more this year. Jo said we're having a record year for tourism and somehow they're hearing about her place now. She didn't seem too pleased about it."

"She needs a bigger place and more help if that keeps happening," I say.

I take a seat next to Felicity and take my first bite of chili. My moan is obscene and I realize it because Felicity's eyes fly to mine when she hears me, and her red cheeks are back. I grin and wrinkle my nose in apology.

"This is the best chili I've ever had in my life," I tell her. My eyes widen. "Sorry, Grinny. Your chili is so good."

"It's okay, my boy." Grinny laughs. She stands up. "That settles it. I've gotta try some of that. I couldn't decide what I wanted at Sunny Side because after smelling this, it's all I wanted."

She grabs a bowl and ladles out a small portion. When she tastes it, she closes her eyes and nods.

"Oh, that *is* good," she says. "Really good."

Felicity's face is radiant. "Thank you. You guys are so good for my ego. And you're really the best to cook for—Weston is fun too, but my parents are very meat and potatoes, and my sister doesn't do any carbs. I've tried to make it for her without the beans and it was too spicy." She waves her hand. "I can't get it right for her." She looks down at her bowl, deep in thought for a second.

"Try the cornbread, Grinny. It's delicious too," I add. "I've had to work out more, having Felicity's cooking every day."

Felicity's eyes track over my shoulders and chest, and I'm tempted to flex for her to make her laugh. Talking about her sister brings her down.

"Girl, you have got a gift," Grinny says. "You must enjoy cooking."

"I do." Felicity brightens up, and I just stare at her for a few seconds, memorizing her face until I catch myself and take another bite of chili. "I started cooking more in college. It took my mind off of all the stress."

"I used to feel that way too. I can't say that I enjoy it as much as I used to, but I still like cooking big meals for the family," Grinny says. "Since it's just me most of the time, I find that I rarely cook anymore."

My heart aches when she says that. She's been so resilient since Granddad died, and we've all tried to spend time with her and be there for her, but I know it's still not enough. She's still alone a lot of the time.

I reach out and pat her hand. "You should come over for dinner more often. Every night, if you want. Or if you don't feel like getting out, I can bring the leftovers to you."

She smiles at me, her eyes shining. "You've always taken care of everyone," she says, squeezing my hand. "When are you gonna let someone take care of you?"

I swallow hard, feeling that more intensely than she probably meant for me to. I smile to cover up the emotions and joke the way I usually do.

"The family just keeps growing—what'll happen if I stop making sure everything runs smoothly?"

"You've made sure they're the independent adults they need to be," she says. "They'll handle it just fine. It's time you focus on you." She points her finger at me with those last words, her grim look showing me she means it.

"Don't worry about me, Grin. I could be saying all of this to you. And in fact, I am. You focus on *you*."

Her head falls back as she laughs. "I get out way more than you do," she says, taking her bowl to the sink and washing it. "Peg and Helen keep me busy, and—" she pauses, her eyes flying to mine.

"What is it?" I ask.

She's quiet for a second and then shakes her head. "Nothing. It's nothing."

"Doesn't sound like nothing," I say.

She laughs. "Nah. Sometimes I think this old woman's imagination is getting carried away."

"Well, tell me and I'll let you know."

She dries the dish and puts it back in the cabinet. "I promised that boy a book and then it's bedtime."

She taps the counter and walks back to the couch, cuddling next to Owen and looking at the book he's reading. He hands it to her and she starts reading it aloud.

What is she not telling me?

For a second, my mind flies to the worst-case scenario. Is she sick? Was she trying to tell me she's not well? No, she was talking about being busy and getting out more than me. That can't be it.

I listen to her reading for a few minutes and she eventually looks up. "I can hear you thinking from over here, Sutton Henry," she says. "I'm sorry I did that. I hate it when people start to say something and then don't." She laughs and the knot in my chest loosens.

"You'd tell me if it was anything of concern, right?"

"You have my word," she says.

The tension in my shoulders lessens somewhat and I glance at Felicity, who's watching us with amusement.

"What?"

"You guys are so cute," she says, low enough that only I can hear. "I love how close the two of you are, how you communicate. I love my grandparents, but I don't feel like I know them very well. Not like the two of you. Were you close with your grandpa too?"

"Very." I nod. "But it was different. He was gruff and

didn't dive as much into feelings…he could when he wanted to, but it wasn't as constant like it's always been with Grinny. But the man could get downright flowery when it came to her. He worshipped the ground she walked on and demanded that everyone treat her with that same respect…which was easy to do. It was important to him that I was a man of character." I lean my elbow on the island and think about that.

What would he say about what I'm doing with my son's nanny?

I clear my throat and wipe my hands on the napkin. I don't want to think about what he'd say. I have a feeling I know and I'm enjoying it too much to stop, so why go there?

"Where are you right now?" Felicity asks.

I look over at her and smile. "I'm right here, enjoying this dinner with you."

She smiles back at me. "I'm glad."

"Hey…why did you stop eating dinner with us?"

She looks down, her lips puckering. When she looks up again, her expression is sheepish. "The truth?" She checks to make sure Grinny and Owen are engrossed in their book.

"Always."

"I didn't think I could hide my attraction to you if I kept hanging around here with you guys. I was trying to keep it professional."

"Are you saying you've wanted to rip my clothes off for a while now?" I whisper.

"Sutton!" She looks over my shoulder again and relaxes. "Yes," she says, smirking.

"For how long?" My voice is low and raspy and her tongue dips out to lick her lips, which makes me even harder.

"Since the day I met you…and it's only gotten worse since I've gotten to know you." She sighs.

I laugh. "You say that like it's a hardship."

"It is! It's been exhausting."

"Well, let me exhaust you in other ways," I whisper. "And please, always stay for dinner."

CHAPTER TWENTY-NINE

WRONG SIDE OF EVERYTHING

FELICITY

Weston calls while we're cleaning up and I'm about to ignore it when Sutton says, "Take it. I'll finish this."

"I don't want to leave you with a mess."

"It's hardly anything. And you made dinner, I should clean up."

I smile at him and wave at Grinny and Owen before I walk outside, answering the call.

"Hey. We've been playing phone tag," he says. "How ya been?"

"I'm great. The question is, how are *you*? Are you still somewhere up in the clouds?"

He laughs. "Yes and no. It's been insane. So much press, and the coach is not letting up on us for a second."

"I've seen you in a few interviews. You've done great. Some of them get a little personal." I laugh.

He groans. "I'm so tired of all the interviews, but it's just part of it. I feel like I'm repeating myself though."

I open the door to my place and sit down on the couch, propping my feet up, but quickly move to lie on my side. My backside is feeling tingly where Sutton's hands have been, in the best way.

"Well, they seem to love whatever you're saying. '*Oh, you are so funny and so intelligent,*'" I say, mocking the last interviewer he talked to on a popular sports show.

He laughs. "She was hot."

"Mm-hmm. She thought you were too, which is so gross to see on national television, by the way…watching your brother flirt."

"I was just being nice," he says. "She was the one flirting. Thank you for reminding me though—she gave me her number."

"I knew it!" I cackle and he laughs too.

"Okay, enough. I'm calling to see if you want to bring anyone with you to the Super Bowl."

"Really?" He's said he has extra tickets between what they've given him and what he's bought, but I thought he might run out with all his friends.

"Yeah. I've got two extra—I wish there were more, but they're yours if you want them."

"Thanks, West. I know Jamison and Scarlett are already

going, which will be fun. Can I let you know for sure who I'm bringing tomorrow?"

"Sure. Let me know. I've already reserved two-bedroom suites at the hotel, so you'll either have a massive one to yourself, or there are two bedrooms if you bring guests."

"You're such a good brother," I squeal.

"I purposely called you *after* Olivia, so I could balance out your love with her hate," he says, laughing.

"Ugh. She needs to find a man...or a woman. Something to chill her out."

"Agreed. It's like happiness angers her." There's noise in the background and he yells that he'll be right there. "I've gotta run. We're gonna go find some fun."

"Have fun. Be safe," I tell him.

"Same to you, but more of it," he says. "Love you."

"Love you too."

I set my phone on the coffee table and rest my eyes for just a minute.

When I wake up on the couch, I stretch and then pause. It's brighter outside than I would've expected. I reach for my phone and see the time and all the missed messages and groan. I can't believe I slept through the night. I jump up, throwing clothes on and rushing into the bathroom to brush my teeth. It's a messy bun kind of day and I don't bother with makeup. I don't bother with reading my texts either. If I take a second longer, I'll be too late to make Owen's breakfast. I slide my feet into my boots and am still sliding my arm through my coat sleeves as I run to Sutton's back door.

I knock and rush in, pausing when I see Sutton and Owen at the breakfast table...with another woman. She's beautiful, with large blue eyes and light brown hair, and her clothes scream expensive. They're eating scrambled eggs and toast, sipping coffee and juice, and the whole scene is so unexpected, I just stand there staring for a few seconds.

"Felicity!" Owen says, getting up to rush toward me.

His arms wrap around my waist and I smile down at him, still half asleep.

"Good morning, Ace," I croak.

I clear my throat and Owen reluctantly lets his arms drop. He takes my hand, which is more unusual than the hug. He's a little cuddler, but I think he's reached for my hand maybe twice since I've been here, and both times were while crossing the street.

"Morning, Felicity," Sutton says, his voice formal.

His smile doesn't quite reach his eyes and unease builds in my gut.

"This is Owen's mom, Tracy," Sutton says. "Tracy, this is Felicity."

Ah. The mom. Is that why she's looking me up and down, lip slightly curled, like I'm gum on the bottom of her shoe?

"Of course it is," she says.

My head tilts, unsure of what she means.

"Hi, Tracy! Nice to meet you," I say.

She takes a sip of coffee and continues with her staredown. I feel like I'm one of the contestants on *Project Runway* standing in front of the judges and I really botched my project.

Why did today have to be the day when I didn't have time to look decent?

"I've been talking about you all morning," Owen says, squeezing my hand.

I grin at him and he lets go, pointing to the table.

"Come eat. When we found out Mom was coming early,

Dad and I got up and made breakfast." He makes a face. "It's not as good as yours, but—"

"Hey," Sutton says, looking more relaxed when he laughs at Owen. To me, he says, "There's plenty. Join us."

I sit down reluctantly, wishing I could be anywhere but here.

"I'm sorry I'm late," I tell Sutton. "I fell asleep on the couch after I got off of the phone and…" I shake my head. "I didn't wake up until seven minutes ago."

Sutton chuckles. "It's okay. We had it under control this morning."

"Must be nice to be late for your job and then have such a pushover boss," Tracy says, laughing at Sutton like they're in on a joke, but the punch landed where she intended.

"Felicity's always here before we even get up," Owen says, looking from his mom to me.

God, I love this kid. But I don't want him to feel like he has to defend me with his mom. I smile with what I hope is a reassuring smile, even though I feel like crying.

I stand up. "You can deduct it from my pay," I say, nodding to Sutton. His eyebrows lift and he frowns. "I'll just grab some coffee and work on Owen's lunch."

"Don't worry about it, Felicity. It happens," Sutton says. "Eat. Like Owen said, it's not as good as your breakfasts, but it's not all that bad."

I'm already walking away.

"I'm not hungry yet, but thank you," I say over my shoulder. "I'm sure it's good."

The relief I feel when I reach the coffeepot is acute.

I need coffee like I need my next breath.

As soon as I'm alone, I'm setting my alarm to go off at the same time every morning. Never again will I rely on myself to do it the night before.

I jump when Owen pops up next to me.

"I'll help you with my lunch," he says.

I lean down and tousle his hair. "Thank you, but I've got it, Ace. You should enjoy your breakfast with your mom."

"But—" He looks back at the table and up at me and then sighs. "Okay."

Now I feel bad for sending him away. He seems so dejected.

Once I have a little coffee in my system, I'm less rattled. I feel Tracy's eyes on me, but I try to pretend I'm the happy, professional nanny who is *not* screwing her ex-husband.

Can she tell? Is that why she's so hostile?

When I open the refrigerator, the cool blast of air helps. I stand there hiding for a few long seconds before getting to work. I'm glad for the lunch system I set up, it makes the mornings painless. Making Owen's and often Sutton's—if he doesn't have lunch plans—lunches is one of my favorite things to do. The bento boxes I bought for them have five sections—one large, one small, and three medium. Owen's is smaller than Sutton's, but it's the same setup.

I work on their sandwiches first, cutting the crusts off more for the cute factor than anything. I put turkey, cheese, and lettuce between the slices of bread—finely chopped jalapenos on Sutton's—cut the bread into strips, and then roll them until they're little pinwheels. In the medium-sized section, I arrange the carrots, celery, and cucumbers I'd already chopped, and in the smallest section, I add Ranch dressing. I fill the other medium section with raspberries, blueberries, and strawberries that were also ready to go, and in the last medium section, I add their favorite chips. Sutton likes jalapeno potato chips, and Owen likes the plain. For a tiny sweet, I sprinkle a few chocolate chips in the top corner of the fruit section and call it done.

"You're giving my son chocolate and potato chips every day?" Tracy says from the table.

"Tracy," Sutton says, his voice low.

"What? I have a right to know."

Owen jumps up and carries his box to the table. "Did you see everything else? She mixes it up every day. Sometimes we have taco salad, sometimes there's yogurt and granola instead of chips. But Felicity makes me eat my vegetables every day. Dad too. Right, Dad?"

I turn so they don't see my eyes filling. Owen is killing me. He's trying so hard, and his mom seems like a—well, I don't need to go there. I need to get out of here.

"Yes, she does," Sutton says pointedly to Tracy. "Have you ever seen a more beautiful lunch box? But it'd be okay if she threw it into a brown paper sack with baggies and only one vegetable instead of three, not to mention all that goddamn fruit..." He sighs and reaches into his pocket, giving Owen a dollar. "Sorry, son." He takes a deep breath. "Felicity puts time and care into our lunches, not to mention a helluva lot of other things, and you don't get to come in here and disrespect her."

Tracy blinks at the box, her lips pursed. "I didn't see the fruit." She sniffs.

The mood is tense now. Normally, I'd tell Owen to rinse his plate and put it in the dishwasher and then go brush his teeth, but I don't want to give any instructions with his mom around.

Owen brings the bento box back to the island and puts the lid on it.

"I love your lunches," he whispers.

"I'm so glad," I whisper back, grinning. "Are you done with breakfast?"

"Yep." He turns and gets his plate from the table, rinses,

and puts it in the dishwasher without me even asking. "I'm gonna go brush my teeth," he says, dashing up the stairs.

I put the lid on Sutton's box and set it near his bag, and then I start putting the food away and cleaning up. When Sutton stands from the table, I'm worried he's going to leave me alone with Tracy, but he walks over to the island and gives me an apologetic look.

"Thanks for the lunches. They look great."

I nod, my jaw clenching. "No problem."

"Tracy will be taking Owen to school this morning," he says.

"Okay. Sounds good. I'll just finish cleaning real quick and then be out of here."

"Leave it. I need to talk to Tracy before they leave for school."

"Oh. Right. Got it." I practically fly to the door and slip my boots on, grabbing my coat as an afterthought. "Have a good day, you guys."

It's not until later, after I've cried and gotten angry and then calmed down, that I check my messages. There are a few from last night and this morning.

> SUTTON
> Heyyy, come back.

> SUTTON
> Sorry, if you're still talking to Weston...

And later...

> SUTTON
> Owen is in bed. I can't stop thinking about you. Would I be a needy bastard if I said I need a kiss goodnight?

And then this morning...

> **SUTTON**
>
> Tracy's in town. She wasn't supposed to be here until the weekend. I'll take care of everything this morning and keep you posted about the rest of the day. Thanks, Felicity.

Shit. I went through all that for nothing.

No, I take it back. Owen's sweet face smiling up at me flashes through my mind.

I'd do anything for that kid.

CHAPTER THIRTY

TAPERING OFF

SUTTON

I look out the window briefly, sad to see Felicity go. I was worried last night when I didn't hear from her.

Maybe I'd been too rough. Maybe I'd scared her off. Maybe she didn't want this after all.

But she must've not seen my messages because she showed up when I said she didn't have to, barreling inside in a mad dash, apologizing. She looked even younger than her age, with her hair piled on top of her head and no makeup. She tolerated Tracy's bullshit with dignity and brightened Owen's smile just by being here. Dammit, if that didn't make her even more beautiful in my eyes.

I live for those fucking lunches. They're the highlight of my day, seeing what she's going to come up with next. I haven't told her enough how much I appreciate the care she puts into every detail, but I'll make sure I do from now on.

"You were out of line," I say, turning to face Tracy.

I move to the island and lean against it.

"Oh, whatever. You try coming in and seeing your husband and son playing house with a pretty young thing," she says, rolling her eyes.

"*Ex*-husband. She's not a thing, her name is Felicity, use it. And we're not playing house. She's doing a damn good job helping with Owen. Why are you being so petty? I've been nothing but kind to every guy you've dated and especially to Jeff the entire time you were *married*."

"So, there *is* something going on with the girl. Is she even legal?" she snaps.

"That's not what I'm saying. You showed up before you were scheduled to be, and you were rude to Felicity, someone who takes such good care of our son. You owe her your kindness for that alone."

"Work sent me here for a few days, and I would think you'd want me to spend all the time I can with him. You're always harping on me for not spending enough time with him."

"Next time, call before the morning of."

"I want to take him home with me this weekend."

I run my hands through my hair. "Tracy, we've talked about this. He's not ready for that. We need to ease him into it."

"Of course he doesn't want to leave when he has a playmate who makes him fancy lunches and does whatever he wants. I look like the bad guy here, wanting him to spend time where I'm living now, and I'm his mother. He should be with *me*."

"Where is this coming from?" I ask. "You're seeing him every other weekend like you have been for a long time now, minus this past month when you're getting settled in Arizona. All of a sudden, you want to see him more? Insist on changing his routine when I've asked you to give him time?"

"I don't know anyone there, okay? It's been an adjustment." She stands up and moves toward me, and if I weren't against the island, I'd back up.

When she gets within a foot of me and reaches out to touch me, I lift my hand, stopping her.

"Sutton, I miss you. I miss us. I'm so…lonely," she says, her lips trembling.

I shake my head. "*Don't do this*," I say, moving past her when I hear Owen coming down the stairs.

"Have dinner with us tonight?" she asks.

"I'll let you two have this time together," I say.

She swallows and looks at me, tears about to spill over. If I didn't know her so well, I'd be sympathetic to her sadness, but she tries to play me, in one way or another, every damn time.

"Do you have everything, son?" I ask.

He's putting his arms through his backpack straps and nods. "I put my lunch in my bag already."

"Good deal. Why don't you go ahead and get in your mom's car?"

"Okay. Bye, Dad." He hugs me and I bend down to kiss the top of his head.

"I love you," I say.

"Love you too." He smiles up at me and then he's out the door.

"We need to finish this discussion before you say anything to Owen," I say.

"It'd save you a trip flying if he just came home with me now," she argues.

"He's not missing school, Tracy. Just stay here and be with him this weekend like you'd planned. I'm talking to him a lot about coming to see you. He's not ready. Do you want him to go and be difficult and miserable? Or can you be patient and work on convincing him he'll love being there?"

"He doesn't have to love it." She shrugs.

I count to ten and take a deep breath. "I've wanted to avoid this, but you're backing me into a corner. If you want to change our custody agreement, get a lawyer, and we'll discuss it in court."

"You know I can't afford that!" she cries.

"I'll loan you the money *and* refer you to a good lawyer." I grab my jacket and bag and open the door, motioning for her to go ahead. "If you truly want Owen more often and in your new state, let's at least get a mediator."

She opens her mouth and then closes it, eyes flashing as she walks out.

That's what I thought.

During my lunch break, I call Felicity.

I texted her when I got to work, apologizing for the way the morning went, and her text back said: **No need to apologize.**

The rest of the morning, I was slammed, so I didn't text her again.

I'm a little surprised when she answers.

"Hello?"

"Hey. How's your day going?" I ask.

"I'd say it's steadily improved since this morning." Her tone is light, but I can tell she's still uneasy.

"Good. Well, first, let me say that Tracy was completely out of line and I told her so."

"You didn't have to do that. It's a complicated situation. I'm sure it feels weird for her to see me taking care of Owen in the house that used to be hers."

"You're being very generous. None of that gives her the right to be rude to you."

I think of the argument with Tracy and hope to God she's not going to continue fighting me on this. If I thought her desire to see Owen was genuine, I'd feel differently about all of it. She's digging in her heels out of the blue and I don't know why.

"What else?" Felicity says.

"What?"

"You said *first, let me say*, so there must be something else…"

"Right. Second, but of no lesser importance, your lunches are little works of art. Owen and I talk about them often and compare notes, but I realized today that I haven't told you enough how much I enjoy them. You've turned what were boring and uneventful lunches into a daily *experience*."

She giggles.

"I mean it."

"I'm happy you enjoy them. I didn't realize you were so passionate about my lunches."

"I think I'm passionate about everything where you're concerned," I say, and then wince.

"Well, thank you. That…means a lot."

"Was yesterday too much?" I put my head in my free hand but keep going. "I wasn't sure if you really didn't see my texts last night or if you might've been avoiding me."

Might as well just put it out there.

"No," she gasps. "Sutton, I didn't see your texts until after breakfast this morning. Oversleeping won't happen again—I've got a recurring alarm set now. I didn't realize I was so tired, but you must have worn me out." She laughs quietly, sounding shy, and I wish she was in front of me so I could put her at ease. "And then I came in all gross and rushing around, not realizing you didn't need me this morning."

"There is nothing gross about you, ever. And if it had been a normal day without Tracy here, it would've still been fine if you overslept. Things happen. I'd like to think I'm easygoing."

She laughs. "You are. Except in bed. And then you get *bossy*." Her voice changes at the end, playful and sexy.

"Do you like it?" I ask, my voice low and raspy.

"I *really* do. Couldn't you tell?"

I adjust myself under my desk. "It seemed like you did in the moment," I say. "I'm just making sure you're still feeling that way today."

"I haven't been able to get it out of my head. Trust me, I *liked* it."

"*Fuck*," I whisper.

I love the sound of her laugh. It tapers off at the end with a little hum. She does it now and I smile like a fucking kid.

"I better go because you're making me hard as a rock and I have to be in court in fifteen."

"Ooo, plenty of time to pretend that's my fist around you—"

"No, I am not doing that at work," I interrupt, laughing. Although she has me strongly considering it.

"Suit yourself," she says.

"And don't you either. We wait for each other, deal?"

She laughs. "Since when are orgasms negotiated?"

"Since you got in bed with me." I grin when she sighs.

"Okay, fine."

"I'm sorry to say I'll be late tonight. Owen's going to dinner with Tracy, and I'm going to Callum's for a bit. You're welcome to come with me, if you'd like."

"Maybe another night. I need to do laundry and catch up on a few things. Oh, before you go—would you and Owen be interested in going to the Super Bowl? Weston's giving me two extra tickets."

"That would be…incredible." I can't believe I'm even hesitating. What guy in their right mind would turn down tickets like this? "Won't your parents think it's weird if I show up there? It seemed less so when it was close and my whole family came out, but if it's just me and Owen…"

"They might. But I don't really care. Jamison and Scarlett are going since it's in Boston. And it's the Super Bowl. I'd hate for you to miss out because we're worried about that."

"When do you need to know for sure?"

"I told Weston I'd let him know today."

"Okay, I'll look at the schedule too, and see if it's even a possibility."

"Sounds good."

"I'm having a hard time saying bye," I say, groaning.

She laughs. "I can tell. How about this? If Owen's still out when you get back from Callum's, come over. We can chat more then."

"I'll try to make that happen."

"Bye, Sutton."

"Bye, Felicity."

I've always hated wearing the robe, but it's a godsend

right now. I manage to get through court sporting a semi, and no one's the wiser.

CHAPTER THIRTY-ONE

ON THE MOVE

FELICITY

I've stayed busy, cleaning and working on laundry, and my phone stays quiet. I try not to check it like crazy, but I do look a few times to make sure the sound is on and roll my eyes at myself every time.

Around eight, I hear from him.

> **SUTTON**
>
> I'm so sorry it's taken me so long to message you. I got hung up at Callum's and I'm heading home in a few minutes, but I think Tracy will be there when I get back, and we need to talk about Owen.

I sit down and stare at my phone for a few minutes.

It's hard to tell from texts, but it feels like his whole mood has changed from earlier. Meeting Tracy today was bizarre and made me think about things I don't want to think about.

It's weird being on the outside looking in when I've felt so at home with Sutton and Owen from the very beginning. It doesn't help that Tracy isn't very likable. Maybe she was having an off day. Every protective instinct in me wanted to keep Owen from feeling the conflict, but it wasn't my place. I don't get a say about that little boy when both of his parents are around. But did she not see how her attitude was affecting him this morning?

I've gotten attached to Sutton and Owen way too fast. I love that little boy so much already, but I'm not his mom.

I'm not permanent.

This could really break my heart.

I finally text back:

> No worries.

> **SUTTON**
>
> I don't like the way this day has gone for us.

That makes me smile a little bit.

> Well, tomorrow's a new day. <Smile emoji>

> **SUTTON**
> You know what? Count us in for the Super Bowl.

> Really?

> **SUTTON**
> Yeah, it works with my schedule, which rarely happens this close to the date. And the rest? Fuck it. We only live once, and I'd love to see your brother win that trophy.

> Okay! YAY. I'll tell him you're in.

> **SUTTON**
> Thanks for thinking of us. Sleep well, sweetness.

> You too.

Sleep is fitful, and when I wake up—on time—the next morning, I check my phone first thing. A message came from Sutton after I went to bed last night and I stare at it, wondering if this is the beginning of the end.

> **SUTTON**
> I hope you see this before morning so you can rest. Tracy will be here for a few more days and we're working through some things regarding Owen. Consider the rest of the week paid time off.

I will be overthinking this like crazy.

> Tell Owen to have a good day for me, please.

> **SUTTON**
> What about me?

> Have a good day.

SUTTON
You too, sweetness.

Him calling me sweetness helps. It lets me know he's thinking about our time together and hopefully not regretting it.

I take a shower and get ready for the day, uncertain about what to do. I texted Weston last night about the tickets and he filled me in on what his schedule is like today, or I'd go see him. My parents are working, but I could go spend a few days with them. They'd want to know why I'm not working this week though, and what would I say? The ex showed up?

Maybe I'll see if Scarlett or Pappy are at the lodge, and if they're not around, I could go see Sofie or Ruby. I could even stop by the hospital and say hi to Marlow, maybe catch her around her lunch break. I could go skiing. It's the perfect day for it. Fluffy snow and not brutally cold.

Wherever I end up, I'm going to have fun. I can't sit around here thinking about Sutton, Owen, and Tracy. I pack an extra sweater and my ski gloves in a backpack, along with my laptop, and head to my car…just as the three of them are walking out the back door. It probably looks like I planned this, but I had no idea what time it was. I'm kicking myself for not being more aware.

"Felicity!" Owen runs over and hugs me.

"Hey, Ace. How are you today?"

"Good. I've missed you. I didn't see you last night *or* today. Will I see you tonight?"

"I've missed you too. I'll be off for the next few days. Have lots of fun this week, okay?"

"But where are you going?" His face falls.

"I might go see my parents or something, I'm not sure yet. But you're going to be so busy, you'll have lots to tell me about when we see each other again."

He hugs me again even tighter. Tracy calls him, and he looks a bit forlorn as he walks to the car. I wish I knew why he doesn't seem happier that she's here. Most kids would be so excited to see their mom. It'd probably be best if I did go away for a few days and let them all have this time together.

Sutton waves and I return it, and everyone moves toward their cars. The space where I park is to the side of the garage, and Sutton keeps the driveway and my area clear of snow, so there's more room. Tracy and Owen pull out first and Sutton goes next, but instead of going down the driveway, he pulls up next to my car and lowers the window. I do the same and wait for him to say something.

"Hey." He smiles and some of my worry fades just like that. "I'm sorry yesterday didn't go as I'd hoped."

"It's okay. Is everything all right?"

His jaw tightens and a look crosses over his face...and some of the worry is right back.

"Tracy has been pushing for Owen to go to Arizona with her. She wasn't supposed to be here until the weekend, and she showed up with no warning and wants him to miss school and go home with her for a few days. I asked her not to talk about it with him, but she did anyway, so we all had to talk about it last night. He does not want to do it. Not yet. Not without me."

I nod, unsure of what to say. I have too many questions to know where to start.

"Sometimes I don't know if I'm doing the right thing or not." He rubs his hand over his face and looks out his front windshield. "For most of his life, I've begged her to spend more time with him, to make it easier for him when he's with her, and she hasn't. After he was born and she didn't bond with him, she concluded that she's not cut out to be a mother, and I've tried not to force it, but I've also wanted her to make an effort. Now that she's divorced again, she's lonely and thinks Owen should want to be with her more."

I try not to flinch when he says that about her not feeling cut out to be a mother. That's *heartbreaking*. It kills me for Owen especially, but for Sutton too, and even for Tracy.

Sutton looks at me, and his eyes are anguished.

"He cries every time he talks about having to go to her house. This happened when she lived right here, so you can imagine how he feels about going to Arizona."

He lets out a ragged exhale and my heart pinches. I wish I could hug him.

"I agree with her—that a boy should be with his mother. But these aren't normal circumstances. It feels wrong to force him into being with her when it makes him miserable."

"Do you know why it makes him miserable?" I ask.

"When she was married to Jeff, Owen said Jeff spent more time with him than Tracy did." He lifts a shoulder. "Maybe now that Jeff's gone, she'll be able to focus on Owen more."

"Can you go with Owen to Arizona?"

"Not this week, but that's what I was suggesting we do this summer. I don't want to take him out of school and disrupt his life by having him fly back and forth every other weekend."

"I'm sorry, Sutton. It sounds really complicated."

He nods and winces. "Yeah, it always has been with her."

"Am I making it worse? For Owen? For her?"

"What?" His brows crease. "No. Not at all."

"It might be hard for her, seeing him interact so easily with me, especially if they don't have that."

"At this point, I don't really care if it's hard for her, but you could be right. And I don't really mean that. I do care. Because I want more than anything for my son to have a healthy relationship with his mother. But she's being unpredictable—I suggested we revisit the custody agreement if she's not happy with it, but I don't think she really wants that."

I nod. "I'll stay somewhere else while she's here. It'll be better for everyone involved."

"It won't be better for me." He grips the steering wheel and stares at me.

"I'll be back. Figure things out with her and let me know when I'm needed around here again. I can be here whenever you need."

He sighs. "I hate this."

"Owen is the priority. It's important that you work things out with her and that he's at peace with all of it."

"You're right. Thanks for listening. I miss you."

"I miss you too." My lips lift in a smile and his eyes are so sad when he looks at me, but he smiles back.

He pulls away and I follow him, but when he turns to go to the courthouse, I go toward the lodge. I'd rather stay close in case Sutton and Owen need me than be an hour and a half away in Silver Hills. The parking lot is packed and it's probably a longshot that they have a room available, but I go inside and wait in line at the reservation desk.

"Felicity? Hey, what are you doing standing in line?" Scarlett says, walking toward me. "Everything okay?"

"You wouldn't have a room available, would you?" I look around, taking in all the people. "Looks pretty full."

"There's a condo that we try to keep open for family and friends, and you definitely qualify as that," she says, smiling warmly. "Come back to my office. I can get you set up back there."

We walk past the counter and through the door, going down a long hallway until we reach her office. It's beautiful, and the only thing out of place are the rubber toys lying on the floor.

"Ignore the dog toys. My dogs were here earlier and they can't stand to leave the toys in the basket." She laughs, motioning for me to sit down.

"Owen talks about your dogs all the time. I can't wait to see them."

"I can't believe you haven't already. Owen's been so busy with hockey that he hasn't come over as much. Now that he's done for a little bit, maybe the two of you could come over soon."

"I'd like that." I nod.

She taps on the computer keyboard for a minute. "Okay, yes, the condo's cleaned and ready to go."

"Great." I take out my credit card and slide it over to her.

She looks at me like I've just put mud on her desk. "You're not paying."

"Yes, I am! I didn't come here to get a freebie!" I put my hand on my cheek to cool off my burning cheeks.

"Don't be silly. That's the perks of taking such good care of my nephew and brother." She hands me the key card. "Do I need to kill said brother?"

"What? No. What do you mean?"

"Well, there's a reason you don't want to stay there. I'm just seeing if it's because my brother's being difficult."

"Oh. *No*, not at all." I take a deep breath and slowly let it out. "Tracy's in town."

"Ahhh." She shakes her head, her eyes narrowing. "Enough said."

CHAPTER THIRTY-TWO

CLUELESS AND PROPER

SUTTON

The past few days have been hell.

Tracy hasn't been satisfied having one-on-one time with Owen—she's wanted me to be with them. I've gone along with it because the two nights I didn't, Owen came home crying and saying he didn't want to go out with her again.

When I asked why, he said she's mean to everyone, including him.

So I've gone to dinner with them and had her back to the

house until Owen goes to bed each night as a compromise for him not going to Arizona with her yet.

She *is* mean to everyone. Every restaurant we've been to in Landmark Mountain gets a pinched expression of dread when they see her come through the door. Even Sally at The Pink Ski, and she's nice to everyone. I didn't think Mar was going to serve her on Saturday morning, but with Owen there, she softened.

And with me around, Tracy's focus has been on me, not Owen. The few times he's tried to bring up something he wanted to talk about, she shut him down and made him feel small.

She's leaving early this afternoon and I can't wait for her to be gone.

Owen asks every day when Felicity will be back, and I've said I'm not sure. I've texted her every day and she's responded a few times, but she's mostly been quiet. At first, I thought she was trying to give me space to figure things out with Tracy, but now I'm wondering if she's having second thoughts about us. I know from Scarlett that she's been staying in a condo at the lodge, and it's made me feel better that Felicity has been hanging around my family since she's been gone. At least she's had fun. I've gotten texts from my brothers too, letting me know how they feel about her.

The gist: They love her and think I'd be the world's biggest idiot if I didn't try to date the woman. Even Callum said, "She's quality, man. Don't miss out by trying to be all proper."

What we are doing behind closed doors is anything but proper, but I don't tell my brothers that. I'd never hear the end of it.

When Tracy pulls up in her rental, I brace myself for one

more interaction. I need the two-week break before I have to deal with her again.

"Owen, your mom's here," I call up the stairs.

Tracy steps in the back door, another thing that drives me crazy, but I've never told her I'd like her to knock.

"Looking good," she says. "Is that a new sweater?" She walks over and puts her hands on my chest.

I stop her hands from moving up to my hair. "Tracy," I warn.

"Sutton," she says, mocking my tone.

"So you'll be back Friday after next?" I turn and walk around to the island, stopping to wash my hands just for something to do to get away from her.

The next thing I know she's behind me, pressed against my back.

I turn around. "Tracy, what are you—"

She leans up to kiss me and I lift her up by both shoulders and move her back.

"*Stop.*" I move across the room, and when she starts to follow me, I lift my hand. "Don't try it again, I mean it. I don't know why you're doing this when I've told you again and again that we're not going there."

Her face twists and for a second she looks like she might cry, but instead she laughs. "I know you want me, Sutton. You've spent time with me this week when you didn't have to. You can't tell me you're not feeling something."

"I've spent time with you and Owen because he wanted me to—no other reason."

She starts to say something and stops, shaking her head. "We always come back to one another."

"No, we don't. Before we were married, yes, but we haven't been off and on again since Owen was a baby."

"I wasn't ready then. I am now," she says, moving closer and smiling.

"When I divorced you, I was done, Tracy. We're not going back to anything. We have a son together and the best thing we can do for him is to be civil with one another, but there's no way I'm having a romantic relationship with you again."

"God, Sutton." Her face crumbles and she really does start crying now. "Why are you being so cruel?"

"Because you've tried to have sex with me multiple times over the years and I've already made myself clear. Why do you keep pushing it?"

"I can be a better mother if I have you by my side." She sniffs, wiping her face.

"Your relationship with your son shouldn't be contingent on your relationship with me. That's not fair. Be a mother to him, Tracy. *Please.*"

She dabs her face with her sleeve. "I've gotta go."

"Let me get Owen. I don't know why he hasn't come down yet."

"I don't want him to see me upset."

"It'll be okay. He's a caring kid, he'll give you a hug." I try to get her to smile, but she glares at me. I hold up my finger. "One sec. I'll be right back."

I go upstairs and find Owen in his closet with his LEGO sets.

"What are you doing in here?"

"Just playing."

"I called you when your mother got here. Come say bye to her."

"Do I have to?"

"Yes."

He gets up, not looking happy about it. I poke him in the

side and he laughs, too ticklish to stay grumpy. We walk down the stairs and look in the kitchen and then the living room.

"Tracy?" I call.

Nothing.

I go back to the kitchen and open the back door. Her car is gone.

Fuck.

I close the door and lean against it, defeated, and look at my son.

"Did she leave?" he asks.

"It looks like she did, yes."

He lifts his little shoulder up in a shrug, and my heart fucking aches.

"I didn't want to see her anyway."

"Son, I'm so sorry. She shouldn't have left this way. She was upset with me. It's not you."

His eyes fill with tears and I'm in front of him in the next second, pulling him to me.

"She doesn't like me, Dad. She never has."

"She does. She loves you so much, Owen. She just doesn't know how to show it." Even as the words are coming out of my mouth, I question them. I don't know if they're true, and I don't know if I should be pretending that they are. I just don't want my son to hurt.

I decide we need a break from Tracy for today. Now that she's heading back to Arizona, there's time to deal with this. I'll call her later, but for now, I don't want to think about her.

"Can we call Felicity and have her come back?" he asks, leaning back to look at me.

I grab a tissue and force him to blow his nose. He grumbles as always. The boy would leave his nose running for days to avoid ever blowing it.

"How about we just see her in the morning? She might be doing something fun tonight."

"Let's see what she's doing," he says, perking up.

"Okay, I'll call, but we can't be disappointed if she's busy."

"Okay," he says, nodding.

But when I call and she doesn't answer, he sighs.

"I'm a little disappointed," he says.

"Me too."

I text the family thread. Maybe they know where she is.

> Tracy just left. <Dancing man emoji> What's everyone doing?

It's about a minute before my phone buzzes.

> MARLOW
>
> They're all skiing. Felicity's with them—did you know she's an incredible skier? Seriously envious of her skills. Do you guys want to come over? I'm watching Dakota tube down the bunny hill. You could get a few runs in while I watch the kids. Or Owen might rather ski.

"Felicity's with the fam skiing. Marlow said Dakota's tubing. Do you want to head over there? You could go tubing or skiing for a little while before they close."

"Yes," he says, bouncing up and down. "I'll tube with Dakota so she's not by herself."

"That's nice of you, but Aunt Marlow's hanging close…"

"But Aunt Marlow's pregnant, so she can't really go tubing right now."

"Good point." I squeeze his shoulder and he looks at me over his shoulder. "Do you know how proud I am of you?"

"Yeah," he says, smiling.

"Good. Because I think you're the best person I know, and I know some really great people."

"Thanks, Dad. I think you're the best too." He tugs on my hand and moves us toward the stairs. "We don't have much time."

I laugh and we run up the stairs. "We've got a couple hours. Get your warm clothes on. Hustle."

He salutes and hurries to his room. I hurry too, throwing on layers as fast as I can.

"I'll meet you in the garage," I tell Owen as I'm passing his room. "I need to get my skis."

"Okay."

But he's out of his room, ready to go before I get all the way down the stairs.

We make record time to the resort and I walk with Owen to the bunny hill. Before we get there, I look over at Owen.

"Wait. Here, let's get your jacket zipped up." I zip up his jacket and unclip his gloves from his coat, guiding his hands inside. Then I tug his hat to cover his ears and bop his nose. "There."

He grins up at me, and then he reaches out and zips up my jacket. Then he pulls my gloves out and nods like *come on*. I chuckle and let him put my gloves on one at a time. When he's done with that, he motions for me to come closer and I bend down. He pulls my hat over my ears and then pats my cheek with his massive glove.

"I think we're all set," I tell him, grinning wide.

"All set," he echoes.

And then he takes off, running toward Dakota, and she yells in delight when she sees that he's here.

"I didn't let her know he was coming just in case it didn't work out. She is so happy right now," Marlow says.

"You sure you're okay watching both of them out here? It's cold."

"I run hot when I'm pregnant. This feels good."

I grin at her. "You look adorable with that little baby bump." I wrinkle my nose. "Is that okay to say? Should I not acknowledge the baby bump?"

"When I'm a whale I might not want you to acknowledge it, but you're still safe right now." She laughs and I nod, laughing.

"Got it."

"The last I saw everyone, they were heading toward that lift and going all the way up to the top." She points to the lift to the left of us.

I turn to look and see Felicity by the lift, looking our way. My heart does a weird flip just seeing her and another when she waves.

"Thanks, Marlow. I've got my phone on me, so call or text if you need me."

"I'll keep a close eye on him," she promises.

I set my skis down and click them into place, and then I ski toward Felicity.

"Hello," she says.

She's smiling, but her eyes are reserved.

"Hi. It's really good to see you."

"You too."

"You going up or are you done for the day?"

"I'm going up. I took a bathroom break and told everyone I'd catch up."

"Perfect timing for me."

Her lips pucker like she's trying to hold back a bigger smile. We move toward the chairlift and wait while a few people get on before us. She looks hot as hell in her blue ski outfit. It makes her eyes stand out.

Once we're on the lift, I look over at her. "How've you been?"

"Good. How about you?"

I groan. "I don't want to talk about me. Tell me about you."

"Well, I've been hanging out with your family a ton. It's been a lot of fun actually…made the time go by faster. I've been to all the houses, met all the animals—I'm obsessed. Oh my God, when Delgado rides on Lucia's back, I can't take it. The only thing cuter was watching you and Owen bundling each other up a few minutes ago." She gives me a side-eye smile.

I laugh. "You saw that, huh?"

"I'm so glad I didn't miss it."

"Why didn't you come say hi?"

Her cheeks are pink from the cold, but they turn even brighter. "I don't know. I wasn't a hundred percent sure Tracy wasn't with you, and I didn't want to be in the way."

"You being in the way was never the issue. I didn't want you to have to deal with Tracy's toxicity." I face her and she won't look at me. "Hey, you believe me, right?"

"Yeah, if you say that's what it was, I'll believe you."

"That's all it was. I'm sorry that I made you feel otherwise."

"You don't need to apologize."

I bump her shoulder with mine. "I'm jealous my family got to spend time with you without me there to enjoy it, and Owen's going to be both thrilled and sad that he wasn't there when you saw Lucia and Delgado."

She makes a face. "I know. I thought about that too…*but*, I know a secret that is going to make Owen so happy, he won't even care."

"What?"

She shakes her head and zips her lips. "Nuh-uh. I promised Scarlett I'd let her be the one to tell Owen and she's waiting until the two of you are together."

"You're really not going to tell me anything?"

She wrinkles up her nose. "Sorry…but no."

I laugh. "You're not sorry."

"No, not really." She tries to keep a straight face but cracks up.

"I've missed you like crazy," I tell her.

She turns to look at me and blinks, her lips slightly parted.

"And it's fucking hard to be this close and not kiss you," I add.

"So kiss me." She grins, lifting a shoulder.

I stare at her, taking in her beautiful face.

"That's not exactly keeping things private..." I wish I could take it back as soon as I've said it.

"Right." She nods, turning to look ahead.

"I've missed you too," she says softly.

We reach the end of the lift and when we ski off to the side, everyone's huddled near the top of the longest run.

"There you are," Sofie says when she sees Felicity and then she notices me. "Hey, Sutton, I didn't know you were coming. This is great. Guys, look who's here."

They all turn and I'm pounded on the back by Theo and Wyatt. Callum's too far or he'd probably be doing the same thing. Scarlett gives me a side squeeze and Ruby grins at me next to Callum.

"It feels like forever since we've seen you," Ruby says.

"I know. For me too," I say.

"Is Tracy gone?" Wyatt asks.

"Yes. And it could not be soon enough. I'm so glad you

guys got to hang out with Felicity though. If I could've escaped, I would have, trust me."

"Why did she come so early?" Scarlett asks.

I shake my head. "I honestly don't know. But I know I don't want to talk about her right now."

They laugh and Theo lifts his fist in the air.

"First one to the bottom buys everyone beer!" he says.

Sofie giggles and he frowns.

"Wait, I mean, last one…" he starts.

"Too late," I say.

I motion for him to go ahead of me and he gives me the bird.

"After you, I insist," I tease.

"Good God, we'll be here all night," Jamison says, laughing. "Beer's on me." He motions for Scarlett to go down the hill with him, and they take off.

Everyone else falls into place and somewhere between the lift with Felicity and skiing down the mountain with her, I shed the heaviness I've been living through for the past few days and feel like everything's going to be all right.

CHAPTER THIRTY-THREE

ANNOUNCEMENTS

FELICITY

We end up at The Pink Ski after we're done skiing. All that exercise worked up an appetite. Grinny meets us there, all smiles. And then Owen walks up to the table with Marlow and Dakota and wraps his arms around me, hugging me so tight.

He doesn't say anything, just hugs me, and it makes me so emotional, I barely hold back the tears.

When he finally pulls away, he looks at me and says, "I'm so glad you came back."

I put my hand on his cheek and lean in close. "Ace, even when the time comes that you don't need me to be your nanny, I'll still be your friend. I will always be cheering you on and loving you and wanting the very best for you. Okay?"

"Okay," he says, his lower lip trembling. "But I'll still need you to be my nanny for a long time, right, Dad?" He glances over at Sutton. "We need Felicity."

Sutton's eyes meet mine, and the intensity in them makes my lungs stall. "We do," he says.

I squeeze Owen's shoulder and smile through my blurry eyes. "Okay then. It's settled."

That seems to put Owen's mind at ease. He goes to his seat and says hi to everyone else. Half the table is talking to the owner of the restaurant, and when she gets around to us, her smile is warm and friendly.

"I'm Sally. If you're hanging out with this crew, you must be good people," she says.

"I can attest to that," Grinny pipes up.

"Hi, Sally. I've heard great things about you and this place. I've been excited to try your food." I glance at the menu and then back at her. "I haven't even looked at the menu yet, I'm sorry. Any suggestions?"

"We have a lemon chicken orzo soup today, and it's a hit," she says.

"Sold, yes, please."

She laughs. "That was easy. Our drink of the day is a Campfire Mule—our take on a Moscow Mule, but instead of vodka, we're using whiskey with the ginger beer, and a touch of maple syrup."

"I'll try it."

She winks at Sutton. "Well, she's a keeper. Are you gonna be that easy, handsome?"

"You know me, Sally." Sutton gives her his megawatt smile, and I see her practically melt at his feet. "I am not an easy man."

"And isn't it a shame," she says, fanning her face and sighing.

The table laughs, Sutton included.

After everyone's ordered and we've chatted about how great the skiing was today, the drinks come, and Scarlett lightly taps on her glass with her spoon.

"I have an announcement," she says.

The volume at the table ceases immediately, and we all turn to Scarlett in anticipation. She told me I'm the only one who knows, and I can tell by the wide eyes and giddy glances between everyone that they think they know what she's about to say. I giggle to myself and cover my mouth with my hand when Sutton glances at me.

"Jamison and I are proud to announce that we are…" She looks around to make sure she has everyone's attention.

"You're killing me. Spit it out already," Theo says, and we all laugh.

"About to become grandparents!" she says, lifting her glass in the air.

It's quiet for a second and then the low hum turns into a loud buzz with everyone talking at once.

Sofie: *"What?"*

Theo, laughing: *"No way."*

Wyatt: *"What do you mean?"*

Marlow: *"I'm not tracking."*

Sutton: *"Explain thyself."*

Grinny: *"Grandparents?"*

Ruby just laughs and looks at Callum. I think they get it.

Scarlett looks at Owen and lifts her eyebrows. "Do you know what I'm saying?"

He opens his mouth and then stands up, leaning his hands on the table as he stares at her. "You don't have kids, but… you have Lucia and Delgado, so…" His eyes grow huge and his mouth drops even wider. *"Are you having puppies?"*

She points at him. "Bingo."

"That's *possible*?" Marlow asks.

"We're having puppies?" Dakota yells.

The table roars with laughter, and everyone throws out their questions. Scarlett shakes her head, laughing, and nudges Jamison.

"Tell them."

"About eight weeks ago, I came home and Scarlett had a surprise for me. It was a mug that said PROUD PUPPY GRANDPA, and I couldn't believe it either," he says, laughing. "We should've gotten them fixed as soon as we found them, but it's been a little chaotic with the lodge renovations, and honestly, I didn't think the little stallion had it in him. I mean…I just didn't think they had that kind of relationship." He wipes his eyes, cracking up along with everyone else. "Lucia's been lethargic for a while, but I've been exercising them more, so I just thought it was that. Turns out, our husky girl and the little stallion have been busy when they have the place to themselves."

"Lucia and Delgado are having puppies!" Owen says, jumping up again. He looks at Scarlett and Jamison. "This is the best news I've ever heard. When are they coming?"

"Well, technically it could be anytime now, probably sometime in the next few days," Scarlett says. She looks at Sutton and smiles and he groans, but he's chuckling.

Owen's attention snaps to his dad. He's so excited he can barely take it.

Sutton grins over at him.

"Looks like we better get prepared for a puppy," he says.

Owen's fists fly in the air and his head falls back. "Yes. Yes, yes, yes!" he cries.

"It'll still be a while before they can live at your house," Scarlett says.

He nods, his voice shaky with excitement. "I know, but I can help take care of them if you need, and they can get to know me, and it's perfect because my hockey schedule isn't as crazy right now..." He runs out of air and takes a deep breath. "I mean, I have to practice for tryouts, but we'll have time, won't we?" He looks at me and then his dad.

I love it when Sutton's eyes are crinkled up. His smiling eyes are right up there as my favorite, tied only with the way he looks at me in bed. They're smiling now, and my breath catches when he includes me in the look, making me feel like I'm part of this decision.

"This is a lot of pressure for you," he says under his breath.

I shake my head, laughing. "No, it's not, I promise."

"You're up for having a puppy around the house?" he asks me. "Tell the truth. We could probably find other options if you're not, but if you say yes, you'd be the one with it during the day."

"I'm so up for it," I say, glancing at Owen and grinning at him. "Scarlett and I were talking earlier this week about how much we wanted you to have a puppy, and she told me about Lucia and Delgado having puppies. I couldn't wait for you to find out."

Owen squeezes my arm and his body twists from side to side. He can't contain it, and I can't stop laughing.

"I can't believe it," he keeps saying.

"Can I have a puppy too?" Dakota asks.

Wyatt groans and then smiles at Dakota. I've learned that this man is putty in Dakota's hands. It's the sweetest thing to see.

"We'll have to think about it. The new baby will keep us busy, you know," he says before sighing. "It's up to your mama."

Marlow's shoulders shake as she laughs. "You just can't say no to her, can you?"

He holds his hands out toward Dakota. "Well, just look at her. Can you?"

Everyone laughs and the food comes. As I eat, I look around the table taking it all in, feeling like the luckiest person to have found people like this.

"I have to say, despite loving this news with all my heart, I was kind of hoping for another announcement," Grinny says to Scarlett, pressing her lips together to contain her smile.

Scarlett laughs and waves her hand, glancing at Jamison. "Yeah, we're still doing things backwards," she says.

Jamison leans in and kisses her, whispering something that makes her cheeks flush.

Sutton nudges me with his elbow. "You're quiet over there."

"Just enjoying your family."

"You approve?" Again with the smiling eyes.

Be still, my heart.

"I absolutely do," I tell him.

"How do I rate in this approval?" he says low enough that only I can hear.

"You and Owen are soaring so high at the top."

He smirks and for a second, I see the bedroom eyes, but he quickly schools it before looking down at his plate.

"You too, sweetness," he says. "You too."

CHAPTER THIRTY-FOUR

FREEDOM AND FRIVOLITY

SUTTON

I buckle my seat belt and my hands brush against Felicity's. She smiles at me and pushes her hair back before sighing.

"We made it," she says.

Jamison and Pappy are sitting across the aisle from us and there are two people missing from this party.

Turns out Lucia had her puppies the same night Scarlett told us they were coming, and as much as Owen wanted to go to the Super Bowl, he wanted to be there to help Aunt Scarlett with the puppies much, much more. He must take after Theo and Callum because the boy is a natural with animals. Scarlett was relieved when I agreed to let him stay with her while we're gone. She said he's been the biggest help, which made Owen the happiest I've seen him in a long time. One of Weston's friends is taking Owen's ticket, so it all worked out.

It'll be a quick trip to Boston, but I'm thrilled to have the breather. This week has been packed between work and Felicity and Owen with the puppies. I've barely seen them with the workload I've had. They've both been troupers, Felicity taking up the slack with Owen and keeping the house running without me, and Owen filling me in on everything I've missed when it's just the two of us at bedtime.

I lean my head back and turn to look at her. "Thanks for everything this week. It should be much calmer when we get home. We wrapped everything up with the case, and next week will be way different. I think I'll be off by the time Owen gets off of school…maybe every day."

"That's great. I've missed you." Her eyes fly to Jamison and Pappy, but they're engrossed in their conversation.

"I've missed you so fucking much," I tell her.

Her eyes flare with heat and I want to kiss her so bad I can taste it.

Tonight, I plan on making up for the time we've lost this week. We'll be flying home late tomorrow night, but I'm going to make our time together count.

Felicity is excited and a little nervous, but we talk on the whole flight, and by the time we land in Boston, she's relaxed and I think a little giddy to be on this trip.

Jamison and Pappy invite us to dinner with their family, but Felicity and I had already agreed that we'd have dinner together in Boston before going to the hotel near Gillette Stadium.

"I think our suite at the stadium is close to yours," Jamison says. "Stop by and say hello, or text us and we will."

"Felicity is dying to meet Zac and Autumn," I say, grinning when Felicity's eyes widen.

"You're not supposed to tell him that!" she says.

"Well, it's true, isn't it?"

"Definitely come by our suite then," Jamison says, laughing. "Summer and Liam will be there too."

Felicity squeaks. "I don't even want to admit how obsessed I am with the two of them. I've seen every movie Liam has ever made and I'm a huge fan of Summer's work."

"They're the sweetest people," Pappy says. "My great-granddaughter Ivy will be there too. She's a hoot."

"Shit, I forgot to have you let Ivy know Owen wouldn't be coming after all," I say.

"I'll prepare her for it tonight, but I'm sure she'll still give you some grief about it tomorrow." Jamison chuckles. "Maybe it'll get them to Landmark Mountain soon though." He rubs his chin, looking at Pappy. "These puppies might even bring the whole family to Landmark Mountain."

Pappy points at him. "You're onto something. I think you're right."

We say goodbye and as fun as their company was, I instantly feel lighter when Felicity and I are alone. It's a constant battle to watch myself when we're out in public. A battle that gets increasingly harder. I see her catching herself about to touch me or stopping herself from whispering something to me, and I remind myself of why it's best that we keep this between us.

Truth be told, the reasons are becoming fuzzier by the day.

"Hi," I say when it's just us.

She grins at me. "Hi. I can't believe we're on a trip together."

"I can already tell I'm not going to get my fill of you."

She lifts a shoulder coyly. "Well, you do get to take me home too, so there's that."

I smirk, my mind already on what I'm going to do to her the second we're behind closed doors.

We catch an Uber and make our reservation a few minutes ahead of schedule. Felicity stops in the restroom and takes my breath away when she walks out a few minutes later in a little black dress.

"Felicity." My voice is gravelly. "You look stunning."

"Thank you," she says, her lips quirking up with her smile.

A clerk tucks our carry-on bags in the coat closet and gives us a tag to pick them up after dinner. We're seated in front of a window overlooking the Bay.

"This is so pretty," Felicity says.

The waiter gives us our menus and says he'll be back shortly.

Felicity lowers her head, but her eyes meet mine. Shyness and seduction war with one another in her gaze and it's a heady combination. I swallow hard.

"Is this a date?" she whispers.

I almost answer with humor. *Do you want this to be a date?* But I don't feel like hiding behind my humor tonight.

"Yes," I say emphatically.

Her smile is my reward, and fuck me, it could generate enough power for this whole city, it's that bright.

"Owen called while you were in the restroom. He said to tell you the puppies are squeaking even more. He wanted me to practice the sound to show you."

She laughs. "Come on then." She wiggles her fingers for me to be out with it.

I glance around, my chest rumbling with my laugh. I laugh a lot more with Felicity in my life; Owen does too. I lean in so the whole restaurant won't hear, and in this upscale restaurant, I mimic the newborn puppy sounds.

Her head falls back and she laughs so hard, her eyes tear up. "Do it again," she wheezes.

I do, and only stop when a throat clears next to me. The waiter stands there, looking stern and very concerned.

I frown, trying to match his seriousness, but can't hold it, and it just makes Felicity laugh harder.

"Did you find anything on the drink menu?" the waiter asks.

"Would you like to share a bottle of wine?" I ask Felicity.

She nods gratefully, lifting her cloth napkin to dab her eyes. The waiter asks to see her ID, and she shows him, and it doesn't escape my attention that he doesn't bother asking for mine.

We go with the waiter's recommendations and go ahead and order our food too, and when he walks away, Felicity fans her face.

"He was having none of that," she says, cracking up again.

"He'd get along very well with Miss Eleanor."

She lifts her eyebrows. "She's that serious?"

"Even more. This guy sort of lifted his lip in an almost smile when he left the table. Miss Eleanor…nope."

"Wow. That is intense. I don't know if I'd be able to handle that level of somberness day after day."

"We get shit done. There's no lingering in the breakroom to gossip or catching up about our weekends. It's wham, bam, thank you, ma'am."

She giggles. "I never knew that's what that saying meant."

"Seemed to fit in a weird sort of way."

Her eyes twinkle in the candlelight, and I can't take my eyes off of her. She looks so beautiful, her hair a shock of color against her black dress.

"You're gorgeous every day, but tonight...God, it's beyond."

Her lips pucker and then she grins. "Maybe it's because you can look at me all you want and not be afraid of what everyone is thinking."

I'm quiet for a moment and then nod. "I think you're right."

When our food and wine comes, it's out of this world. We take bites of each other's meals and then trade because she likes mine more than hers. We talk and talk and talk, barely pausing for breath, and we laugh about every little thing. I feel drunk on her, high on this feeling, barely able to believe how happy she makes me.

We share two desserts and the sounds she makes keep me in an even more painful state than I've been in all night.

It's the longest foreplay I've experienced without ever touching her.

When we leave the restaurant, me rolling both our bags and her walking ahead to make sure we get in the right Uber, I wish that this night would never end.

As soon as we're in the back seat of the car, the driver starts talking. Felicity frowns at me when he says another name and we realize he's on the phone. She grins, as happy as I am to not have to make conversation, and I tug her mouth to mine. It's a long drive to the hotel and we make out until our driver says we're almost there.

Felicity pulls back, her chest rising and falling. I swipe

my thumb over her lips, missing them already, and she makes sure I don't have her lipstick anywhere.

"I hope this is the fastest check-in ever because I feel like I'm going to die if you're not inside me soon," she says in my ear.

"Oh, sweetness. I'll make sure it is. But don't say anything like that for the next minute." I adjust myself and barely hold back my groan when she watches, her teeth tugging on her bottom lip. "Stop that," I whisper, sliding her lip out. "You look like you want to take me in your mouth when you do that."

"That's exactly what I want to do," she says, leaning closer and licking her lips.

My head falls back against the seat and I try to think of anything but her as we pull into the hotel parking lot.

I tug my suit jacket on when I step out of the car, hoping it will hide most of my situation, and we hurry inside. I purposely don't make eye contact with anyone as we walk through the lobby. My sole mission is to get the key to our suite. It's loud and crowded, but the line to check-in is virtually nonexistent since everyone seems to be partying in the hotel bar. When we step into the elevator, I lean against one wall and when she moves next to me, I point to the other side.

"I don't trust myself in this elevator. Over there."

She pouts but giggles. "You're no fun."

"Your parents could be around any corner."

"They're actually staying at another hotel," she says.

I give her a pointed look. "Get over here."

She laughs and crosses her arms, her cleavage tempting me even more than it has been all night. "I'm gonna make you wait just for telling me to go away."

I growl just as we reach our floor and she gets out first, giving that ass an extra sway with each step.

"You're killing me," I mutter.

"You'll live," she sings.

"I don't think I will."

We reach our room and I lift the key card. When it turns green, Felicity opens the door and walks in. The door closes behind us and I roll the suitcases inside, cursing as she lifts her dress over her head and stands in front of me in a lacy black ensemble that was absolutely created to knock me flat on my ass.

CHAPTER THIRTY-FIVE

MORE AND EVERYTHING

FELICITY

"The fuck are you trying to do to me?" he asks, pulling off his jacket and tossing it on the couch.

He runs both hands through his hair, tugging the ends, and takes a deep breath.

"You like?" I ask.

"Hell. Yes." His eyes roam down my body, sending trails of heat through me, and he curses again, his breath ragged. "Turn around."

I do and he lets out a pained sound. He stalks across the room, and his hands knead my backside as he whispers in my ear, "Are you really mine tonight?"

"I'm yours for however long you want me," I answer truthfully.

It might be crazy to be so upfront with him, when my heart is in his hands, but from the beginning, he's gotten the truth out of me, and when it comes to how I feel about him, it's just ready to spill out of me.

He pushes my hair aside and his tongue glides up my neck, making me shiver.

"What would you like first?" he asks. "I'll do anything you want, Felicity."

My head falls back on his shoulder as he continues to place open mouth kisses on my shoulders and neck.

"I want you in my mouth," I tell him.

He stills. "Is that true?"

"I only tell you the truth."

He straightens and I turn, putting my hands on his chest and staring at him before I unbutton his shirt.

"You have too many clothes on." I hurry to remedy that, and my fingers stumble over themselves in my rush.

He doesn't move, his eyes watching my every move, the bulge in his pants letting me know how much he wants me.

His whispers egg me on, encouraging me, praising everything I do. I fall to my knees.

You're so fucking beautiful...

Do you see what you do to me...

I dream about that mouth, that pussy...

I can't wait for it...

And on and on, the husky rasp of his stream of consciousness feeds me.

By the time I lower his zipper and pull him out of his

boxer briefs, I'm trembling. And when my tongue circles his head, we both moan.

"I could come just looking at you on your knees," he says.

I dip my mouth over him, taking him in an inch and then two and he sucks in a breath.

When I take him in deeper, humming when he tugs my hair into his fist, his entire body tenses. He rocks into me, testing how much I can take, and when I look up at him, he curses and gives me more. When he reaches the back of my throat, he can't hold back anymore, and fucks my mouth. His thrusts are sharp across my tongue and lips, and my teeth make him cry out for more.

"I'm close," he says, and I don't let him pull back.

It doesn't take long before he's coming with the sexiest raspy groan.

His fingers are shaking when I pull my mouth away and swallow, and he runs them over my lips.

"That was perfect," he whispers.

He lifts me to my feet and bends down to pick me up, carrying me through the living room and into one of the bedrooms. When he puts me on the bed, he stares at me reverently.

"I want to remember the way you're looking at me right now for the rest of my life," he says.

I lean up and reach out my hand for him.

"*Fuck*," he exhales.

He leans down and licks me over the lace, already ravenous. I whimper and he slides the lace aside, dipping his tongue deep inside like he just can't wait and then coming back out to lick the rest of me thoroughly.

I dissolve into the sheets, writhing and bowing off the bed, I grip his hair with both hands and press him into me.

He laughs against me, his warm breath adding to the

sensation and when I beg him for *more, more, please, more*, he lifts up long enough to ask how to get the lace off.

I show him and help him, untying the ribbons and lifting up as he slides it down my body.

"I love that thing," he says, tossing it over his head and diving back into me.

I laugh and then am moaning in the next second, my cries getting louder and more desperate.

His fingers slide inside while his tongue focuses on my clit, and I don't think I can take it. I arch off of the bed and my orgasm is so long and so intense, I don't know how he can possibly still be giving it to me this good, but he does. When I fall back against the bed, limp as a noodle, he wipes his mouth and kisses his way up my body, pausing to put on a condom.

In seconds, I'm ready for more, and I wrap my legs around him, trying to pull him against me.

"We're just getting started, sweetness," he says, his face hovering over mine.

His erection juts between us, hard and ready, and I'm so wet that with the smallest nudge at my entrance, he starts to slip inside. He gasps and burrows into my neck, leaving a small bite as the rest of his body stills.

"I need a second," he says. "You feel so fucking good, Felicity."

He pulls out and I whimper. He slides back in, a little deeper this time.

"I want to take you in every position, but I want to see your face when you come too much. I want to hear your sweet sounds in my ear and I want to see your eyes when you're squeezing me inside."

"Sutton," I cry, my hands and legs pulling him deeper into me.

More, more, more.

"So greedy." He grins.

It's that diabolical grin that makes every nerve in my body stand at attention.

"Don't tease me, Sutton. Give me everything."

His smile falls and determination takes its place.

"You want everything?" he rasps, bending down to lick my mouth.

His last word is hoarse, and he grips my thighs tight and slams into me. Again and again and again and when his hand snakes between us, pressing against me, my eyes roll back in my head. When we start to get close, he flips me on top of him and I'm so dazed that it takes me a minute to process what's happened.

He licks his lips, the hunger in his eyes all-consuming, and gives me a defiant look like he's daring me.

I think he expects me to ride him, so what I do next throws him off completely. I lift up and we both groan when he glides out of me. But when I start to crawl off the bed, he leans up on his elbows.

"What—" He looks like a sad little boy whose favorite toy has just been taken from him.

I smirk over my shoulder and walk toward the desk in the hotel room, reaching out to grab the pen. I sample it on the little pad of paper to make sure it works and smile when it's a deep black.

"I love a quality pen," I tell him as I climb back on the bed and sit on his thighs, his cock twitching like it's looking for me.

"I feel like I knew this about you based on your planner, but is this really the time—"

I laugh and lean forward, moving his dick over just a bit and smoothing the skin between his hip bone and his deep V.

My hair falls over his abs and lower and he groans as his muscles tense. I find the spot I want and write in pretty handwriting:

I WANT EVERYTHING IF EVERYTHING MEANS YOU.

He leans up, watching as I write and since it's upside down for him, he reads it out loud slowly. When I'm done and he's read the last word, his eyes meet mine and he leans up, his chest against mine. He lifts my hips just enough to slam me over his length. My head falls back and I cry out.

"You're so deep," I say, my chest rising and falling against his.

"Look at me."

I do and what I see in his gaze is almost too much. I want to believe what I see there, but I'm scared to trust that I'm right.

"I'll give you everything until you're ready to find your everything elsewhere," he says, pushing my hair back, his hand lingering on my cheek. "Okay?"

"What if you're all I want, everything I ever want?" I whisper.

He doesn't say anything, but the slow way he presses into me, the deepest long strokes taking my breath away as our eyes never waver from each other, gives me hope that he's listening.

And hope that maybe I'm all he wants too.

CHAPTER THIRTY-SIX

MY OWN MIND

SUTTON

She can't possibly know what she wants at twenty-two, can she? I just thought I knew what I wanted then, and if I'd stuck with what the younger version of me wanted, I'd be a miserable bastard now.

It's a resounding thought as I make love to her all night long.

She wants everything with me.

No, she just thinks she wants everything with me.

But I'm like a man possessed. I promised her everything, and I intend to fulfill that promise, whatever she means by it. I know I tried my best to do that last night. We fucked on the bathroom counter, in the shower, against the bedroom wall, and back in our bed. I lost track of how many times she came, but I know it didn't stave off the desire, it only stirred the craving in me for *more* of her.

She's asleep with her head on my chest now. I've dozed here and there, but my body is so aware that we're in bed together, I feel like a live wire. She's insatiable and so am I, and the problem is, I know myself well enough to know that this isn't a temporary feeling for me.

I got up to go to the bathroom and brush my teeth a while ago and she curled back into me when I got back in bed. It's been so long since I've woken up with a woman in my bed, and it feels too right. I force myself to let her sleep, and when she wakes up and stretches against me, her thigh bumps into my hard-on. She reaches out and grips me with her hand. Her eyes lift to meet mine and she grins.

"Morning," she whispers, kissing my chest.

"Morning."

"How long have you been awake?"

"A while."

I smile at her when she lifts her head back up.

"Why didn't you wake me?" She kisses down to my stomach and presses a kiss on my tip, making me jerk against her mouth.

"I thought you deserved some sleep after being kept up all night. Today's a big day."

"We still have a long time before we have to be ready," she says, smirking.

"Time that you can catch up on sleeping," I start.

She shakes her head. "You weren't sleeping...I don't want to sleep."

I growl and she laughs, licking up the length of me.

"Come here," I tell her, straddling her hips over me.

She sits up and rocks over me, her teeth sliding over her bottom lip as she gets the friction she craves.

"I love waking up with you," she whispers.

Her hair is wild and her lips are swollen from our kisses and she looks so beautiful it hurts.

"I love waking up with you too," I admit.

I love it too much. I love it so much it's messing with my head.

Because what do I do now?

What do I do when she's ready to move on?

"Sutton?" Her lips pucker with her slight frown. "What's wrong?"

Her hips pause their seductive roll and my dick twitches against her wetness, making her breath hitch.

"Nothing," I lie.

I'm determined not to ruin this. I'm not going to grieve the ending while she still wants all of me. *What the hell is wrong with you?*

"Um...I didn't say this last night because I wasn't sure if it would freak you out...or maybe make you think I'm taking this more seriously than you want me to, but—" she pauses, and I frown.

"What? You can say anything."

"I know. I just...I'm on the pill." She lifts her shoulder. "You don't have to do anything with that information, but—" Her lips lift in a shy grin. "I've never had sex without a condom. My tests have always been all clear, and...well, I just wanted you to know."

My hands grip her hips and I rub her against me, making her gasp.

"I don't make it a habit of having sex without condoms," I tell her. "I did with one woman during a limited time, and that was Tracy. My tests are all clear too, I can show you a picture of my results if you'd like to see."

"I trust you're telling me the truth."

I nod. "I appreciate that, but I'll show you anyway," I say, grabbing my phone to pull up a picture of my last test in a starred folder. "And in the future, you should make sure your partners show you as well."

Her brows furrow in the center and she leans back, her hips still. She slides my hands off of her hips and climbs off of me, moving toward the bathroom.

"Felicity, wait. I—"

She closes the door and I hear running water, the toilet flushing, running water again, and still, she doesn't come out. Ten minutes go by, and I get up and knock on the door.

"Felicity, talk to me…"

"I'm going to take another shower and get ready for the day," she says.

But I hear her sniffling.

"Sweetness. Talk to me first. I'll let you get ready, but let me see you."

"I don't feel like talking," her voice breaks.

I turn the knob and it's not locked, so I walk in. Tears are running down her face. She grabs a towel and wraps it around her and I ease toward her, feeling so bad that I've made her cry.

I put my arms around her and hug her. She lays her head against my chest and my chest gets wet with her tears.

"I'm so sorry I upset you."

She sniffles and wipes her face, leaving her head against me.

"It hurts that you didn't take our night seriously," she says, choking back more tears.

I pull back and lift her chin up to meet my eyes.

"I took our night very seriously."

She shakes her head, tears spilling over her long lashes. Her eyes look like a swirling ocean, the depths of blues and greens colliding.

"If you had, you wouldn't have brought up my future partners." She leans back and slides her thumb over the words she wrote on my body. "I told you I want everything if everything means *you*. I meant that. I know you don't want to hear that I want this to be something real. It's only supposed to be fun, and I'll try to keep it light after I have a good cry, thank you very much. But that doesn't mean you should diminish my feelings or toss out future partners like we're nothing."

I put my hand on her cheek, my thumb clasping her jaw. "I don't want to diminish your feelings, ever. Please, forgive me for making you feel that way. We're *not* nothing. Not even close, trust me. All night I've been trying to show you how much you mean to me… not make you feel like you don't matter."

"I don't want anyone else," she says, looking up at me, her lower lip trembling.

"For now, you don't. But you might, and I want you to know it's okay. You have your whole life ahead of you, and you'll want to get married one day, have kids of your own, not be with an old cynic like me—"

She pulls away, and my hand drops. She wipes her face, and her expression closes off.

"I'd like to take a shower now, and then maybe we can

find some food?" she says. "If you'd like to explore a little bit, I can call my parents and see if they want to meet up."

"Would you rather I find something else to do while you see your parents?"

"I'd rather us still be in that bed, but we don't always get what we want," she says, her eyes firing up for a second.

I tug on her hand. "Well, come get back to bed then. That's easy." I try to make her smile, and she almost softens, but not all the way.

"Sutton?"

"Yeah?"

She grips the top of her towel with her free hand and moves a little closer to me.

"Don't tell me how I should feel. It's condescending. And I don't like it when you call yourself old or when you act like I'm too young to know what I'm feeling. I do know, and if you don't feel the same, it's okay and I'll deal with it, but stop putting what we have down because of our age."

Her hands are shaking a little when she takes a deep breath and tugs her towel up again.

"Do you…see marriage in your future again? More kids?"

There's tension in her eyes and mouth. I can see the risk this question cost her, and I want to applaud her for having the courage.

"I haven't believed I'd have that again, no. But not because I don't want it." It takes something out of me to admit that too, and she breathes out a sigh that rings of relief.

"Just promise me that if you start feeling more for me, you won't push me away, thinking you're doing what's right for me…okay?" Her gaze is old-soul weary, like she's just been exposed to the secrets of life and it hurt too much to learn the brutal truth.

"Okay, I promise." My voice echoes in the bathroom and she shivers.

I pull her against me and she sighs and stays there for a few beats before lifting her head again.

"Because I make up my own mind, and you don't need to try to do it for me."

"Got it." I press a kiss on the tip of her nose and smile at her.

She smiles back and I can breathe again.

I want to tell her I already do feel more for her. That I've already wondered if I should push her away. And I've thought I probably *do* know what's right for her.

But I don't do any of those things.

I pick her up and carry her back to bed and just hold her for a while, my fingers tracing circles over her back.

Eventually, we fall asleep, and when we wake up a couple hours later, we get up and get ready. The spell from last night is broken, but the hurt from this morning is gone, and there's a new tentativeness in its place.

CHAPTER THIRTY-SEVEN

UNREACHABLE

FELICITY

I try to shake off the mood from earlier, my conversation with Sutton wreaking havoc on my emotions, and by late afternoon when we're arriving at the stadium suite, I've almost succeeded.

After giving me a night I never even knew to dream of, I should've expected a withdrawal from him today. And it wasn't even that he withdrew as much as he still treated us like we were a casual thing, when I was thinking last night had changed things for us.

It still doesn't feel resolved. He still believes I'm too young to decide anything and that I'll eventually need more than him, and I don't know what to say about that beyond what I've already said. All I can do is prove it to him over time.

It still stings, though, and I try not to let my wounds show. I was honest with him about it hurting me, and if I take it beyond that, I feel like I'll prove his point. He'll think I'm an immature kid unable to take it when things don't go my way.

He's treated me carefully since our talk this morning, extra sweet. I want to pretend like I didn't have a tearfest in front of him, and yet, I'm glad he knows how I feel.

The festivities are already well underway in the stadium. Laughter and the sounds of people cheering and talking and music coming from the suites make it feel like the game has already started. Weston called while I was getting ready and he's nervous, but ready. I look for him out on the field and see him tossing the ball with one of his teammates.

"Felicity, there you are," my mom says, coming over to hug me. "I can't believe we haven't even seen you this whole weekend until now!"

"I know. It's been a quick trip," I say.

As I'm letting go of my mom, my dad reaches out and shakes Sutton's hand.

"Good to see you again, Judge Landmark," he says.

"Call me Sutton," Sutton says, smiling.

"Hi, Dad." I hug him next and he squeezes me extra tight. "Where's Olivia?"

"She'll be coming closer to game time," Mom says. "We just wanted to avoid the traffic as much as possible.

I nod.

"Where's Owen?" Mom asks. "I thought Weston said he was coming."

"That was the plan. My sister was coming too with her boyfriend Jamison—"

"Zac Ledger's brother," I say with wide eyes.

Sutton laughs. "Right, Zac's brother. But Owen's greatest wish is to own a puppy, and my sister's dogs just had puppies. He was excited about the Super Bowl, but the puppies knocked it down a notch."

Everyone laughs and we pause when a server comes by with a tray of drinks. "Vodka tonic, lemontini, or old-fashioned," she says, pointing out the array of drinks.

"Ooo, I'll have a lemontini," my mom says.

"Me too." I grin.

My dad takes an old-fashioned, and Sutton does too.

My proper judge who can be so very sinful.

I see him leaning over me, his muscles straining as he tells me to *take it, all of it*, our bed slamming into the wall in perfect time like a metronome.

My cheeks feel hot and I press my drink to one side, letting it cool me down.

"How's work going? What have you got this one doing for you this week?" Dad asks, grinning at Sutton.

"Oh, I—" Sutton looks at me, and I square my shoulders.

"I watched Owen. Sutton had an especially hectic week, so I took Owen to school and picked him up, and then most days, we went to Scarlett's to see the puppies. He's getting ready for hockey tryouts soon, so next week, I'll try to get him to the rink more, but this week, it was all about the puppies."

My parents stare at me in stunned silence and then at Sutton.

"I'm Owen's nanny," I add.

"But we thought you were working at the courthouse," my mom says.

"I let Weston think that when he first heard that I was working for Judge Landmark and just never corrected anyone. I knew you wouldn't love it if I was taking this time off of school to be a nanny."

"Why are you doing this?" Dad asks. "No offense, Judge, but Felicity, if you just wanted a job, you could've worked at Shaw & Shaw or something closer to home. A nanny—" He laughs and pinches the bridge of his nose.

"I needed something besides law. Henley told me Sutton was looking for a nanny, and you know how much I love kids. And Owen is a dream child. It's been amazing. I don't have any regrets. It's been the best thing I could've chosen." I take a deep breath and Sutton smiles reassuringly at me, encouraging me to tell them the rest.

But then I look in the doorway and gasp. Everyone turns to see what has my attention and sees Zac and Autumn Ledger walking into our suite with an adorable little girl about Owen's age. Ivy. I've heard a lot about her from Owen. Sutton smiles and waves at her, and she beams and waves back. And then I see Liam and Summer Taylor behind them. Wow. Jamison and Pappy come in last, smiling wide.

"I feel a whole lot of starstruck right now," I say under my breath and hear Sutton's laugh next to me.

"We'll continue this conversation later," Dad grumbles, but he's perked up considerably since seeing one of his favorite NFL players walk into the room.

"Hey, I tried texting you a little bit ago, but the service isn't great in here," Jamison says, using sign language for Ivy's sake. "Everyone wanted to meet you, Felicity."

"Me?" I ask in surprise.

The women hug Sutton and smile at me, and the guys fist-bump him, before doing that bro hug thing guys do.

"We all know Sutton pretty well by now," Zac says. "We had to meet the woman who…he trusts with Owen." Zac's eyes are laughing as he grins at Sutton, and holy star power.

I'm suffering from hot man overload. Jamison, Zac, Liam, and last but not even close to least, Sutton…my eyes don't know where to land.

And I could swear they're all looking at me like they think I'm Sutton's woman or something.

It's a good thing I told my parents about Owen.

The introductions begin and when Jamison isn't signing, Zac or Autumn take over so Ivy always knows what we're saying.

"It's been too long since you've been in Landmark Mountain," Sutton says when everyone's met each other.

"Now that the season is over for us, we'll be up there, don't worry," Zac says.

"You won't find a bigger fan of your playing than our son, Weston," Dad tells Zac. "And maybe this one." He points at me.

My cheeks flush. "You're all right," I say, lifting a shoulder.

Everyone laughs and Autumn and Summer tell me they love my teal dress. Coming from the two of them who look like supermodels, I'm beyond flattered.

"I didn't know until recently that you're sisters," I say.

"Yep, it's just the two of us, but we've gotten into our fair share of trouble," Autumn says, laughing.

"Speak for yourself," Summer says, bumping Autumn's hip. When they both laugh, the two of them look more alike than I'd originally thought.

Ivy puts her hand near my arm and I smile down at her.

"Owen?" she says out loud and then signs his name.

I wish so bad I could sign back to her, but I try to repeat what she did for his name.

"He wanted to see you so much," I say, and Autumn interprets. "And he said to tell you to please come to Landmark Mountain soon. He wants you to meet the puppies."

Autumn shoots me a look when I mention the puppies, but she signs it anyway, and then continues signing as she says, "Ivy has big ideas about those puppies."

Ivy nods her head emphatically and we all laugh.

Ivy places her hand near her chest and moves it in a circular motion. I don't know much sign language, but even I can tell that it's the sign for *please*.

We all laugh again and I tell them to hurry and come to Landmark Mountain. The puppies will need new homes. Autumn signs it all, but she keeps shooting me looks that have me cracking up.

Liam comes over and pulls Summer's back against his chest, clasping his hands over her stomach. I just take them in for a moment, still not believing that I'm meeting such talented people. And I *like* them, all of them.

Pappy chats with my parents and I talk with the girls a little longer before tuning into the guys' conversation with Sutton. Jamison is talking about the ski season at home, and how great the snow has been this year.

"And that one is quite the skier," Jamison adds, pointing at me.

"Is that right?" Zac says. "So the athletic gene is in your family, I take it."

"Me? No." I laugh and wave him off.

Sutton shoots me a grin and nods. "She looks like a pro out there, and I grew up on those mountains."

"Nice. Well, you'll have to show us how it's done when

we come for a visit. See if you can get this one out there," Zac says, tucking Autumn into his side. "She's always working so hard at the lodge when she's there."

He looks at her with such pride and adoration, it's staggering. I take a drink of my lemontini and swoon.

"The lodge is gorgeous. Scarlett can't say enough amazing things about what you've done for the resort," I tell Autumn.

"It's true," Sutton says. "You've made the resort what it should've always been."

"I couldn't have done it without Scarlett and Jamison," Autumn says, smiling fondly at her brother-in-law.

I glance over at Sutton, and he smiles briefly before glancing away. I feel a pang of envy, wishing we weren't hiding our relationship. I miss his hand in mine, his lingering touches, the way he looks at me when we're alone. When we're in public, it's like he puts on a friendly, reserved persona that feels unreachable.

"Well, we should probably move to our suite, so the people joining yours will have room when they get here," Zac says.

"I'm sure they wouldn't mind meeting you," my dad says, his laugh so loud my mom jumps.

He pats Mom on the back in apology and takes a long swig of his drink. I've never seen my dad nervous around anyone. I guess Weston and I aren't the only super fans in the family.

Zac smiles at him warmly. "It was great meeting all of you. And we'll see you soon in Landmark Mountain. Count on it. I'm trying to convince Summer and Liam to come while we're there too. They need a vacation."

He clasps Sutton's hand. "Good to see you, man."

"You too," Sutton says.

I stare at the guy I used to obsess about when I had to watch football with my brother, next to the guy I swooned over at the movies, standing face-to-face with the man I spent the night with, the man I think I love…and as hot as Zac Ledger and Liam Taylor are, neither of them hold a candle to Sutton Landmark.

Not for me anyway.

CHAPTER THIRTY-EIGHT

A SIP HERE, A SIP THERE

SUTTON

After my night with Felicity and the way this morning went, I'm not as excited about being at the Super Bowl as I should be. I feel terrible about making her cry, and if it were any other circumstances, I'd be able to make sure we really are okay.

Being away from home in a beautiful suite with the woman I can't seem to get enough of…that's where I want to be.

Things are unresolved, and I never deal with that very well. I can hardly focus on anyone but her, and around her parents is not where I can let down my guard.

When everyone leaves our suite, the space is considerably quieter. David resumes his stern dad stare at Felicity, and Lane shoots anxious glances between the two of them.

"I'll give you all time to talk," I say, gesturing to the seats and moving to sit down.

"No, don't go," Felicity says, reaching out to touch me and then dropping her hand before it touches me. Her cheeks flush and I move back to where I was standing before.

"I shouldn't have chosen today to tell you about my job," Felicity tells her parents.

"No, you never should've lied to us," her dad says.

"I've been trying to figure out a way to tell you a few things. Now isn't the time, but I'll call soon or come home so we can talk about all of it."

"Just tell us." David throws his hands up. "What could be worse than you not wanting to be home before your schedule picks up even more? You just thought Georgetown was difficult. Law school will far surpass that." He looks at me for agreement, but I keep my mouth shut.

I'm here for support, nothing else.

Felicity swallows hard and her gaze meets mine. What she sees in my expression seems to steel her nerves.

"About a year ago, I started to reconsider what I wanted to do with my future. Before that even, I was questioning it, but I tried to press on anyway. I know how important it is to you and Mom that I'm a lawyer, that I come to work with you at Shaw & Shaw one day. But I haven't been able to make peace with it." Her voice is shaky, but it gets more confident as she keeps going. "I'm not going to law school in the fall."

"What?" David's voice thunders and Felicity winces.

Lane touches David's arm and he takes a deep breath.

"Honey…you were overworked," Lane says to Felicity. "You graduated early. It's no wonder you reached burnout—you need a break. I didn't want you to work at all before you start back to school, but you had this job before we even knew about it," her mom says, shaking her head. "By the time fall rolls around, you'll be ready."

"I won't be ready," Felicity says. She gives her mom a sad smile. "It was never my dream to be a lawyer. It was your dream for me. And I've spent my entire life, from the time I realized it was your dream for me, trying to fulfill that for you. But I can't do it. I don't *want* to do it."

"This is nonsense." David tosses his hand up in frustration. "You've been talking about being a lawyer since you were a little girl."

"Because you let me know that's what was expected of me," Felicity says softly. "I don't have the competitive streak that Olivia and Weston or the two of you have. I'd rather keep the peace than argue facts in court."

"But you were outstanding on the debate team," Lane says, her eyes welling with tears. "I still just think you need time."

"Do you know how much anxiety I had doing the debate team?" Felicity laughs. "I've put an agonizing amount of thought into this decision, and I've dreaded telling you so much because I didn't want to disappoint you and let you down, but I hope you'll let me figure out what my passion is and encourage me through it."

The only sounds now are of the crowd filling the arena, the suite is silent.

"Hey, what's going on in here?" Olivia walks through the door and comes to a stop where we're all four standing. "What's wrong?"

"We've got a game to watch," Felicity says. "And I need another drink."

She lifts her empty glass in the air and walks past us, pausing when the guy walks toward her with the tray of drinks.

"What the hell did I miss?" Olivia asks, but no one answers. Her eyes narrow on me. "Why are you here?"

I wondered when one of them would get around to asking that.

"Don't be rude, Olivia," Felicity calls from across the room. "I invited him."

"Weston didn't offer *me* any free tickets." She scowls.

A couple walks in and a few guys that the family doesn't know. I'm introduced to Francis and Ken, family friends, and then we meet the guys Weston went to college with—Jeffrey, Connor, and Sam. It breaks the tension to have them in the room, and since the game is about to start, David and Lane move toward the seats. David looks like he wants to keep talking to Felicity, but she's staying by the food for now. When David sits down, I walk over to Felicity.

"How are you doing?"

"I feel much better!" she chirps, taking a long gulp of her lemontini and piling a small plate with appetizers. "That has been hanging over my head for so long, I feel like a weight has just flown off my chest." She sets her drink down and flutters her hands up in the air.

I laugh. "Was that supposed to be a bird?"

She points at me. "Perceptive."

"Thank you. Did you have another lemontini when I wasn't looking or is this what two does to you?"

She presses her lips together and nods, her expression serious. "Yes and yes. I'm a lightweight. Don't judge me. Ha!" She points at me. "That can be our catchphrase from now on. Don't judge me, Judge Landmark," she says in a high voice. "Don't judge me since I'm already a judge, Felicity." She lowers her voice into a ridiculous impression of me.

"I do not sound like that."

She giggles and picks up her empty glass and tips it in her mouth to get a drop out. "You kinda do." Her eyes widen and she curses and then slams her hand over her mouth. "Whew, I would've owed Owen at least a dollar for that one. We've gotta go watch the game."

I nod. "I thought you might want to, yes."

She loops her hand through my arm and then drops it, lifting her finger. "We shall not have impropriety," she says in that voice.

"Okay, if I actually sound like that, you have permission to punch me in the face."

She laughs and grabs a lemontini from the tray that goes by. My eyes widen and she waves her finger back and forth.

I lift my hands up. "I'm not judging."

"Very good." She takes a deep swig and then holds it out for me. "Come on, try a sip. I think you'll like it."

"You're making it look delicious," I say, and she cracks up like that's hilarious.

When she presses it to my lips, I take a sip mostly to space out her drinks.

"Right?" she asks, happily.

"Yes, you were right. I like it. Here, have some of this bacon-wrapped shrimp. It looks good." I lift it and instead of taking it with her hand, she leans in and covers it with her mouth, her lips bumping into my fingers.

"You're being very improprietous this evening," she says, lifting the bruschetta up to my lips.

"Is that a word?" I take a bite and chew. "And I'm just trying to keep up with you."

"It is now. The word works for you. Are you trying to keep up with me because you feel sorry for me?"

"What? No. Why do you say that?"

"You've been all cautious around me since this morning. I won't break, you know." Her eyebrows crease in the center and she eats the last bite of the bruschetta.

"I know you won't break, Felicity."

"Today was the day to own my truth and I did it." She wipes her fingers with the napkin and lifts her glass in the air.

"Yes, you did."

"I wish you had a glass to clink. Here." She grabs another lemontini as the guy makes his way back from serving the rest of the guests. She hands it to me and I clink her glass.

Her smile is radiant.

"You've heard that women mature faster than men, right?" she asks.

"Oh yeah." I laugh.

She nods and winks at me, clinking my glass.

"I can't wait for you to catch up."

CHAPTER THIRTY-NINE

PROACTIVE

FELICITY

My brother won the Super Bowl and I was almost too lemontini'd up to enjoy it.

Or I enjoyed it a little too much *because* of the lemontinis.

Whatever means I'm so proud of my brother and I drank way too many lemontinis—that's what I am.

"I've never had that much to drink." I rub my stomach as

we go back to our suite to get our things. "And you kept plying me with food."

"Because you had that much to drink," Sutton says, laughing. He sobers quickly and gives me a sympathetic look. "Will you be okay on the plane?"

I groan.

We hung out long after the game ended, celebrating with Weston and the Mustangs fans. It's late and the last thing I want to do tonight is get on a plane.

He goes into the kitchenette and comes back with crackers, cheese, ginger ale, and bottled water. Next, he finds the pain medication in his bag and sets it next to the food.

"Aw, for me?" I try to smile and his smile back is much more genuine.

"Are you okay?" he asks again, putting his hand over mine.

"You keep asking me and I can't tell anymore if it's because I drank too much or because I was upset this morning…"

"Both," he says.

I rip open the package of crackers and eat a few before swallowing the tablets. I try to drink as much of the water as I can and don't feel too bad. My tongue is numb and I can't stop talking, but I don't feel terrible.

"Hmm. Well, I'll have to let you know about the hangover tomorrow. Do you know I made it through college without a hangover?"

"Impressive."

"Or sad." I laugh. "It might've helped to let loose a little occasionally. I did…just not with alcohol."

"I'm glad I'm here to see it then." He leans against the wall and watches me eat the crackers. "Would you rather we fly out early in the morning? Scarlett will still have

Owen and will take him to school. I just have to be at work early."

I'm already shaking my head. "No. We shouldn't change our flight."

"It wouldn't be the end of the world."

"I'm ready to go home."

He likes it when I say that. I don't miss the longing in his eyes, the way they lit when I said *home*.

"Are you sleeping in my bed tonight?" he asks.

My lips pucker and I lift my eyes up to the ceiling like I'm contemplating it and then look at him directly to say, "No."

"No?" He frowns. "Why not?"

"In case I don't wake up feeling my finest."

"All the more reason you should sleep in my bed tonight."

I shake my head and he looks like he wants to argue with me, but he doesn't. I finish the crackers and cheese and take a few sips of ginger ale. Standing up, I toss the packaging in the trash and wash my hands before zipping my luggage and grabbing my purse. I tuck the bottled water in my bag and pick up the ginger ale.

"You look ready to go," he says.

I nod and he takes my bag from me and grabs his, wheeling them toward the door.

"Thanks for bringing me, Felicity. I enjoyed our time here. I hope I didn't wreck it for you this morning."

I make a face. "I'll try to just remember the orgasms instead."

A loud laugh erupts out of him and we're both laughing as we walk toward the elevator.

It doesn't escape my notice that he hasn't kissed me since this morning, but he did want me in his bed later.

It's probably best all the way around if I retreat a little bit, protect my heart. It's one thing to share my truth and another to be stupid and not pay heed to all the red flags he's throwing around.

I dove into this headfirst with him, but I'm still going to take care of myself.

Even if I'm already in too deep.

The flight back is not even half as fun as it was flying here. At times I feel like I'm going to throw up, but I end up closing my eyes and at some point, the meds kick in. I manage to fall asleep and it's the best thing I could've done.

I wake up to Sutton lightly nudging my shoulder.

"We're here," he says softly.

I sit up and whimper.

"Is it bad?" he asks.

"It's not great, but not awful either."

His low, husky laugh skitters over my skin, and I rub my arms.

"Feel like getting out?" He motions toward the door and gets out, turning around to face me.

I give him a droll look. "Yes, I feel like getting out."

"Those lemontinis made you a sassy little thing," he teases.

"I think we both know it was in there all along." But my words don't have any heat behind them. My body feels like it's moving two feet in front of me at all times.

He holds out his hand and I take it. When I step out off of the plane, I'm dizzy. We stand there for a second before he tucks my hand in his arm and walks me through the airport and to his car.

"It feels like the middle of the night," I say hoarsely.

"It is."

He opens the car door and I get inside, leaning my head back to look at him. "I like your car."

"Thank you. It's been good to me." He shuts the door and I wince at the loudness.

When I open my eyes again, he's driving and we're almost at his house.

"I think you'd miss me," I say.

"I'd miss you if what?" He turns to look at me, the light from the streetlamps flashing over his face as we pass them.

"You'd miss me if I ever left."

He lets out a long exhale. "I'd miss the fuck out of you if you left, Felicity."

I nod and close my eyes. I'm so, so tired.

I'm not sure if I dream it or if I really hear him say, "Please don't ever leave me."

The next morning, I wake up in Sutton's massive bed with the bajillion thread count sheets and the plushest comforter I've ever felt.

My head hurts.

It really, really does.

My eyes are slits as I crack them open and groan. Shit. It's eleven o'clock! I gingerly sit up and see a bottled water with more ibuprofen and a little packet next to that. I pick up the packet and a note flutters onto the bed.

Felicity,
I miss you already.
Call me if you need anything.

I wish I'd had these chewables last night for you, but Cecil's wasn't open yet. They're supposed to make a hangover feel better. Sunny Side breakfast would probably also help. Wish I was there to eat it with you.

Sutton

I smooth the note with my fingers, admiring his handwriting and loving that he wrote this note for me.

Did he really go out early this morning before work to buy me a hangover remedy?

I start with the chewables and water, taking my time getting up. After I go to the bathroom and get a shower, I almost feel human again. I look at Sutton's note again and, on a whim, I call and place a large order from Sunny Side. About fifteen minutes later, I pick it up and drive to the courthouse.

This is around the time he usually calls me, unless it's when he's done for the day, and I wasn't up to pack his lunch this morning. It's possible he went out, but when I pull into the parking lot, I see his car and park a few spaces down.

Olivia thought the courthouse was run-down, but I think it's pretty. It's brick with white trim, the details are ornate but not gaudy. Two white columns are at the top of the stairs leading to the entrance, and there's a small room in the center of the top floor, with three windows on the three sides. The dome on top makes it a distinguishable building whenever you're near Landmark Mountain. The trim could use a touch-up in a few places, but it's not run-down at all. And inside, it's even more beautiful. The woodwork is intricate, and everything is shiny and clean.

There's a small check-in that almost has me second-guessing this decision, but it's painless, and I'm through the door in less than a minute with instructions to go up the stairs to the left to reach the offices. Once I've done that, the woman at the desk looks up and I see from her placard that it's Miss Eleanor.

"Hello, I'm Felicity Shaw. I have Judge Landmark's lunch." I lift the bag and she nods before picking up the phone and reciting what I said to presumably the man himself.

When she hangs up, she looks at the files in front of her as she says, "His office is behind me. You'll see his name on the door."

"Thank you."

She nods and I walk past her desk just as Sutton opens the door to his office.

"Hey," he says in surprise.

I hold up the Sunny Side bag and he laughs.

"Great idea," he says.

"You have some good ones."

He motions for me to walk inside and closes the door behind us.

"I see you haven't lost your sass. Hopefully, you lost the hangover?"

"Thanks to your bedside care, I am feeling fine."

He takes the bag and motions for me to sit at the couch near the windows.

"Your office is beautiful."

"Thank you, and thanks for the food. I was about to leave to grab something."

I nod and feel as stiff as Miss Eleanor.

I sit and he sits in the chair across from me. He watches as I pull food out of my bag and then he does the same with his. When we've started eating and it's still quiet between us, I clear my throat and finish the bite I'm chewing.

"Do you have to be in court this afternoon?" I ask.

"Not today. It's a light week and mostly mornings in court."

"Oh, that's right."

I take another few bites and then can't stand it any longer.

"Why are you being so weird?" I ask.

"Am I?" After he says it, he winces.

"You know you are."

"I just...after yesterday and everything that happened…I thought you might need time to process some things." He sets his food on the side table and leans forward, his forearms on his thighs.

"Quit trying to proactively make up my mind," I say, closing my food container. I've lost my appetite.

He frowns. "That's not what I'm doing."

"Yes, it is. If I want to process things, I'll process things. I don't need you backing off because you think I might need to." I lift my fingers in quotes with my last few words.

He nods. "You're right."

"Damn right, I am."

He tries not to smile. "Get over here."

I lift my eyebrows haughtily. "I thought you might need time to go without."

His mouth falls open and he starts laughing. When I don't budge, he lifts his eyebrows.

"If I want to go without, I'll go without. Isn't that how this works?" He crosses his arms, mimicking me.

"Is that how you want to play this?" I stare him down.

He grins and my stomach bottoms out.

"Not even a little fucking bit," he says. "Please, get over here."

And this time, I do.

CHAPTER FORTY

SUCCEEDING

SUTTON

We kiss until we're both breathless. I have a grip on her hips and grind her over me. Her head falls back and she comes in for another kiss, her hips moving in little circles, making me so hard I can't see straight.

The next thing I know, she's on her feet, gathering her bag, and blowing me a kiss.

"I'll see you in a little while, Judge Landmark. I'll pick up

Owen and see if I can talk him into skating for a while, since he's had all weekend with the puppies."

"I'll come with you," I say. "I'll come home before you leave to pick him up."

I can't stop grinning at her.

She's not completely let me off the hook yet though, and she lifts a shoulder.

"Very well," she says.

I nod and stand up, leaning an inch from her face and stealing a quick kiss. "Very well, sweetness."

Her hips sway enticingly as she walks away and I swipe a hand over my face and adjust myself before she turns around. It's hard not to smirk at the way she lifts an eyebrow at me. Her eyes flicker down my body and now she's the one smirking.

"Good luck hiding that when Miss Eleanor comes up in a few seconds," she says.

"What—"

She turns and leaves, and the next thing I know, Miss Eleanor is flying into my room, looking more frazzled than I have ever seen her.

"Are you okay, Judge?" she asks, her eyes trailing over the room until they're back on me.

Fortunately, just seeing her running into the room cured my dick.

"I'm fine, Miss Eleanor. Are you—"

She takes a deep breath and clutches her chest. "I must have misunderstood. I thought your guest said you were having heart trouble…"

That girl. I hold back my chuckle and lift my hands.

"She's probably right, but as you can see, I'm fine."

Her features shift back to primness, and she nods briskly.

"Miss Eleanor, I'm touched that you came to my aid so quickly."

"I pride myself on being a conscientious employee," she says, moving toward the door.

"You are certainly that, Miss Eleanor," I call after her, her heels already clacking across the hall's wood floors. "Extremely conscientious."

When she's gone, I sit at my desk and have a good laugh.

The level of anticipation I feel as I pull down my long driveway is ridiculous. I'm acting as if it's been weeks since I've seen Felicity and not just a couple of hours. I'm excited to see my boy too, it really does feel like a long time since I've seen him, and it reminds me to call Tracy later. She hasn't let me know exactly when she's coming to town this weekend.

When I enter the back door, Felicity glances up from her laptop, surprise covering her features.

"Hey," she says.

"You seem surprised that I'm here."

She lifts her shoulder slightly. "I guess I didn't really think it would happen—this is the first time you've been home this early."

I tsk under my breath and walk until I'm right behind her, and then I bend to kiss her neck.

"I do what I say I'm going to do, sweetness."

I feel her lips quirk up as I kiss closer to her face, and I smile against her skin.

"Is there time to finish what we started?" My hands wander down her neck and over her breasts, stopping to palm them.

"No," she whispers.

"Damn." I lower one hand and cup her between her legs, loving the way her head falls back with a sigh. "Come to my bed tonight," I whisper.

She turns and tugs my hair until she has my mouth where she wants it, kissing me with such fire, I pull her out of the chair and back her into the wall. I lift her thigh and dip my fingers under the waistline of her pants, cursing when I feel how wet she is.

"Let's have a sample of what's to come," I tell her, my fingers dipping over and into her most sensitive places.

Her head falls back and for a few minutes, I stare at her in wonder as she starts to tremble. Her cries do something to me —a rightness, a calm—as she detonates at my touch.

When she opens her eyes, I slowly pull my fingers up to her mouth and rub her lips until they're glossy with her before kissing it off. Her eyes are glazed when we break apart, and I reach back and smack her backside before squeezing it.

She laughs and rolls her eyes. "You're looking awfully sure of yourself all of a sudden."

"I just love making you come."

Her breath hitches and her cheeks turn pink. She takes a deep breath and starts to move past me but pauses to run her hand down my stomach and right over my dick. Her eyes brighten when she feels how hard I am.

"Sorry to leave you this way, but it's time to go."

"I'm *this way* all the time now that you're around," I say to her back as she grabs her coat and tugs it on.

She laughs. "Good."

I groan and follow her to the car. We're early enough to park and get out, and it's worth it when Owen comes out with the rest of his class and takes off running when he sees us.

"Dad!" he yells.

I lower and he jumps into my hug, letting me lift him off his feet, highly unusual behavior for him anymore, but I think he missed me.

"Felicity!" he says when I lower him to the ground. He hugs her just as hard and beams up at us. "I'm so glad you're back. Aunt Scarlett and I had so much fun, but I missed you guys."

"I missed you too," I tell him. "The Super Bowl wasn't the same without you."

"Aw, yeah," he says, his face dropping slightly. "But wait until you see how big the puppies have gotten. You're not gonna believe it, Felicity."

"I can't wait, but I thought maybe we'd go skate for a while today, maybe at Uncle Callum's rink? You haven't been skating as much and tryouts will be here before you know it," she says.

"Yeah, I should. And *then* can we go see the puppies?" he asks excitedly.

She laughs and wraps her arms around him again, leaning her head down by his. "Let's see how the night goes. Oh, wait…how much homework are we talking?"

"Just one math sheet!"

She holds up her hand and he slams it into hers before we get to the car.

If I wasn't crazy about her for how she makes me feel, the way she is with Owen would do it. The combination of the two is almost more than I can handle.

Felicity Shaw is dismantling my life one brick wall at a time and in a way that makes me want to yank my heart out of my chest and say, "Here, take it. It's yours anyway."

I'm just not sure what to do about it.

I know she deserves better than this, but I'm not ready to

face the scrutiny we'd get if we were ever open about our relationship.

And I'm still not certain that she doesn't deserve better than me, period. As hard as it is and as sick as it makes me to think about, I imagine her with someone like Penn Hudson, a young, successful guy on the cusp of greatness.

I didn't miss the way he hugged her like he wanted there to be more, and I can't help but believe she'll wake up one day and realize that too. If not Penn, someone else equally as young and virile, someone who has a clear rap sheet that doesn't include a difficult ex-wife.

Annoyed with myself, I start the car and head to Callum's.

Felicity's right here by my side, and I'm not going to let a day go by without enjoying the time I have left with her.

CHAPTER FORTY-ONE

THE RIDE OF OUR LIVES

FELICITY

I should have known Sutton would be sexy on the ice. It's just not right how good-looking that man is.

Callum and Ruby's rink is the best of both worlds: we can skate freely without any other lessons in the way or other kids flying past, and we have unending entertainment as we skate with the animals. A couple of the emus look at us longingly, like they wish they could ice skate more than life itself, and Dolly, the most outgoing of them all, does just that eventually. Ruby puts on music and skates out on the ice, and Dolly follows her, slipping and sliding, but managing to remain upright the whole time.

The sight has all of us, even Callum, laughing until we can't breathe.

When the sky starts to fade into pinks and purples, Owen gets tired and we all take a break.

"I could order takeout if anyone's hungry," Ruby says.

"I've been thinking about the snowmobiles," Sutton says. "We haven't taken them out once this year."

"You have snowmobiles?" I try to taper off some of the excitement in my voice, but I can't. I sound giddy. "It's my favorite thing to do."

He holds his hand out. "Come on. We have to do it then."

"Were you hungry though?" I ask Ruby.

"Not yet, actually." She laughs. "I was just trying to be a good hostess."

I put my arm around Ruby's waist and squeeze her, and Sutton's face softens as he watches us. I smile at him and then laugh at Owen who's looking up at his dad with pleading eyes and hands clasped.

"What?" Sutton laughs. "If we do this, you can go too."

"*Yes*," Owen says.

"I bet your dad would even take you first when you look at him like that," I tease.

Sutton smirks. "Don't tell my secrets, Felicity Shaw," he pretends to growl. "It just so happens we have enough for everyone to go." He holds a finger up when Owen jumps up and down. "You'll be riding with an adult."

"Can I ride with Felicity?" He goes back to the clasped hands and Sutton ruffles his hair before sliding his hand over his face, making Owen crack up.

"How about I take a loop around first, just to get used to

the snowmobile?" I suggest. "Weston and I take ours out every Christmas, so I can handle them. I just would want to be certain I felt comfortable on yours before I take out precious cargo."

Sutton gives me a smile that is full of such longing, it makes my lungs stall. I don't miss the look Callum and Ruby exchange and widen my eyes to Sutton as a hint to maybe tone it down a little if he wants this to remain private, but he doesn't get the message or doesn't care.

I'd like to believe he doesn't care, but it's one step forward, two steps back with this man.

"Good idea," Callum says and motions for us to follow him.

"Callum has our snowmobiles from last year. We usually ride here or at Theo's place. All of us are paranoid about the water at my place, even though it's mostly frozen by now. One of the kids Callum and I went to high school with went out before the ice was fully frozen one year, and he nearly didn't make it." Sutton shakes his head.

"Oh no! Was it on your property?" I ask.

"No, but it put the fear in us for life. Theo has a lake at his place too, but it's not as deep and freezes faster. Anyway, sorry to bring up that horror story. I was mostly trying to explain why our snowmobiles are here," Sutton says sheepishly.

"That's awful," I say, squeezing his arm.

There's a small outbuilding not too far from the barn and the snowmobiles are in there. Sutton and Callum get four out, and I'm happy to see they're like mine.

"I'll go out with you," Ruby says. "Oh wait. I need to make sure Dolly's in her stall or she'll be trying to keep up with me."

We all laugh and Sutton points out the ones that are his.

"She can ride ours too," Callum grumbles.

Sutton laughs. "I know. Settle down. I just thought you and Ruby might be more comfortable on yours."

Callum lifts a shoulder and I giggle. I'm learning he's more bark than bite. The family contributes his softening to Ruby, but Ruby says it's who he is—he's all heart behind his grumbles. I tend to believe the truth is somewhere in the middle.

I get on one of the snowmobiles Sutton pointed out and tilt my head toward Sutton and Owen. "You coming?"

"Why don't you go while Owen's getting his helmet on and all that?" Sutton says.

"Okay, see you soon." I wave and then take off behind the barn and down the long driveway.

It's a beautiful night, not too cold out, and I'm dressed warm enough to enjoy being out in the elements. I ride along the side of the street, seeing where Callum's property turns into Theo's and then where Sofie's aunts are living now—the house where Sofie grew up, and alongside that is Sutton's house and Grinny's in the distance. Going between everyone's houses while Tracy was in town gave me a better lay of the land than I'd previously had.

I turn back and drive to where they're all waiting.

"How did it feel?" Sutton asks.

"Great." I grin. "It's the perfect night for this!"

Sutton gives me a big smile. "You look pretty comfortable on that thing."

"I am. It runs even smoother than mine." I glance at Owen who's practically jumping up and down. "You ready for a ride?"

"Yes," he yells.

Sutton helps Owen get on the back of my snowmobile and tells him to hang on tight.

Owen nods. "I will." He demonstrates by gripping my sides as tight as he can.

I laugh. "Yep, he is."

They get on their snowmobiles and Callum leads the way, Ruby goes next, and Sutton motions for me to go ahead of him. We go to the back of the property, way past the barn and before the line of trees thickens in front of the mountains. There are still a lot of trees, so we stay in a single line with a safe distance between us. It's so peaceful out here, and we take our time, enjoying the ride.

When we reach Theo's property, it opens up and Callum motions that we can spread out now instead of riding single file, and we all fan out, going a little faster than before. I'm still going slower than I normally ride with Weston, but there's no way I'm doing that with Owen on the back. And it seems just fine with him—he's loving this. He cackles as we dip here and there, and I laugh too, reminding him to hang on tight.

Ruby screams and points out something and I turn to look and see it at the last second, a fox running near me as fast as it can. To avoid hitting it, I move the wheel sharply and hit a rock or something bigger. I hear Sutton yelling. Whatever it is, we hit it and everything happens so fast.

"Owen! Hang—"

The snowmobile turns like it's going to land on its side or flip all the way, and my head hits something hard before everything goes dark.

CHAPTER FORTY-TWO

NEVER AGAIN

SUTTON

"I'm calling 911," Callum yells.

"Owen, Felicity!" I yell, over and over.

"Dad," Owen cries, and relief floods through me.

Felicity is quiet.

The second I'm off my snowmobile, I'm rushing toward Owen and Felicity. Ruby and Callum are closer to Felicity and the looks on their faces terrify me.

"Is she okay?" I yell.

"Her pulse is strong, but she's not opening her eyes," Ruby says, crying.

I reach Owen first and he's whimpering, tears running down his face. I check him for broken bones or any signs of harm, but it's hard to tell in the snow.

"I'm right here, son. Don't move yet, okay? We're calling an ambulance. Does anything hurt?"

"Everything hurts," he says. "But especially my arm."

My eyes fill with tears. "I'm so sorry. Just hold as still as you can. I can't tell with your coat on if anything's broken yet. We're going to the hospital. Do you hear that siren? That's for you."

"What about Felicity? I tried to hang on, but I couldn't," Owen cries.

My God.

My whole world flashed before me when I saw the fox running toward Felicity, and then they hit something and Owen flew in the air, and Felicity went seconds later, her head hitting a rock big enough to jut out of the snow.

"I'm going to go check on her. Okay? Will you be okay while I see about her? I'll send Uncle Callum over here."

"I'll be okay." He cries harder. "Go check on her, Dad."

I run to Felicity and don't even have to ask Callum to go to Owen, he's on it. I pick up Felicity's gloved hand and squeeze it.

"Felicity, wake up. Felicity, please, sweetness. Owen's sore, but I think he's okay. The ambulance is coming, but I really want to see your eyes. Please open them and let me know you hear me."

Her head is turned toward the rock her head hit and the night sky has darkened just in the past few minutes. Ruby has her phone flashlight on and keeps it aimed on Felicity, and the lights from the snowmobiles are still illuminating us enough to see the blood trickling down Felicity's temple.

It feels like forever, but help arrives in record time. I'm grateful that it must be an otherwise quiet night in Landmark Mountain because two ambulances pull in as far as they can and then they come running with stretchers the rest of the way.

I stay to ride with Owen to the hospital, but my heart is torn in two when I see them putting oxygen on Felicity and riding away with her first. Ruby's with her.

"I'll call Wyatt and have him meet us there if he's not on tonight, and I'll follow in my truck," Callum says.

I nod gratefully.

"Please, hurry," I tell the paramedics as they put a neck brace on Owen. I've seen them around town before, but I don't recall ever meeting them, and I hope they're qualified. "I'm worried about my son, but I'm also worried about Felicity. She isn't waking up. Please, *please*, just get us to the hospital." My voice cracks and I pat Owen's leg, trying to reassure him when my own heart is breaking.

They nod.

"We'll get you there as soon as we can," the guy doing Owen's vitals says. "I'm Charles and that's Evan. You're Dr. Wyatt's nephew, aren't you? He's not going to be happy to see you rolling in on this stretcher, so let's get you better fast, okay?"

Once they have his coat off, they put his arm in a sling. His vitals are good, and they keep checking the rest of him on the way to the hospital. My head hangs down as I grip Owen's hand. I can only pray that Felicity is going to be okay.

When we pull in, Wyatt rushes toward us and looks Owen over.

"You scared us, buddy. Am I ever glad to see your face," Wyatt says, shooting me a concerned look before he glances over the chart. "Looks like a broken arm is all we have to worry about right now, but we're going to do all the tests to make sure you're okay."

"My arm hurts a lot, and I'm kinda sore, but I'm all right," Owen says, his gritted teeth letting me know he's hurting more than he's letting on.

"How's Felicity?" I ask. "Have you seen her?"

"I was with her for just a minute and Dr. James and Dr. Emma are with her now. I just had to see Owen for myself." His eyes are glassy as he ruffles Owen's hair and then grips my shoulder. "Are you okay?"

"No."

He gives me a sympathetic look and motions toward the back. "I'll come see you after the nurse has been in there."

He looks at Owen and I can tell he's still assessing him as he talks. There's no one I trust more than him in this hospital or any other hospital, for that matter.

"Linda will take you to do a few X-rays, for sure on that arm. You'll like her a lot. We'll get some pain meds going, and you just tell Linda if you'd like a popsicle or something special to drink." Wyatt pats Owen's leg. "We'll have you feeling better in no time, I promise."

"Thanks, Uncle Wyatt."

He grins at Owen and looks at me. "I'm going to check on Felicity, and I'll give you an update as soon as I can."

"Let me know when I can see her," I say, my voice cracking. I swipe my hand down my face and look at the ceiling while I try to catch my breath.

"I will," he says.

The fact that my brother walks away from us so quickly

lets me know two things: he's confident Owen is going to be okay, and he's concerned about Felicity.

When we're in one of the ER rooms, I call Tracy and tell her there was an accident. She talks to Owen and he reassures her that he's fine, he's just worried about Felicity. Tracy is fuming mad when I get the phone again. She goes off about me letting our son ride on the back of a snowmobile with anyone besides me, and especially with an irresponsible *child* like Felicity.

I tell her no one regrets that either one of them rode snowmobiles tonight more than I do, and that if Felicity doesn't recover fully, I'll never forgive myself. That seems to shut her up for five seconds and I choose that time to tell her I'll text with updates about Owen and hang up.

Next, I get in touch with Felicity's parents by calling their law office and speaking to Olivia. She gives me David's number and he sounds as panicked as I feel when I explain that Felicity was injured and still hasn't woken up. He says they'll be here as soon as they can and I promise to update him too.

Dr. Emma sticks her head in the door when we get back from X-rays.

"I have two people looking for you," she says, smiling warmly, as Ruby and Callum step into the room behind her. "Hi, Owen. Hi, Sutton," she adds. "I was looking for you earlier, but you were out getting X-rays. Wyatt asked me to come let you know that Felicity is awake and she's asking about you." She smiles at Owen when she says that last part. "She's two rooms down."

I sag against the back of my chair in relief. "Is she okay?"

"I'll let Wyatt be the one to fill you in on that. He's with her now. We'll be running more tests now that she's awake."

"Can I see her?"

"Yes. It'll put her mind at ease about Owen."

"We'll stay with him," Callum says.

"Thank you. Is that okay with you, son?"

He nods. "Yes. I wish I could go too." His lip trembles. "Can I go?"

My eyes meet Dr. Emma's and I shake my head. "Not yet. But I'll let her know you're asking about her."

"Tell her I love her, Dad. Please. Tell her I love her and I'm sorry I didn't hang on tight enough."

I pat his cheek. "You do not need to be sorry about that for even a second. Okay? Owen, I promise you, this is not your fault."

A tear slides down his cheek and I wipe it away, leaning down to kiss his forehead.

"Okay, Dad," he whispers. "Go see her. I want you to."

I straighten and nod, thanking Dr. Emma, and I walk out of his room to Felicity's. Wyatt and a nurse, I think her name is Pam, are in there, blocking her at first.

I peer around them to see Felicity as Wyatt is saying, "Ah, there he is."

It takes every effort I possess to smile at her rather than cry like a baby, the way I want to. She's wearing a neck brace and has a big patch high above her left temple. She's wearing a sling on her left arm and when I walk over and lean close, she blinks and tears run down her cheeks.

"I'm so sorry," she cries.

"I've tried to tell her Owen is okay. His name was the first word out of her mouth," Wyatt says, smiling at her as Pam secures the tape on Felicity's IV.

"You don't have anything to be sorry about," I tell her, wishing I could touch her but so scared I'll hurt her. "This accident could've happened to anyone. Owen wanted me to tell you he loves you, and he's sorry he didn't hold on tight enough, so there's entirely too much guilt going around." I reach out and catch her tears, my finger caressing her cheek for a second afterward. "We're worried about you. What's going on?" I glance at Wyatt and he lifts his eyebrows toward Felicity.

"You can tell him everything," she says.

"We're going to run more tests now that she's awake, to make sure there's no internal bleeding or anything going on that we're not seeing. She has a concussion. And eight stitches up there for a nasty cut," he points to her bandage, "but I did the stitches myself, so the scar will be minimal and her hair will cover it again in no time. She broke her arm…"

"Same one as Owen," I add.

"He broke his arm?" Her voice wobbles and more tears fall.

I grab the tissue next to her bed and she takes it with her right hand, wiping her eyes and nose. Pam hands her a little bag to put the used tissue in.

"Does your hand hurt?" I ask, pointing to the hand she just used.

"No."

I reach out and hold it and she gives me a teary smile.

Wyatt clears his throat, smiling at our hands before he looks at Felicity again. "Are those meds kicking in yet?" he asks.

"I think so," she says softly.

"Good. I'd like to take you to get X-rays now, okay?"

"Okay." She glances at me and squeezes my hand. "Tell Owen I love him too, and I'm so sad he broke his arm. I'll try to get better fast so I can make all his favorite things."

"You just get better fast," I tell her. I stand and kiss her forehead, lingering there for a second. "Please, get better," I whisper.

CHAPTER FORTY-THREE

LUCKIEST GIRL

FELICITY

I'm moved into a new room after the tests are done. They want to keep an eye on me during the night and Wyatt says I'll be more comfortable here. I drift in and out of sleep, the headache and grogginess pulling me back under. But when I hear Sutton and Owen talking quietly, I force myself to wake up.

"Sorry to wake you," Sutton says sheepishly.

"Don't be, I'm so happy to see you guys."

I reach my hand out to Owen and he hurries over. Sutton moves behind him and I wish I could erase the worry from both of their faces.

"Hey, Ace. I'm so sorry you got hurt. I feel awful about what happened," I tell him. "How are you feeling?"

He holds my hand and leans on the bed carefully. "Don't feel bad. It was an accident, and I'm okay. See?" He holds up his arm and I smile when I see his cast. "I got green because it's our favorite color," he says, his voice still quiet and shy.

I let go of his hand to pull the blanket down and show him my green cast. He grins, so pleased. My eyes well with tears and his widen.

"Are you hurting?" he asks.

"I'm okay too," I tell him. "I just think I'm the luckiest girl in the world to have you in my life."

He leans over like he wants to hug me but then pauses. I hold my good arm out and he comes in, nuzzling into my neck. The tears fall then, and I glance at Sutton to see him fighting back tears too.

He brushes my hair back and his hand caresses my cheek. He starts to say something but stops when he hears something behind him. His hand falls and I miss his warmth.

Footsteps shuffle in and my mom rushes to my bedside, gasping when she sees me. Owen leans up and I pat his back before he moves to make room for my parents.

"Sweetheart," Mom cries, her face crumbling.

My dad puts his hand on my foot and is at a loss for words.

"I'm okay," I assure them both.

"You have a concussion and broke your arm. That doesn't sound okay to me," my mom insists.

I smile at her, and my eyes find Sutton's again. He's quiet and still looks racked with worry. My mom turns to see who has my attention and she grabs a tissue, wiping her nose.

"Thanks for calling us," she tells Sutton.

"Of course," he says. "I'm sorry it was such a scary call, but I knew you'd want to know."

Mom nods and her eyes snag on Owen's cast. "Were you in the accident too?"

He nods. "Yes, ma'am."

The tension in the room immediately leapfrogs to insane levels. I can feel my parents' eyes on me, and I know *lawsuit* is flashing in their minds in huge red letters.

"Owen has already been discharged. Besides the broken arm and being sore, everything else looks good," Sutton says, his eyes still on me. "Now, we just need to get Felicity feeling better."

My heart warms with his words. Does he really not blame me for the accident?

I blame me enough for both of us.

"Thank you," my mom says. "And thank you for looking out for her until we got here. We can take it from here."

Sutton's mouth opens to respond, and I smile at him and Owen.

"You should get this boy home. It's past his bedtime," I say. "Come here, one more hug." I hold my hand out to Owen and he's there in seconds, his hair tickling my neck as he leans in.

I'm surprised when Sutton steps closer after Owen moves, and his head lowers to kiss me on the cheek.

"Call me if you need anything at all, no matter the hour," he says in my ear. "I *hate* leaving you." He straightens and says louder, "My brother's promised to watch you like a hawk." His smile is sad, and he lingers near my side for a few moments before stepping back. "We'll come back to check on you in the morning."

"Thanks for everything," Dad says, shaking Sutton's hand.

"Yes, thank you." My mom hovers near Sutton before sitting on the edge of the chair by my bed. "You're a busy man. Too busy to be here in the morning, I'm sure. We can send an update if there are any changes," she says.

"I'm not too busy," he says. His eyes flash to mine again before he nods politely to my parents and leads Owen to the door. "Good night."

"Good night," my parents echo.

"Night, Felicity," Owen says.

"Night, Ace. I love you."

"I love you too." Owen smiles at my parents and he and Sutton walk out the door.

I miss them as soon as they're gone, but my parents visibly relax when they leave.

"How are you really doing?" Mom asks.

"I'm pretty sore."

She snorts. "For you and Weston, 'pretty sore' means you're in bad shape. Do you have any idea how much Olivia would be milking this?"

I laugh and shake my head, regretting it instantly. My eyes close to see if that curbs the dizziness. "I have some idea, yes." I open my eyes and squint at her. "I'll be fine. You don't have to stay. Get some sleep. I'm sure I'll be released tomorrow."

They both let out a sound of surprise or frustration, I can't tell which.

"We're not going anywhere," Dad says.

"And you're coming home with us."

Again, I turn my head too fast. "No, that won't be necessary, I—"

"You are going to need time to recover from the concussion," Mom cuts in. "The broken arm will slow you down too, but the concussion is the most concerning."

"My doctor—Wyatt, remember you met him at the game?—he'll let us know if there's anything to be worried about after he gets the results of the tests. Until then, let's not jump to any conclusions, okay?"

"Is this really the best place to receive care?" Dad huffs. "You should've been airlifted to Denver."

I groan. "No, Dad, I shouldn't have been. This is an excellent hospital. They've been very thorough."

"Well, no matter what the doctor says, you need to let us take care of you. Work will have to wait, your health is most important," my mom says firmly.

Her tone offers no room for argument, and I'm too tired to argue right now anyway. I rest my eyes, opening them when I hear Wyatt come in. He exchanges pleasantries with my parents and then focuses on me.

"I have good news about your arm. It's as I thought, no need for surgery. It should heal nicely in six to eight weeks. If everything is looking good in four weeks, maybe we can switch over from this cast to something a little more comfortable." He smiles and studies my face, stepping forward as he pulls out his little light. He's used it on me a couple of times now. "I'm going to check your pupils. How's your head feeling?"

"It hurts."

"Any dizziness?"

"Yes."

"Pupils look good. There's no hematoma or signs of edema in your scans, which I'm happy about, but since you were unconscious for fifteen minutes or so, I want to keep watching for swelling. I'm also happy to say your ribs are bruised but not broken. I'm sure it's still hurting like crazy, but if they were broken, it'd hurt to breathe." He makes a face. "With the way you're banged up, it probably already does, but the fewer things broken, the better. It's okay for you to sleep, but we will be waking you up often to ask simple questions and assess your condition. Sorry about that in advance."

I return his smile.

He checks my water. "Drink more water if you can, even while we're getting fluids in you with the IV. Just use that call button when you need to use the bathroom and one of the nurses will be right in to help you."

"I'll be staying here tonight with her," my mom says.

He nods. "That'll be fine. I just ask that you let her rest and not have the TV on." He looks at me again. "It'll be important that you avoid all screens, especially in the next forty-eight hours, but really…it might be a while before you can watch TV without getting a headache. I'd prefer you to avoid them for three weeks and then we reassess."

"Okay."

"*Okay,* easiest patient ever." He grins at me again.

I'm really glad he's here. I was already fond of him, but as a doctor, I trust him to know what's best for me. And bonus: he's got great bedside manner.

"All right, you know what comes next. The walk. I'm sorry to do this to you. Pam was going to do it soon, but I'd rather you not be woken up any more than you have to be."

I take my time getting out of bed, waiting until my head clears somewhat before I stand up.

He offers his arm and we walk from my bed to the door and back again.

"One more time on your own?" he says.

I let go and walk even slower across the room. My head hurts, but I make it across the room and back to bed. In the next second, I grab the little bag on the tray and hold it up, afraid that I'm going to throw up.

I breathe through it and it passes, and I lean my head back. "Sorry, thought I was going to lose it there for a second."

"Have you thrown up since the first time I walked with you?" he asks.

"No."

"Good. Let us know if you do, and please, wait for a nurse to get up, okay?"

"I will."

"All right. I'm going to let you sleep." To my dad, he says, "We have a couple of rooms for family that need to stay close. During tourist season it's often full, but not tonight. I can show you those if you like. They're all open right now, so there's no risk of getting booted out." He grins and my dad looks at me.

"Go sleep, Dad. You too, Mom." I barely have the energy to say it. "I just want to sleep and I'll feel bad if I'm keeping you up."

"I'm not leaving you," Mom says.

I sigh.

"I'll sleep a few hours and then come relieve you," Dad tells my mom. "Would you let me know if anything changes?" he asks Wyatt.

"Absolutely. We'll take good care of her." His phone buzzes and he checks it, shaking his head and laughing quietly. "My brother and nephew have already left at least three messages since they left, so I have a lot of people to answer to about this patient." He smiles pointedly at me. "Rest."

I grin and close my eyes, thinking about Sutton and Owen.

CHAPTER FORTY-FOUR

OPINIONS AND DISCONNECTS

SUTTON

"She's okay, brother," Wyatt says. "I've just been with her, and while I love you dearly, I can't answer the phone every two minutes."

"I haven't called that much," I grumble. "It killed me to leave her."

He laughs, but it just as quickly fades. "I know it did. I saw the look on your face. You're a whipped puppy, aren't you?" He doesn't wait for me to respond, sliding right into doctor mode. "Her scans look good. No surgery needed for her arm..." His pause grows and I slow down my pacing, holding the phone tight against my ear.

"But?"

He sighs. "But concussions are tricky. We're learning more about them all the time, and it can be hard to know right away how long-lasting the effects will be."

"What are you saying?" I've been researching traumatic brain injuries since I put Owen to bed and it's fucking terrifying all that can happen. But I want to hear my brother tell me *his* opinion.

"Normally we'd release her tomorrow, given the results of her scans, but I'd like to keep her another day for observation. I have a feeling her parents will want to take her back to Silver Hills and I'd rather her not even travel that short distance right now."

"What? No, she doesn't need to go back with them. I'll take care of her." My thoughts jump into action, picturing the room I'll set up for her. The guest suite on the main floor that hardly gets used. That way she won't have to take the stairs if she's still dizzy at all.

"Good luck telling them that." There's a muffled sound as he speaks to someone else. "I've gotta go, Sutton. But I'll let you know of any updates, I promise. Try to sleep, okay?"

I mumble something back and the call disconnects.

I walk into my room to check on Owen. I just want to have him close even though I can't stop moving yet. He's sound asleep, thank God. It took him a while to settle down when we got home. He was exhausted but kept asking about Felicity.

Instead of going to bed, I go downstairs and strip the bed, throw the linens into the washer, and while I'm waiting for that to finish, I dust the furniture and clean the bathroom.

For the first six years or so after our parents died, Grinny and Granddad stayed in the upstairs bedroom I'm in. It's the largest, with the massive bathroom I'm sure Grinny missed once she moved into this room. This bathroom has a nice tub and shower, but one sink instead of the two upstairs and very little counter space. They moved down here when Scarlett and Theo were old enough to not need them as close during the night and so none of us would have to share a room anymore. Just one more thing my grandparents sacrificed while making it sound like it was their joy to do so.

When I've put the clean sheets and comforter back on the bed, I look over the room with a critical eye, trying to imagine anything Felicity might need. From what I've read, she should probably avoid reading or watching TV. Room-darkening shades—that's what we need. And maybe a gift card for audiobooks. I bring a large vase for the flowers I'll buy before she gets here and set it on her bedside table before calling it done. Next, I order the shades and gift card online, and all of this while checking my phone religiously.

I sent Felicity a few texts when I got home, telling her how I hated to leave her, how grateful I am that she's okay, to please not ever scare me like that again...and reminding her that she can call or text at *any* time. And then I remember she's supposed to avoid screens and I feel bad that I texted at all.

She finally texts back around three in the morning, just as I'm heading upstairs.

> FELICITY
>
> Thank you for not hating me. And it's okay if deep down you do. I'll never forgive myself for putting Owen in danger like that. I'm cured of snowmobiles forever. I hope he's not hurting too much.

An anguished sound comes out of me before I can stop it, the weight of all of it hitting me all over again. I try to get it together before I check on Owen again, relieved that he's still sleeping well, and I hurriedly text Felicity back.

> There's no part of me that hates you. Please let this guilt go and know that I still trust you with my son now as much as I did before this happened. Remind me to tell you about the time he stood on the back of the chair and fell right on his face before I could reach him fast enough.

FELICITY
I'm so sorry I woke you up!

> You didn't. I'm awake. Why are you? And why are you on your phone?!

FELICITY
Can I call?

> Please.

I move into my bathroom and shut the door. The phone flashes her name and I answer. I hear her sniffling and it hurts to hear her upset and not be there to touch her, to reassure her.

"Sweetness, don't cry. He's okay. He really is."

"I just can't stop thinking about how much worse it could've been," she cries.

"I know. That's all I've thought about too, but about both of you." My voice cracks at the end and we're quiet for a moment.

"My dad will be back soon. He went to the bathroom and to get more water. I just needed to hear your voice."

"How are you feeling?"

"My head's weird, but I'm okay."

"You wouldn't say even if you were feeling awful, would you?"

She laughs softly. "You sound like my mom."

"Oh no." I laugh.

"I'll let you go," she says. "You should be sleeping."

"*You* should be sleeping. Try to, okay? I'll be there in the morning…or in a few hours now, I guess."

"Okay, I will…I have. They just keep waking me up." She's quiet for a beat. "I miss you." Her voice breaks, and it fucking kills me to not be there.

"I miss you too. So fucking much."

"Good night."

"Night, sweetness."

I'm woken up to my phone ringing and I fumble around to answer, heart thundering.

"I'm outside," Tracy says.

"Here?" I squint to see the time and rub my fingers over my eyes when I see *6:53*.

"That's what I said," she snaps.

It's not what she said, but I don't argue. I'm not in the mood to deal with Tracy for a second longer than I have to.

"Just a minute," I say and hang up.

My alarm was set to go off in a few minutes and I showered only a few hours ago, so I throw on my clothes for the day and check on Owen—still sleeping soundly—before I jog down the stairs. As soon as I open the door, Tracy rushes in, already spewing her toxic.

"How could you let this happen?" She turns on me,

pointing her finger. "You better have fired that girl. I knew she was too inexperienced to take care of him when I saw her."

"Do you want to know how our son is doing?" I pour water into the coffee maker and the beans, and for a minute, the sound of the beans grinding is the only noise.

"Of course I do," she spits out when the noise stops. "But you're acting like what she did was nothing, and I'm here to tell you—"

"Owen has slept through the night. I'm sure the pain medication has helped him sleep more than anything, but he was up late last night, so that also plays a role. He—"

"Do not act like I don't care about my son because I'm talking about her—"

"You haven't once asked about him, so I thought maybe you'd want an update."

She scowls at me and sits at the kitchen table. "You're avoiding talking about her."

"I'm not. I'm telling you about Owen first. Besides the broken arm, which Wyatt says should heal completely based on the break, he has a bruise on his hip and his cheek was a bit raw from landing in the snow. I was there, Tracy. Felicity is a seasoned driver. I watched her before she took him out. If I'd been driving him, it still could have happened. It also could've been so much worse. A fox came out of nowhere, and Felicity turned to avoid hitting it. I watched her turn to grab Owen and it was to her detriment because he had a better landing than she did."

"If you don't fire her, I'm suing her," she says, her eyes tired but still flashing up at me.

"Do you hear yourself?" I lean back against the counter and sigh, pinching the bridge of my nose. "Go ahead. You'd lose and I wouldn't help you pay for this lawsuit. There would be two witnesses who were actually there to corroborate my testimony. Not to mention, Owen, who, by the time a hearing took place, would be healed and singing Felicity's praises. You don't have a case, and it'll just make him dislike you in the process."

"He already dislikes me, but I'd be keeping him safe." She sighs and leans her head against her propped-up hand.

"The way he feels about you is no one's fault but yours." I stare at her when I say this, and she blinks back her surprise. "And only you have the power to change that."

It's quiet for a moment and I hold up the full coffeepot. She nods and I get two mugs and fill them. I take hers to the table with the cream before I go back to mine. I close my eyes when I take a sip, exhaustion catching up with me.

Hearing footsteps upstairs, I set the coffee down and go up there. Owen is getting done in the bathroom and he washes his free hand.

"Hey, Dad. How's Felicity?"

"Good morning, Ace."

He grins every time I call him that, and it makes me even happier that Felicity is in our life. God, to think she almost wasn't.

I get a sudden zing of clarity. I've tried to curtail my future with her because of her being young and what that means for my reputation.

How utterly fucking stupid.

If one day she doesn't want me, then so be it, but I'm going to love her every day between now and then, and beyond.

"The last I spoke to her, she was doing all right. Mostly worried about you, and I think her head is bothering her more than she's saying. How are you feeling?" I lift his chin in my fingers, studying the cheek that was red and raw last night. "Your cheek looks a little better."

"Yeah, it just feels a little hot still, but it's better than last night. My arm hurts," he says, frowning.

"Well, it's time to take some medicine. Let's get something in your stomach first."

"And then we can go see Felicity?"

"Your mom is downstairs and would like to see you."

His face falls. "But I need to see Felicity. We said we'd be back this morning."

I put my arm on his shoulder. "Give your mom some time and I'll make sure you see Felicity too. I'm not positive when that will be since I didn't know your mom would be here this early, but I'll get you there."

He looks at me with dread and I pat the cheek that isn't sore.

"I'll be right here with you, okay?" As much as I want to rush to the hospital, I'm not leaving Owen with Tracy when she's in this mood.

He nods, and we go downstairs.

CHAPTER FORTY-FIVE

MEDICAL JOURNALS, OH MY

FELICITY

It's hard to tell morning from night in the hospital, but my mom comes in looking refreshed after sleeping a few hours, and a different nurse comes in, announcing a new day. I feel like I've been dragged by a horse and stomped with combat boots or something else that equals *brutal*.

Wyatt checked on me before he left and Dr. James has been in this morning. I was surprised to find out that they're not releasing me today and maybe not tomorrow either. It must be a really slow week at Pine Community Hospital.

Sutton and Owen show up after I've eaten a few bites of breakfast and they're a bright spot in my morning. They don't stay long, but Sutton promises they'll be back. He explains that Tracy is in town and he doesn't say it, but I get the impression that she's not happy.

Shit. I wouldn't be either if I were her.

My parents make a few comments about how nice Sutton's being, and they ask if I think he'll sue. I tell them he won't and if I were feeling better, I think they'd probably be saying more, but they let me rest.

When Sutton comes back alone around lunchtime, saying Scarlett and Grinny are at the house with Owen and Tracy, he looks like a man on a mission.

"I was hoping I could have a word with the three of you," he says, looking at me first and then my parents.

My mom shoots me a look like *here we go—lawsuit!*

"I talked to Wyatt last night and he let me know about them keeping you longer. First, I want to assure you that your job is secure with us as long as you want it." His eyes heat through me when he says this, and it's obvious to me that he would say this a lot differently if my parents weren't here. "Best-case scenario and what I'm hoping for with all my heart, is that you recover completely and right away, and that has nothing to do with the job. I want you to take as much time off as you need to recover. I insist on it, actually. Owen will be covered." He leans in, his forearms dropping to his thighs. "That being said, because Wyatt also said that ideally, he wouldn't want you to make the trip to Silver Hills for a while, or anywhere else, for that matter, I've gotten the guest room on the main level ready for you. With the size of my family, there will be someone who can help with whatever you need, whenever you need it." He looks at my parents. "And the room above my garage where Felicity has been staying is available to you at any time…or the whole time she's recovering, should you want it."

My parents look at him, stunned, and my mom speaks first.

"That's very generous of you. But don't you think you should come home, honey? I'm sure you'll be better in no time, but it'd feel good to be home, wouldn't it?"

"I'd like to stay here. This is my home." My eyes shift from my mom's to Sutton's. "I won't need a babysitter though. I'll be fine."

My mom lets out a long-suffering sigh and nudges my dad.

"Well, we'd rather you be home," he says. "But since you're an adult—"

"How about you let us talk about it with Felicity," my mom interrupts.

"Mom—"

Sutton is already standing. "Sure. I'll give you time. I just wanted you to know the offer stands." He smiles at me and moves toward the door, turning to look at my parents one more time. "I really care about your daughter."

And with that, he leaves.

"Felicity?" My mom faces me. "What did he mean by that?"

I close my eyes. "He's a generous man."

My mom sputters and I could put her mind at ease by downplaying my relationship with Sutton or I could tell her everything, but I'll wait to see where Sutton stands when it's all said and done. It took a lot for him to say what he did to my parents, but will he ever let himself love me completely?

I'm just not sure. All I know is that my feelings for him... they're vast.

He makes me wish for forever.

I fall asleep and dream of him.

Two days later, Sutton and Owen lead me into their guest room. Since seeing it once, I haven't been back, and it's evident that they've added some loving care to it just for me.

A massive bouquet of flowers sits next to the bed, and on the dresser, there's an overflowing basket of goodies. I gasp when I see the soft pajamas, cozy socks, a green zip-up hoodie, one of Ruby's emu water bottles and a mug, snacks galore, and a gift card for audiobooks.

"The girls helped us with the pajamas and socks...and Ruby's merch, obviously," Sutton says, hovering over me like I'm about to fall.

"And I picked this out," Owen says, touching the hoodie.

"I love it. This is so sweet. All of it. And the flowers are beautiful." My voice wobbles and Owen stares at me and then his dad in alarm. "I'm okay. Remember they said I might be a little extra—" I point at my face and the tears starting to fall. "Don't worry," I tell them both.

"Everyone wants to help," Sutton says. "Just tell us when we're too much. Wyatt had a family meeting last night after he talked to you...we all just want to make this as easy for you as possible."

That makes me cry harder, which makes my head hurt more, but I keep that to myself.

"I can't believe how great you are. The whole family. Thank you." I wipe my face. "But I really don't want to be a bother to anyone."

Sutton waves me off. "You aren't. We all care about you, and this is what the Landmarks do when we love." His eyes gleam when he says *love* and my stomach flip-flops.

He doesn't take the word back either.

For the first two weeks, when Sutton's not here, there's someone else in the house at all times. My parents and Weston are here all the time. Olivia comes once with my mom. And everyone in Sutton's family, and I do mean everyone, even Pappy, comes and sits with me while Sutton or another family member takes care of Owen. They're quiet and let me rest, but they also keep me fed and stay after me to drink my water.

The recovery is taking longer than I expected. I'll feel better one day and then go backwards and have to spend the next day in bed.

By the end of the third week, I feel quite a bit better as long as I stay off of my phone and don't watch TV. Audiobooks and podcasts have been a lifesaver. I still have daily headaches, and I've been surprised that it's taking this long to fully recover. Wyatt and Sutton keep reminding me that recovery time is different for everyone, and that it could take a long time for me to fully feel like myself again.

Sutton's schedule is slower this week and it's been nice to spend the afternoons with him, but the guilt I feel over everything is becoming all-consuming.

We're on the couch. After school, Owen went to play with Dakota. Sutton's behind me, my back against his chest, and his legs are on either side. It's a big couch, but he's a tall, muscular man, so we're leaning a little sideways to fit. His fingers trace light circles on my arm, and even though I've tried to make out multiple times with him in the past few weeks, he hasn't let it go beyond fevered, passionate kisses.

"I hate that I'm still taking everyone's time." The words rush out of me like a waterfall.

His fingers stop.

"I'm fine to start doing more around here, and I saw that you paid me even though I haven't worked in weeks. You can't do that, Sutton."

He kisses my head, and his fingers resume their light tickling up and down my arms.

"I can," he says, his voice light and teasing. "And you're not rushing through this recovery. Owen and I are fine, and everyone is happy to help."

"If I'd known I'd take this long, I would've never come here." I groan when I start to cry.

He shifts, leaning until his eyes are on mine. "I love you, Felicity."

My eyes widen. I've hoped he might, but I haven't dared believe he actually does. Even though he's done everything he possibly can to show it.

"I love you," I whisper back.

His eyes soften, and his thumb caresses my cheek and over my mouth.

"I love you so much, I don't even know how to put it into words," he says. "I've teased my brothers and sister mercilessly for how fast they fell in love, but I'm having to eat every word because I'm right there with them. I knew it but didn't want to admit it before the accident, but talk about clarity—when I saw you lying in the snow, bleeding and not waking up, I fucking wished I hadn't wasted any time." He chuckles under his breath. "And the only reason I haven't told you sooner is because Wyatt told me not to get you too excited about *anything*…" He laughs again.

"Hmm. You thought this would excite me, huh?" I tease, laughing when he pretends to scowl. "Wyatt knows?"

"Oh yeah, he knows. Not because I've said it though. I've been waiting to tell you first, but I'm certain they all know. They've watched me be a basket case about you for the past three-and-a-half weeks."

I laugh and turn so I can see him better. I reach up and put my hand in his hair, tugging his lips to mine.

"I love you," I whisper against his lips.

He groans and kisses me, getting even harder beneath me. I turn to face him and he pulls back slowly, his hands on my face.

We're both breathless, hearts racing.

"I want you," I tell him, unbuttoning his shirt and kissing down his neck and chest.

"Felicity," he says, his voice hoarse, "I read somewhere that it takes twenty-six point three days for a woman to be ready for sex after a concussion."

I blink at him for a few seconds. "It's been…twenty-four days."

"Trust me, I know exactly how long it's been." He adjusts himself, trying to distance his lower half from me.

I don't let him.

"I'll be okay." I go back to kissing his chest and he shakes his head, stopping me.

"When you go a day without being in pain…when you can do strenuous things without paying for it later…we'll talk about it." He smiles at me so sweetly that it almost takes away the sting.

I growl, which only makes his smile grow.

"I want forever with you, sweetness. Or however long you'll give me, but what I want is forever. And if you'll let me, I'll spend the rest of my life showing you just what you mean to me. In every way," he adds, giving me a light kiss.

I grind against him and he laughs, shaking his head.

"I'll negotiate about everything with you, but not this," he says.

"Dammit," I say, swatting his chest. "You're so stubborn."

"Stubbornly in love with you," he says, kissing me again.

I can't hold back the grin that takes over my face.

"Well, when you put it that way…"

CHAPTER FORTY-SIX

LONGER THAN 26.3

SUTTON

It's been two weeks since I told Felicity I love her. It's been pure bliss. It's like we're doing a relationship backwards, having all the conversations we didn't have before we started sleeping together.

I love her more every fucking minute.

We still haven't had sex.

Yes, it's killing me.

Yes, I'll live.

She had an appointment with Wyatt today and he liked the improvement with her balance and that she's having fewer headaches.

We're having the family over in about fifteen minutes. They've avoided all coming at once so she's not overwhelmed or around too much noise, but Wyatt keeps telling her to just take it in small doses. If she's not feeling well, listen to her body. She's sworn she'll go to her room if she starts feeling bad.

Tracy hasn't been here since right after the accident. She didn't even stay that whole weekend. I think she's embarrassed about how she acted, and I hope she'll come around and be the mom Owen needs her to be, but if she doesn't, between my family, Felicity, and me…we're doing our best to make sure he knows how loved he is. It's all we can do. I still want her to do the right thing, but it's up to her.

I find Owen in his room. He got his cast off yesterday, and the kid was a pro at maneuvering with a cast, but he's damn happy to be free of it now.

"Got a minute, Ace?"

He turns and grins at me. "Sure." He holds up a LEGO figure. "I can finally make these again."

I hold up my hand and he slaps it.

"I wanted to talk to you about Felicity."

He puts the figure down and stares up at me. I hold out my hand and we walk to his bed, sitting down.

"She's not leaving, is she?" The look in his eyes kills me.

"No, she's not. If I have my way, she'll stay here forever."

His face lights up. "Yeah, me too!"

"How would you feel about her being my girlfriend?"

He laughs, bashful but happy. "I'd like it. Do you think you'll marry her?"

"Maybe one day."

"You better do it soon. You're the oldest and Uncle Callum and Uncle Theo are already married…Uncle Wyatt will be soon too."

"It's not a race." I poke him in the side, laughing when he cracks up. "I'd marry her tomorrow, but I'm trying to take this slowly and enjoy all of it."

He nods. "Okay. As long as she stays forever, I'm good with waiting on a wedding. But I like the dancing," he adds.

I pull him into a hug. "Well, start telling me the songs you want to dance to, so we'll have a head start. We can start a list."

He jumps off the bed, unable to sit still. He reaches for my phone to look at songs, and I hand it to him.

"The family will be here soon. I wanted to talk to you about it before I talk to them." I get up and walk to his door.

He nods, lost in the list of songs. I laugh and he glances up and nods again.

"I'll come down when they get here."

"With my phone," I call as I walk down the hall.

Everyone starts trickling in, at first quietly because Wyatt and I have them all scared of making Felicity relapse. But Felicity is there in the middle of them all, radiant and chatty, acting more like herself than she has in so long.

Scarlett, Jamison, and Grinny are the only ones missing and when Scarlett and Jamison walk in, her face is red and she's fanning her face.

"You okay?" Callum asks, his hand on her elbow.

"You guys are not going to believe what we just saw."

She looks back at Jamison and he looks amused but doesn't say anything.

"What?" Theo asks.

"Out with it," Wyatt says.

Scarlett points between herself and Jamison, back and forth, back and forth, eyes huge.

"Our *grandparents* just kissed."

She drops those words and then stares at us. We're silent for a minute and then the questions start flying.

Grandparents?

What do you mean?

Where?

"Grinny and Pappy were in the car together and they didn't see us pull up," she says, winded from saying it so fast. "And we were going to tap on the window, but then they started *kissing*!"

The door opens behind Scarlett just as she yells, "*Grinny and Pappy were kissing!*"

Grinny's eyes widen slightly, but she stays fairly reserved. It's Pappy who turns every shade of red, his neck and ears and face painfully flushed.

"I guess the cat's out of the bag," Grinny says, elbowing Pappy.

Again, the questions fly.

How long has this been going on?

When were you going to tell us?

Her eyes meet mine and she smirks. I return it and wink.

"Way to go, you two. It's about time," I say, moving forward to hug them. And because I can't resist pulling shit with my family, I say, "Pappy, you gonna put a ring on it?"

Grinny swats my backside and I jump out of the way, laughing.

Everyone hugs them, and I'm glad that they all seem truly

happy for them. I know I am. Now that I have Felicity in my life, now that I know what true love really is, I want everyone to experience it…even those who have experienced it before, like Grinny and Pappy.

Grinny holds up her hand and I'm across the room by now, but I can see the mischief in her eyes from here.

"So when are you gonna fill us in on your love life, Sutton Henry Landmark?" Her voice is a mixture of a tease and a dare.

I move next to Felicity and put my arm around her, leaning in to kiss her hair. Everyone makes a loud whoop and then apologizes to her in whispers the next second.

"I was planning to fill you in tonight, actually," I say, smiling at her and then looking at my family. "I'm in love with this woman right here."

"Duh!" Sofie says and everyone laughs.

"Yeah, I think you were all on it like bloodhounds from the very beginning. I was a little resistant, overthinking it all…"

"No, not you," Theo chimes in.

I roll my eyes but can't stop smiling like a crazy bastard. Owen comes over and wraps his arms around both of us, and Felicity looks at me over his head, her eyes filling with tears.

"Do you love him too?" Owen asks, lifting his head to look at her.

"I love him so much," she says, nodding tearfully. She leans down and kisses his forehead. "And I love you."

There's not a dry eye in the house after that. Lots of hugs are handed out and it's one of the best nights I can remember.

When everyone leaves and Owen is tucked into bed, I follow Felicity to her room and pull her against me for a kiss near her door.

"Oh no, you're not," she says, pulling me into her room.

"You're not going to declare your love for me in front of your entire family and then kiss me good night like a chaste little soldier.

I crack up. "Chaste little soldier?"

She nods, her lips puckering. She tries to undo her zipper but still has her cast for another week. Her arm has taken a little longer than Owen's to heal.

"Help me out of this," she says in frustration.

I laugh and unzip her dress, and the surprise underneath makes me choke out a sound between a cough and a groan. She grins at me over her shoulder.

"How did you manage to get this on by yourself?" I ask, my fingers trickling down her shoulders and back, until I'm squeezing her perfect ass peeking out of the delicate lace.

"It took way too long," she admits, laughing.

She turns around and I lean down and kiss her nipples through the lace, one at a time.

"I almost hate to take it off of you since you worked so hard to get it on," I say, looking up as I wrap my tongue around her peak.

She reaches behind with her free hand and undoes the ribbons, making me laugh against her.

"You're so beautiful, Felicity," I tell her, straightening to kiss her mouth.

It quickly turns from sweet to sinful, and I can't get close enough. I pull back and sound winded.

"Tell me if it's too much," I tell her.

"I'll be fine. You've made me wait longer than twenty-six point three days, you jerk. I am more than ready."

I laugh and slide the lace off of her, careful around her arm. "How would you like it?" I ask, kissing her bare shoulders and up her neck.

She lies back on the bed and spreads her legs, and I curse when I see her desire.

"Fast this time, slow the next," she says.

"*Fuck*," I grind out.

"Please," she says, her face pure seduction.

I undress quickly and stalk to the bed, so hungry for her. I remind myself to slow down even if she wants fast, but I'm afraid it'll be faster than I want it to be, no matter what.

"Hurry," she says, her fingers gliding down her body until they're between her legs. She slides the wetness around and I lean down and lick it. "See? I'm ready."

She tugs on my head and I pause, looking up.

"I want you inside me."

"I love it when you say what you want. I don't want to hurt your arm though…"

"You won't," she says, smiling. "I can't wait."

I climb over her, not putting my weight on her as I settle between her legs. I stare at her until she gets impatient. She arches into me, and she's right.

"You are ready."

She grins and I slide in, hissing with how good it feels to be bare inside of her. She moans too, already twitching around me as she lets me in deeper.

"You feel so good," she whimpers. "I want it all."

I pull out and then go all the way in, and her head falls back.

"I've missed you," I tell her.

"Not as much as I've missed you."

It takes too much focus to not spill into her, so I don't argue, but I think it's obvious that we're both desperate for each other.

"I'm not going to last long," I tell her, when she clenches around me.

"I don't need it to, I'm there," she says.

I slide out one more time and then keep my thrusts shallow until her whole body is trembling, her walls clamping around me. When I thrust in as deep as I can go, that's when we both free-fall into heaven.

CHAPTER FORTY-SEVEN

P IS FOR...

A few weeks later

FELICITY

"Today's the big day. Are you ready?" I ask Owen.

"Yes!" he cheers.

"Beyond ready, right?" Sutton says.

"Right." Owen laughs.

"I'm so proud of you, son. I know how badly you've

wanted this day to come, and you've been especially patient the past few weeks while we got everything ready."

"Thanks, Dad. It's been hard, but I perseversed."

I try not to giggle as Sutton says, "Yes, you have persevered," without so much as a hint of laughter in his voice at Owen's attempt at the word, even though I know he wants to.

We pull in front of Jamison and Scarlett's condo.

The biggest news around here is that Jamison proposed last week. She said yes—woohoo, there was no doubt she would—and we had a big surprise engagement party for them. I'm happy to be feeling more like myself every day, and I'm so excited and honored that she asked me to be in the wedding.

We've also let my family know about Sutton and me. None of them were surprised. Weston said he felt the sparks the day he helped me move into the room above the garage. Likely story. Olivia is not pleased, but that's also not a surprise.

And I've been looking into a career in mediation. With the struggle between Sutton and Tracy to come to a conclusion about Owen, it's become something I'm not only interested in, but I'm invested in finding solutions. The only problem is, there's not much need for this in Landmark Mountain, but I think I'll still have work. Between that and my side jobs of organizing everything from Cecil's stockroom to Ruby's merch, and life with my favorite guys, I'll stay busy.

Oh, and Owen made this season's hockey team. We had chocolate cake with peanut butter frosting to celebrate and had him open the packages we'd wrapped of all the puppy supplies he'd wanted. He got choked up, and of course, that made me cry.

A lot has been going on in Landmark Mountain.

Scarlett flings the door open before we reach it.

"Are you ready?" she asks Owen, beaming.

He nods ecstatically, his little body about ready to take off like a rocket with all the energy zooming around inside. But when we walk inside and he goes near the puppies, who are weaned from their mom by now, he calms down and sits down by them. Sutton has his camera out—he's been taking pictures a lot more lately—and he looks so cute grinning behind that lens.

They run over to him, but there's always one who, from the time he could, he's crawled into Owen's lap like he's claiming him and warding off the rest. Out of the litter of five, two have been given away, and a few weeks ago, Owen claimed this one.

"Hi, Chewbarka," he says, grinning up at me.

When we were spitting out puppy name ideas, I thought Owen was going to hurt himself, he laughed so hard when I said Chewbarka. The next time we went to Scarlett's to see the puppies, he tried it out on the puppy who's claimed him and it stuck.

"You ready to come home?" he asks, scratching the puppy's ears.

He falls out on his back, wanting stomach scratches.

The joy on Owen's face when his head falls back, laughing, brings tears to my eyes. I don't know if I cry more now because of the concussion or because these two move me every day with their love and their exuberance for life.

I've never been happy like this, not this *so happy I can't keep it in* kind of happy.

"I think he's been ready for you from the beginning," Scarlett says. "He's just the kind of dog you deserve, Owen."

Even *her* eyes are a little misty. She's told me how everyone's been rooting for Owen to have a puppy for so long.

Owen leans down and kisses the puppy's head, loving it when the other puppies clamor for his attention.

"I think they'd all go home with you," Scarlett says.

"Step back," Sutton says, eyeing her.

She giggles. "Right."

She grins at me. She knows I'd take them all if I could get away with it, but one is enough for now.

We gather the things Scarlett has for him, a small crate and a toy that he likes, and we take Chewbarka home.

Later that night, we've played with the puppy all day and laughed endlessly at the clumsy way he runs. Owen started calling him Chewy by the evening, and that has also stuck. Owen is in bed, and he's agreed to leave Chewy in the crate so they'll both sleep better, since that's what Chewy is already used to. He looks up at Sutton and me as we kiss him good night and make sure he's all tucked in.

"Now I have almost everything I've ever wanted," he says, his eyes swimming with happiness.

"Almost? I thought a puppy was the top of the list," Sutton says, throwing his hand above his head to demonstrate the top of the list.

Owen shakes his head and sits up, undoing all our burrito-wrap tucking. He puts his hand above his head and says, "Puppy," and then he stands on the bed and throws his hand up as high as it goes and says, "Marrying Felicity."

Sutton and I are both stunned speechless. Obviously. I think I recover first, laughing and tugging Owen's hand to lie down and get tucked back in.

Sutton's quiet when we go into his room. I moved into his room a few weeks ago, although I still try to be downstairs by the time Owen gets up. Sutton assures me I don't need to keep doing that, but I've wanted to ease Owen into this one step at a time.

He doesn't say anything as he makes love to me either, but the passion is next level. He makes me come three times before he ever enters me, and the way he works me over is earth-shattering.

I fall asleep wrapped in his arms after a second round, hearing him whisper, "I love you so much," against my skin.

EPILOGUE

Six months later

SUTTON

My insides do a tumbly twist when Felicity walks down the grassy, petal-filled aisle toward me. We're in front of the water at the Summit House, and it's the most perfect day for our wedding. But I'd think that even if it were stormy.

I asked her a week after Owen made his proclamation. I was struck speechless that night, but I got my act together enough the next day to buy a ring and come up with a decent proposal plan. Owen helped me pull it off. We went to Tiptop for dinner and asked her out on the balcony with twinkle lights surrounding us. Later, in bed, I showed her where my tattoo artist had added her walking with Owen and me in the compass. Not because I assumed she'd say yes, but because she's it for me. That made her cry, but she loved it. She still stares at it in wonder.

And now here we are. She's marrying me.

There's a lump in my throat and I can't believe it, but I'm crying. Never thought I'd be one of those men crying at my wedding, but then, I never thought I'd be getting married again either.

Until her.

This love is something brand new for me. It's something I will never take for granted.

She takes my breath away, her hair cascading down her bare shoulders, the veil skimming lightly down her back, and the dress is stunning, but I can't get past her eyes. Her face. Her happiness. How much love she shows with one simple look or smile.

Her hands clasp mine as we stand in front of our family and friends, and Pappy marries us. He talks about how much he's loved seeing our love story develop right in front of his eyes, and how it's already grown so big, he knows we'll last forever. When he says that, he also looks past us to wink at Grinny in the front row, which makes everyone say, "*Awwww.*"

I know Felicity and I will last forever too.

As long as I'm breathing, I will love her.

My brothers are standing up with me, but Owen is my best man, and he has been so excited for this day. Everything has gone as planned, except for when Felicity lets go of my hands to reach out for him before our vows. He looks surprised too, but he steps forward and takes her free hand.

His expression is one of complete awe as he looks at Felicity.

You and me both, buddy.

"Owen, I couldn't marry your dad today without making some promises to you first." Her voice cracks and she takes a moment to regain her composure, dabbing her face with a pretty handkerchief.

I'm already a mess. Callum passes me a hanky and everyone laughs, but they're crying too.

"From the day we met, we've had a special bond…which is no surprise because you're such a special person."

Owen's face crinkles up and he starts to cry, which makes Felicity cry harder, but she keeps going.

"You've loved and accepted me. We've had so much fun together. We've laughed and cried together. We've potty-trained a dog together."

We all laugh again, but there are sobs going on out there too, and not just from me and Owen.

"You are the best boy I have ever known, and I know you're going to be an even more amazing man. There will be times that aren't as easy. We might have to work through some things when you become a teenager and don't like what I have to say anymore."

"That'll never happen," Owen says through his tears, and he laughs too when the crowd does, but the tears just keep falling.

I hand him the hanky Wyatt passes. More laughs.

"But here's what I promise you, no matter what, okay? And I want you to hear this part especially. I promise to love you always. I promise to respect you. I promise to listen when you trust me with your stories. No matter what, I will love you."

"I love you too." His little shoulders shake and when she bends down to hug him, none of us can hold it in.

I wipe my eyes, and when Felicity turns and puts her hands in mine again, I'm overwhelmed.

"Thank you," I whisper.

I clear my throat and take a deep breath.

"Felicity, every day I know you, I love you more. The love

you show Owen, the love you show me, my family, it makes me so happy, so full, and I can't believe that I almost let fear take this from me. I vow to show you every day how much I love you. I love you so much, I will take the chicken out of the canned chicken noodle soup because you don't like it."

Everyone laughs and it's good because I was about to weep again.

"I will fill your vases with hydrangeas and peonies and dahlias because you love them. I will make trip after trip to the thrift store when you're purging and organizing. I will respect you and honor you and support all of your endeavors, the ones you're going after now, and the ones that will come in the future. I'm already old, but I want to grow old-old with you."

I even laugh at this, and I kiss her hands.

"For as long as I live, I want to spend each day laughing with you, hearing your voice, seeing your smile, loving you completely. I want everything if everything means you. Till death do us part."

Her lips tremble and she takes a deep breath.

"Sutton, loving you and Owen has been the best thing I've ever experienced, and just when I think it can't get any better, it does. I vow to always fix your color-coded calendar if I accidentally mess it up."

Owen laughs so hard at that, it makes everyone else laugh.

"I will never stop being curious with you. I will always be ready for our next adventure. I will only say *never* and *always* in positive ways. I will be content with the way things are and I'll also work to keep things new and exciting. I will tell you my secrets, my hopes, my fears, and I will hold yours safe too. I vow to love you forever." Her voice shakes when she adds, "I want everything if everything means *you*. Till death do us part."

"Beautiful," Pappy says. "By the power vested in me by the state of Colorado, I now pronounce you husband and wife. You may share your first married kiss!"

Oh, I'm all over that. I have my mouth on hers in the next second and dip her back to seal it in good and proper. When I lift her back up, she looks dazed and so, so happy.

"I love you, Mrs. Landmark," I tell her.

She looks at me and smiles that smile that will always make me weak in the knees. I kiss her again and hear her telling me she loves me against my lips.

It feels like my life has truly begun.

Would you like more Sutton and Felicity?
   Bonus scene:
https://bookhip.com/WHPSBHH

The Single Dad Playbook is coming out soon! Keep reading to sample chapter one of *Mad Love*, Weston and Sadie's story, or preorder here: https://geni.us/MadLove

Do you need to go back to the beginning of the Landmark Mountain series?
https://geni.us/UnforgettableLandmark1

COMING SOON, THE SINGLE DAD PLAYBOOK SERIES
MAD LOVE

Chapter 1

Coffee With The Dads

WESTON

The bathroom mirror is too fogged up to see anything when I get out of the shower. I wipe it down with my towel and turn to see if any bruises are fading yet. Tomorrow will be a week since my team and I won our second Super Bowl, and it does not get old, even though my body is paying the price.

I'm young enough, I can handle it.

I'm doing what I've always wanted to do, playing professional football. After a couple years of doing this, I'm still in shock that I'm living out my dream.

My phone buzzes and I check it. Penn Hudson. We started playing for the Colorado Mustangs at the same time. I've made a lot of great friends on the team, but Penn and I are probably the tightest.

> **PENN**
>
> Should we bust the dad group this morning?

>> Why not? It's always entertaining to hear them vacillate between how great their kids are and how hard they have it as single dads.

> **PENN**
>
> I'm in the mood to annoy them.

>> You just want an excuse to hang with the greats.

> **PENN**
>
> You're not wrong.

The biggest draws of coming to play for the Mustangs were Henley Ward, the best wide receiver in football, and Bowie Fox, my favorite linebacker. Bonus was when tight end Rhodes Archer was drafted along with Penn and me. All of them have been at it longer than we have, and they've accepted us with open arms in every way...except for this little single dad club they have.

>> I'll see you there in fifteen.

> **PENN**
>
> Word.

The mountains look close enough to touch on this beautiful, sunny February morning. I'm lucky that I was drafted from college to play for my home state. I'd miss Colorado if I had to live anywhere else. The snow is crunching beneath my feet, and Silver Hills is just starting to wake up for the day.

It's only been a week since Valentine's Day, but every

heart and cupid that took over the town is gone, and now there's green and silver everywhere I look for St. Patrick's Day. Silver Hills goes all out for the holidays.

I love relaxing mornings like this, maybe because they're rare for me. I'm usually rushing off to practice or still working out at this time. I walk into Luminary Coffeehouse with Penn on my heels, both of us scouting the place for the guys.

"Did we miss them?" Penn asks.

A perky brunette walks up and puts her hand on my arm. "Weston Shaw and Penn Hudson at the same time? Pinch me," she says to the girl next to her.

I look at the two girls and smile, holding back my laugh when they both sigh. It's hard to tell who they're into more, Penn or me—I think they could flip a coin and be happy.

As much as I enjoy a good time, I'm still exhausted from playing so hard last weekend, the parade in downtown Denver, and all the partying that ensued afterwards.

I really just want to chill with my boys.

Or give them shit. Same difference.

You'd think I wouldn't miss the team since we've been together nonstop for months, and I don't miss all of them, but this week, with all the interviews and parties and hangovers, I've actually missed chatting with my favorite bastards.

"Is it me or is it more crowded than usual?" Penn asks under his breath.

"It's not you," I answer.

"Oh, it's you," one of the girls says, winking. "Word got out that this is where you guys meet for coffee and everyone wanted to get in on the action. We drove all the way from Boulder."

I smile politely and motion for her to step forward in line.

She turns and I exchange a look with Penn. When he

looks forward again, his face lights up and I look to see what changed. He waves at Clara, the sassy owner who's my mom's best friend. She's the reason this is our place. She motions us over to the pickup line and lifts up our usual: flat white for me, caramel macchiato for Penn. Just one of the things we love to razz him about.

"Clara is too good to us," Penn says.

Clara is my parents' neighbor and decided to open this coffeehouse after her husband Clarence died. This place has given her a reason to smile again, which is a relief. Clara is good people and seeing her brokenhearted was awful.

"Morning, Clara. You're looking lovely today," I say, taking the cup from her.

"You don't have to sweet-talk me to get your coffee," she says, but she's smiling and her cheeks are pink. She leans in and tilts her head. "I put your boys in the back room so they could have some peace."

"Ahh. We wondered if they saw this crowd and got out of here," Penn says.

"They haven't been here long," she says.

"Thanks, Clara," Penn and I say in tandem and I lift my foot to knock the back of his knee like my sister Felicity always does to me, laughing when it buckles.

For some reason I can never pull it off with my sister, but it works on Penn every time. He didn't have siblings growing up, so he's still caught by surprise when any of us try to torture him.

He curses under his breath and shoots me a glare as we make our way through the crowded coffee shop. It's too small for all these people, but I guess it's good for business. Clara knocks once and enters a code into the door, before cracking it open.

"I have two rugrats here who think they should be invited to the party," she says.

Penn and I step into the cozy room with the large round table and a reading chair on the side with a small bookshelf of books. Clara says it's a room for meetings, but I think this is where she comes to hide and read when it's slow out there.

"Yeah, why you gotta be so exclusive?" I ask, mostly kidding.

Bowie smirks. "Have a kid and we'll let you in," he says.

Henley and Rhodes high-five, and Penn snorts.

"I hate to tell you, but you *need* us in this little club you've got going," Penn says.

Henley raises his eyebrows. "Oh yeah? Why's that?"

"You call yourselves The Single Dad Players…and you guys just high-fived. Enough said."

Henley and Bowie look embarrassed for exactly zero seconds.

"Come on, what do you talk about in these weekly meetings anyway?" Penn says. "We've heard you when we're on the road. It's not entirely parent talk, from what I can tell."

"We go easy on ourselves when we're on the road. Then it's mostly about how much we miss the kids, and we're talking about how great they are…or how difficult," Rhodes says.

"And when you're not on the road?" I ask, playing along.

"Well, I was just telling the guys that Cassidy started her period last night when she was with me, and I had nothing in the house," Henley says, with the same gleam he gets when he intercepts a pass from the opposing team and runs the ball to a touchdown.

Penn and I shift on our feet, obviously uncomfortable.

All three of them fold their arms and look pleased.

"I had to go to the drugstore and get pads and walk her through how to use them through the door." He scrunches his brows and it's the universal sign for when Henley is about to dig deeper, be it on the field or when he's talking shit with us. "She wanted to know how to use tampons, so I talked her through that too, and then I set her up with a heating pad and—"

"Okay, okay," I say, lifting my hand.

Henley's an old dog, who has some good tricks. He knows how to dish it out like a pro.

Okay, he's not that old. He's thirty-five, and the guy gets just as much attention from the ladies as we do when we go out. Not that he's interested in any of them. His ex-wife did a number on him.

But he's a damn good wide receiver. The very best.

Henley grins. "Have a seat."

He waves his hand to the seats around the table and we sit down, not so sure we want to be here anymore but also pleased that we passed.

"Was her flow heavy?" Bowie asks, giving me the side-eye.

"Come on!" I groan.

They laugh like crazy.

"I'm mature enough to talk about periods," Penn says proudly. "I just don't want to know when Cassidy has started hers…" He sticks his lip out and does sad eyes. "She's just a baby."

"Exactly that," I say, pointing at Penn.

For some reason, that resonates, and there's a sad air that comes over the room.

"I can't believe my little girl is so grown up," Henley says sadly. "I was testing you. She hasn't started her period yet. I'd never tell you guys about that. She'd murder me in my sleep if did. I'd be breaking dad code all over the place if I broke that news. But it *could* happen...any day now."

Oh God, maybe I'm not cut out for this. I glare at Henley, but he has my mind rolling now. I love Henley's girls. I can't stand the thought of Cassidy being that grown up either.

My phone buzzes and I look at it, frowning when I see Presbyterian Hospital across the screen. My family would go to Silver Hills Hospital if anything went wrong...

I waited too long to answer, but it rings again right away.

"I'm sorry, guys. It's from Presbyterian Hospital." I stand up and start to leave the room, but then remember the crowd out there.

"Take it in here," Penn says. "I don't think you'll be able to hear out there."

I nod and answer. "Hello?"

"Mr. Shaw?" A woman with a no-nonsense voice waits for my response.

"Yes?"

"Weston Alexander Shaw?"

"This is Weston Alexander Shaw. Who is this?"

"Your son was admitted into the ER at Presbyterian Hospital this morning," she says.

My stomach takes a dive, and I shake my head even though she can't see me.

"I don't...have a son," I say.

I'm facing the wall, but the low chatter in the room goes silent, and I can feel four sets of eyes on my back.

"Your name is on the birth certificate. The baby was born in this hospital a couple months ago, and we hoped that you were the next of kin."

I swallow hard, my vision blurring and thoughts flying at rapid speed. I've never had sex without a condom. I've had women say they're having my baby before, but my lawyers proved the allegations were false.

"Mr. Shaw?"

"This is a joke, right? Who put you up to this? Who the fuck is this?"

"Mr. Shaw, I assure you this is not a joke. There was a car accident this morning, and if you really are Weston Alexander Shaw, your son was involved."

"Okay, I'll play along. Where do I find him?"

"Presbyterian Hospital. Come to the ER and ask for Wanda Dixon," she says and hangs up.

I stare at the phone and turn in slow motion toward the guys. They're all staring at me in concern. Bowie is closest to where I am and he stands and puts his hand on my back.

"What was that about?" he asks.

"That was the hospital. They said my son is there. This isn't funny." I point around the table. "If I find out you guys were behind this, I'm kicking your asses."

Henley frowns. "Weston. Slow down. We wouldn't mess with you about something like this. I'd call the team's lawyers if I were you though."

"I need to get to the hospital. She said my name is on the birth certificate. That can't be right."

Bowie squeezes my shoulder and lowers to meet my eyes.

"It'll be okay," he says. "You've got this, whatever comes. Okay? I'm sure it's just a mix up."

I nod and they all stand.

"We'll come with you," Henley says.

"No, it's okay. I wouldn't want to give the nurses a heart attack when they see all of you coming." I try for light, but my heart is racing.

"Let us know what's going on, if we can do anything," Rhodes says.

"I will. Thanks."

Penn opens the door and leads the way. "Coming through. We've got an emergency," he says.

We weave through the people still hoping to see Mustangs players, pretending we don't hear when we're asked for autographs. When we're outside, I take off in a jog.

"Call me," Penn yells, as I get in my SUV.

The ride to Denver feels longer than ever, but it's really only forty minutes or so. It may as well be another world from the idyllic streets of Silver Hills.

My thoughts are at war, divided into two camps: I can't possibly have a child, and what if I do?

Pre Order Mad Love here! https://geni.us/MadLove

FIND OUT WHAT'S NEXT

Linktree @willowaster
Newsletter http://willowaster.com/newsletter

All your fun Landmark Mountain merch can be found here: https://willow-aster-store.creator-spring.com/

ACKNOWLEDGMENTS

I can't believe we're at the end of this series! I've loved every minute of writing about this town and these characters, but what has been even more incredible is hearing from readers from all over the world about how you love Landmark Mountain too. Thank you so much for going on this journey with me! And don't worry, you'll still hear about some of these characters in my series to come.

So much LOVE and GRATITUDE for the following and many more that I'm sure I'll forget:

I'm so thankful for my husband and kids: Nate, Greyley & Kira, and Indigo. Thank you for putting up with my scatterbrain and pretending with me that this town is real. Thank you, Greyley and Kira, for the amazing artwork and help with creating merch!

Thank you, Kess Fennell, for all the amazing artwork. Every new piece you create, I think, "Oh, *this* is my favorite now!"

Laura, you are a godsend, you truly are. So thankful for you. I love all the places our chats go. :)

Catherine, thanks for your love and the many laughs. I have an endless record of hilarity to recall now when I think of our voice messages.

Nina, I don't know what I'd do without you. You've changed my life in the best ways and I adore you.

Christine, you're stuck with me forever. Thanks for always having my back and for caring all the time.

Natalie, I'm so glad to have you in my life. You've made my life so much better. Thank you for everything!

To the authors who sprinted with me on this one and helped me finish: Laura Pavlov, Amy Jackson, Lauren Blakely, Rebecca Jenshak, and at several critical points, Catherine Cowles—thank you!!

Emily Wittig, you created my favorite covers ever, and I'm so grateful for your friendship too.

Thank you to the entire VPR team—Nina, Charlie, Valentine, Kim, Christine, Sarah, Kelley, Meagan, Amy, Josette, Ratula, and Erica! Your professionalism, your kindness, your cheering me on, your love—it means so much!

To my extended family, thank you for loving me in spite of these spicy books! :)

To Tosha, Courtney, Christine Maree, Savita, Claire, Tarryn, Kalie, Debbie, Steve & Jill—whether you're in my life because of books or were here long before, I know I can reach out at anytime and you'll be there, and I'm so grateful for that!

And last but not least, thank you to everyone who read this series, shared, reviewed, made amazing collages, or told a friend about it—thank you with all of my heart!

ALSO BY WILLOW ASTER

Standalones

True Love Story

Fade to Red

In the Fields (also available on all retailer sites)

Maybe Maby (also available on all retailer sites)

Lilith (also available on all retailer sites)

Miles Apart (also available on all retailer sites)

Falling in Eden

Standalones with Interconnected Characters

Summertime

Autumn Nights

Landmark Mountain Series

Unforgettable

Someday

Irresistible

Falling

Stay

Kingdoms of Sin Series

Downfall

Exposed

Ruin

Pride

The End of Men Series with Tarryn Fisher

Folsom

Jackal

The G.D. Taylors Series with Laura Pavlov

Wanted Wed or Alive

The Bold and the Bullheaded

Another Motherfaker

Don't Cry Over Spilled MILF

Friends with Benefactors

FOLLOW ME

JOIN MY MASTER LIST…
https://bit.ly/3CMKz5y

Website willowaster.com
Facebook @willowasterauthor
Instagram @willowaster
Amazon @willowaster
Bookbub @willow-aster
TikTok @willowaster1
Goodreads @willow_aster
Asters group @Astersgroup
Pinterest@willowaster

Landmark Mountain merch:
https://willow-aster-store.creator-spring.com/